I0524604

Storm Stayed

Musgrave Landing Mysteries, Volume 4

Yvonne Rediger

Published by Brown Wolf Publishing, 2025.

Published by Brown Wolf Publishing
Saskatchewan, Canada

Dedication

For Luke and Leslie

Chapter One

JANE BIRCH GAZED DUBIOUSLY up at the stone exterior of Highmere House as she sat in the borrowed car. Looking through the rain-streaked windshield, her green eyes shifted to the second-floor windows, with relief she saw no one.

It was silly really. Being haunted by the image of a man in the upstairs window from over twenty-five years ago. Back then, the place was shuttered, with the ground floor boarded up and looking for all the world as though the place were abandoned.

Except it wasn't.

As a preteen, Jane was paid by her aunt to clean the coffee shop after homework was done. Visible from across the street, the three-story sandstone house had looked back at Jane as she swept the outdoor patio where customers could sit. The huge stone blocks which made up the exterior walls were much different than any other building in Musgrave Landing and older than most. The house had been built in 1899 and the corner window on the second floor across the way drew the eye.

To this day, Jane swore she'd seen a man looking out the window on several different occasions, even though no one was supposed to live there anymore.

Her Aunt Ethel said it was probably Mr. Willard, the groundskeeper. Jane's gut told her something different.

The mansion sat there waiting until it's mistress, the now late Mrs. Olivia Frost-Highmere, decided it was time to reopen the house.

Maisy Wyatt said she thought the second floor really was haunted. "The hallway is always cold, and I get the weirdest feelings up there sometimes."

Jane had automatically laughed, albeit nervously. The old story among Musgrave Landing villagers went that someone murdered the former millionaire, Mr. Allister Highmere, and now he haunted the place. The actual truth behind the story was even stranger.

Jane's lips flatlined as she grabbed the door handle. "Get over yourself," she muttered and exited the late model Forrester station wagon. "There is no such thing as ghosts." She closed the driver-side door. "You are a mature businesswoman, act like it." She had a customer waiting and an order to fill.

Her running shoes made little sound on the gravel as she walked around to the rear of the station wagon.

At least the worst of the predicted bad weather had yet to arrive. The temperature hadn't dropped like the app on her phone promised either. Still, the chilly December wind was up, trying it's best to fling rain, and drips from overhead branches at her from the surrounding trees. Not the nicest of early winter mornings.

The now refurbished Highmere home was a business opportunity for Jane. That was where her thoughts turned. She was curious about the first party of guests booked into Highmere House Conference Centre. It wasn't everyday her inherited business, Jane's Eats and Treats, supplied three kinds of cheesecake for a business conference.

Jane hadn't bother changing out of her work clothes to make this delivery. It was more important to be on time. She opened the borrowed vehicle's heavy back door and slid the first tray to the tailgate. The red calf-length raincoat covered Jane's jeans and long-sleeved white shirt protecting her from the worst of the moisture. She'd made sure her long dark brown hair was secured in its usual braid down her back. She was neat and clean and that was all that mattered. Well, besides the desserts of course.

Maisy had told Jane the expected group was seven people. The thought made Jane nibble her bottom lip in doubt as she reached inside the car. She hoped she'd made the cheesecakes large enough to accommodate all the guests. It was better to have more than enough, rather than not enough in her mind. She wanted Mrs. Roque to come back to her for more food items for the next conference.

Lifting out the first creation, she was glad Arlie had taken over wrapping up the food while she'd put on her coat. There was no way the wind and rain could penetrate the cellophane wrap, not after her father-in-law was done constructing the barrier.

Leaving the car open, she carried the tray toward the back door of the house. Or as the housekeeper referred to the old Highmere mansion, the HHCC. She should have parked closer and certainly would next time.

It wouldn't matter what the estate's manager/housekeeper, Mrs. Roque, called the place. The residents of Musgrave Landing would always refer to the palatial mansion as 'the big house'. These days the three-story sandstone edifice looked less abandoned and haunted, and more like the original photos Jane had seen in the village museum.

The owners had set the place to rights almost two years ago. The furniture was back, the priceless artwork rehung, and the grounds were meticulously maintained. The place looked like it belonged to the owner of a big corporation, and they lived here. Although that fact was only true a couple of times during the year.

None of the family lived in the village full-time now that their matriarch, Mrs. Frost-Highmere had passed on.

Shifting her load to a more comfortable position on her hip, Jane turned the corner on the brick path to arrive at the kitchen door. She was thankful the wood and metal awning afforded some cover from the precipitation while she waited for the doorbell to be answered.

She glanced down at her burden. This tray contained the raspberry-topped decadent dessert. Whole cakes, not cut up, just as Mrs. Roque requested. The housekeeper would look after the final presentation of the desserts. Still, Jane had made a special effort with the three cheesecakes.

Two more waited in the back of Gladys Wyatt's station wagon. One, a rich creamy chocolate confection with dark chocolate curls on top, and the other was the same as the first, except with blueberry topping.

The black glossy-painted portal swung open, and the blocky figure of Aggie Roque beamed a smile at Jane from across the threshold. Large square hands were folded over her middle, and her brown hair peppered with grey was in it's usual tight roller curls. No makeup graced the housekeeper's lined face or around her navy-blue eyes. The older woman's regular day dress was enshrouded by a starched heavy-cotton white apron. The over garment was something Jane would have thought a butcher might use for cutting meat rather than someone working in a commercial kitchen. However, everyone knew Mrs. Roque made her own rules.

"Thank you, Jane. I'm so glad you are here early. Oh, and the raspberry cake looks perfect. Just as I knew it would be."

"I thought you might want everything delivered ahead of time." Jane nodded.

"Absolutely." Mrs. Roque turned to call behind her. "Tiffany, come take this dessert and put it in the cooler, please. Maisy, you can help Jane unload."

"Yes, Mrs. Roque." A twin chorus of voices chimed. Tiffany, a tall slender red-haired young woman appeared to take the dessert from the café owner.

Jane raised her eyebrows at the long black skirt and crisp white long-sleeved blouse Tiffany wore along with a ruffled white apron over top. She glanced up, but there was no maid's cap on the girl's head. Although Tiffany's wiry red hair was pinned to the back of her head and still gave the impression of a turn of the 19th century housemaid.

Tiffany Zach's fresh face, liberally covered with freckles curved into a smile for Jane and a soft 'ooh' was emitted for the cheesecake. Jane decided right then Tiffany had good taste.

Maisy popped out of the kitchen pantry behind the tall red-head. She too was dressed in the same black and white uniform. Her mid-length blonde ponytail bounced as Maisy scooted past Mrs. Roque.

Jane and Maisy exchanged a smile as the other young woman went by. The café owner followed and had to sharpen her pace to catch up to the taller Maisy. The twenty-one-year-old had a fit, athletic build and was at least an inch taller than even Tiffany. Jane moved her much shorter frame sharply and finally fell into step with the younger woman.

Maisy was on loan from Jane's café to Highmere House for this conference. Partly as a favour to Mrs. Roque, and partly because Jane knew Maisy was saving up money for her own future. Winter was a slower time at the café and Jane couldn't give Maisy as many hours as she would like.

Highmere House had employed Maisy before to serve at several dinners for local groups, and they paid well. It helped that Maisy had been instrumental in bringing in Jane's catering business for the elaborate extras Mrs. Roque felt were necessary for her guests. Jane hoped this trend would continue for some time. She had her own renovations to think of. The roof over the café wasn't going to fix itself.

The relationship was beneficial for all since Highmere House only boasted a staff of two full-time people. When guests were expected, the housekeeper would call in part-time people, like Tiffany and Maisy.

Seymour Willard was the only other full-time employee. His role as groundskeeper meant he was not expected to work inside and that was no doubt for the best. Jane had only ever seen Mr. Willard from a distance, and yet found his long stares unsettling.

"I left the tailgate down. We just have to grab the other two." Jane said as she and Maisy headed to the back of the car. "How's it going?" She said this in a lower tone as they arrived back at the station wagon. She carefully picked up the blueberry cheesecake.

"Not bad." Maisy waggled her head. She balanced the chocolate dessert in one hand and closed the tailgate to the ancient Forrester station wagon with the other. "Mrs. Roque is very precise, and wants everything done a certain way, perfectly. Not that I blame her."

"She does have a formidable reputation to uphold." Jane and Maisy walked side-by-side again to the back door.

It was good, Jane noted, Maisy was proficient with carrying large trays of food. The twenty-one-year-old had to use her other hand to pull up the hem of her long skirt to allow her feet freedom of movement, and to keep the muddy gravel from the hem.

By the time they got back to the kitchen entrance, Mrs. Roque had disappeared, so Jane followed Maisy to the pantry and the walk-in cooler. The first cake was on a shelf by itself. There was room for two more, side by each.

"Have any guests arrived yet?" Jane held the stack of trays from the café, used to transport the desserts. She watched Maisy close the heavy door to the cooler after they exited the enclosure.

"Nope, we don't expect them until the noon hour ferry." Maisy smoothed a wrinkle out of her apron. "Almost everything is ready. We hope the guests will be here well before the rain begins."

"I hope so too. Arlie thinks the ferry will be cancelled this afternoon because of the weather."

"Did he feel the barometer change in his bones again?" Maisy wrinkled her nose as she grinned. "He always says that." Arlington Birch had a fondness for Maisy and not merely because he dated her grandmother, Gladys. Jane's father-in-law had trained Maisy in the running of the café, and she was the only other person he trusted to run his espresso machine. He hovered when Jane ran the thing.

"True, but he's usually right." Jane smiled as she looked at her young employee. "He was reciting something close to poetry this morning about the weather."

"No?" Maisy's amber eyes sparkled as she grinned. Arlie had a way of getting into people's hearts.

Jane frowned slightly. "Let me see if I can remember what he said. Something like; 'When the cat lies in the morning sun, she will creep behind the stove by noon. If she sleeps with all four paws tucked in, close the windows and bolt the doors, a blow from the southwest will be on our shores.'"

"Not the best poetry I've ever heard, but still sounds ominous." Maisy lifted her eyebrows. "Was Ruby complying with Arlie's words?" She named Jane's adopted feline.

"Oh, yes." Jane tipped her head again in a nod. "She was curled up in front of the heater with her feet tucked under her like a loaf of bread. Just like in the poem." After the words passed her lips, Jane had the oddest feeling wash over her. Her smile faded as they left the pantry, and a frown puckered her brow.

Then Jane blinked and gave her head a shake to escape the disturbing feeling. She shifted her eyes to the high kitchen windows.

Gloomy charcoal clouds were creeping across the sky above the treetops. Maybe the storm was the cause of her unease?

"Is something wrong, Jane?" Maisy followed her back into the kitchen proper.

Jane tucked the trays under her arm and waved off her reaction. "I hope the weather system will blow through quickly and leave my roof shingles where they are." She gave an awkward smile.

They found Mrs. Roque slowly stirring a large cast aluminium pot on the six-burner gas stove. The woman's shorter stature forced her to be up on tiptoe to perform the task.

The room was a comfortable oasis of delicious aromas and warm light. All the counter surfaces were stainless-steel with light dove-grey painted cupboards. In contrast, the walls were a shade darker grey with bright white trim on the baseboards and ceiling. All the appliances installed around the perimeter of the room were commercial grade, oversized, and would be at home in any restaurant kitchen.

Maisy walked briskly across the room and snagged a small step stool by the kitchen door. She brought it over to the housekeeper and placed it on the floor at the older woman's feet. "You might find this helpful, Mrs. Roque."

"Why thank you, Maisy. So thoughtful." The housekeeper mounted the step and sighed. "It certainly removes the strain from my shoulders."

Maisy glanced a Jane. "I have to finish dusting the library."

"Of course, you've got work to do." And then the younger woman was gone.

"That girl is a gem. No wonder you won't let her go. I'd hire her in a heartbeat to help me run this place full-time if I get my budget approved."

Jane chuckled. "Maisy is free to decide where she wants to work." She changed the subject to avoid a discussion on the topic, again. "Your soup smells amazing."

"Mm, thank you. It's my own recipe. It's call Wild Mushroom Surprise. I picked the mushrooms yesterday. I thought it would be a good choice since two out of the seven people coming for the conference are vegetarians."

"Good idea." Jane crooked an eyebrow. "What's this conference about?" Jane watched the older woman sprinkle fresh green parsley onto the soup's creamy surface.

"Dunn Wolf Publishing has booked six rooms for the weekend. The guests are writers and editors I was given to understand. The head editor's assistant, Hazel Dell, booked the HHCC weeks ago. Some kind of writing retreat she said."

"Sounds interesting."

"I hope so. Sylvia Highmere said she was going to be here this weekend too. Ms. Dell and Miss Sylvia knew each other from school I'm given to understand. She was interested in meeting the senior editor, so I suggested she come and act as hostess this weekend." Mrs. Roque put the large wooden spoon down on a ceramic spoon rest shape like a tomato slice. "Still, Miss Sylvia can become...distracted. Quite easily, actually." There was resignation in her tone.

Mrs. Roque spoke of all the Highmere children like they were her own, but then she had known the three of them from birth.

Jane nodded but kept her thoughts to herself. The youngest Highmere child was said to be flighty at best. If she actually showed up as announced, it would be a first.

"Which reminds me, I must review the guest list with the girls." Mrs. Roque patted her apron pockets as though she were looking for something.

"I'll leave you to it then. I have to return Gladys' car to her and get your finger sandwiches ready for lunch. Gladys will be bringing them over along with the roast of beef she's prepped. Oh, and Gladys said she'd compile the lunch dessert flans and cheese boards when she gets here."

"Lovely, they will be fresh then. Thank you, Jane." Mrs. Roque braced her right hand on the edge of the stove and climbed down from the stool. "Any word on your van?"

"Ben's waiting for distributor parts, Arlie says." Jane had been dubious about the vintage Ford Econoline when Arlie had taken her to look at the vehicle. At over forty years old, she worried the thing would be unreliable. However, once her father-in-law pointed out the age was a plus, as it could be licenced as an antique at a huge cost savings, she was sold. After two years of consecutive service, 'Bluebell' as Jane called the two-toned van, had earned her keep. The distributor malfunction was the only issue so far. "I'll have it back on the road before Christmas."

"Good news, thanks again."

"No problem, we are all happy to help." Jane felt like she'd been dismissed, which amused her as she moved to the back door.

With her hand on the nob, Jane looked back at Mrs. Roque with a small frown. She wondered about her bad feeling and hoped the sensation had nothing to do with the mushrooms.

Chapter Two

MRS. ROQUE TURNED THE flame under the soup pot down to a low simmer. Then lifted the kettle next to the pot to check the water. Finding the level satisfactory, she put it on the back burner and turned it on to heat.

The housekeeper crossed to the two-way door which led to the dining room and turned left to open a second door which led to the rest of the house. "Tiffany, Maisy, come sit with me for a minute. I'm making us some tea." Mrs. Roque called into the main part of the house.

Minutes later when both young women arrived back in the kitchen, they found Mrs. Roque standing at the central island. The brown ceramic everyday teapot was in front of her, at the ready to receive the hot kettle water.

The older woman looked over at them. "I've got the list of guests here." Mrs. Roque dug in her dress pocket under the huge apron and extracted a handwritten list. "We should go over this so you know which room to put each guest in." She unfolded the paper and flattened it on the island countertop.

Tiffany picked up cups for tea from a side counter and followed Maisy. They each took a stool on either side of Mrs. Roque.

The housekeeper slid the paper up so the two young women could read it. She then carried the teapot over to the stove just as the kettle whistled. "I can tell you a bit about each one." She poured a small amount of water into the pot.

Maisy scanned the list and frowned. "I don't recognize any of these authors."

Tiffany squinted at the names. "Me, neither." One strand of red hair had escaped from the clip on the back of her head and looked like a wayward spring.

"Well, you probably wouldn't. These aren't popular fiction writers. They are considered a bit more highbrow, or so I'm told, although I'm not sure that is strictly true." Mrs. Roque took the warmed teapot and emptied it into the sink.

"Which to me means 'literary'." Tiffany gave Maisy an eye-roll. "Another word for boring. Or at least that's what I thought when I was at school."

The housekeeper lifted one eyebrow at Tiffany's words but said nothing. She wiped the outside of the ceramic pot with a tea towel and then spooned loose tea into it before returning to the stove and adding the water.

For her part, Maisy bit her lip and then cleared her throat. "Ziola Nutt?" She prompted the housekeeper, determined to keep a straight face. "What does she write?"

"Ms. Nutt is a bit more than an author. She is the chief editor and one of the owners of Dunn Wolf Publishing. Mr. Bryce gave me some background on her and the others." Mrs. Roque poured the brew into the cups.

"Mr. Bryce? Who's that?" Maisy asked as she accepted a teacup balanced on a saucer from Mrs. Roque.

The housekeeper blinked at her. "Mr. Bryce Graham is Mrs. Alicia's husband."

"Alicia Highmere?"

"Thank you." Tiffany accepted her cup.

"Yes, dear." Mrs. Roque took her own teacup and joined them at the island placing the milk and sugar tray between the girls.

"Alicia kept her maiden name?" Maisy sipped her tea.

"Yes, Mrs. Alicia built her business reputation with her family name."

The older woman eyed the third stool and then took a kitchen chair with a straight back, this she placed opposite the girls before she sat.

"Is your back giving you trouble, Mrs. Roque?" Maisy asked.

"It's more my knees. I'd rather be lower to the ground. Now," Mrs. Roque nodded at the list, "let's begin." Mrs. Roque said this as if it explained everything as she looked longingly at the sugar bowl.

Maisy slid the cut-glass container over to the older woman, but she shook her head. "I'm off sugar, it causes my joints to swell." She then waved the statement away. "Anyway, as Highmere Holdings chief of security, Mr. Bryce has lots of contacts. Mrs. Alicia and I thought he should vet the guests before we allowed strangers to stay on the estate, and especially in Highmere House. We are not one of those Air B & Bs, you know. We have standards."

Maisy winked at Tiffany, who's mouth turned into a smirk, but she held in her mirth. Mrs. Roque could be a bit opinionated.

It was rapidly becoming apparent to Maisy the older woman was a bit of a snob. She was fairly sure some kind of check was done on Air B & B guests too, although it might only be a credit check or something. "Probably a good idea." Maisy kept her voice neutral. "There are lots of valuable things in this house."

"Exactly, so you can't be too careful." The housekeeper took a sip of tea. "As I was saying, Ziola Nutt, I know who she is. She wrote a sweeping series of books dealing with the discovery and settlement of British Columbia. The historical side sticks mostly to the true account of our provincial history. Except the novels are actually a romance of a sort and did take some historical liberties with how women and immigrants were perceived back then." She waved this statement away too.

"Artistic licence, I suppose." Tiffany poured herself and Maisy a second cup of tea.

The housekeeper declined as she continued. "Ms. Nutt wrote those books from the point of view of a young woman from England. She arrives with her family who settle outside of Victoria. They make and lose their fortune, a bunch of them die in various tragedies. The heroine goes through lots of trials and tribulations before conquering all and coming back out on top with the man of her dreams by the end of book nine."

"Nine, how many books are there in the series?" Maisy ran an index finger over the name.

"Ms. Nutt is supposed to be working on book ten currently. She's made her whole career with those novels."

"Is the heroine a spunky red-head?" Tiffany's eyes sparkled with mischief.

"Yes." Mrs. Roque blinked, somewhat surprised.

"With flashing green eyes?" Maisy too, grinned joining in with Tiffany.

"How did you know?" The older woman's expression became quizzical.

"I haven't read these books, but that's the usual description of the heroine in a lot of other historical romances I've read." Maisy shrugged.

"It's a stereotype, for sure." Tiffany nodded. "I could play her in the movie." Her tone completely dead-panned and made Maisy laugh.

Even Mrs. Roque chuckled. "You do have the hair for it and the complexion of an English rose." Mrs. Roque agreed.

Tiffany rubbed at the freckles on her nose. "Maybe by January, once these freckles fade. Maisy looks dark and exotic in comparison." She nudged Maisy's shoulder with her own. Her tone a bit envious. "You can be *my* good-natured sidekick or best friend."

"I credit my mother for my dusky features, and you can be my sidekick." The pair wrinkled their noses at each other.

"All right, girls, we digress." The housekeeper got them back on track.

"You've read all her books?" Tiffany carefully placed her empty teacup back in the saucer.

"Oh, yes, and quite entertaining they are too. Mr. Bryce told me Ms. Nutt bought into the publishing company with the proceeds of her books. I understand she's quite rich now."

Maisy dug out her mobile phone. "Let's see how rich."

"Is that really necessary?" Mrs. Roque frowned and pursed her lips in disapproval.

Maisy's coworker leaned over to shoulder surf. "Ziola Nutt's net worth, at least publicly, is listed at a million."

"Not too shabby." Maisy put her phone away sensing Mrs. Roque was none too pleased with her. "Still no where near what Highmere Holdings is worth."

"True." The housekeeper seemed somewhat mollified.

Tiffany looked down at the list. "Bertram Nutt, is that her husband?"

"No, Bertram is her brother. Mr. Bryce said he drinks a bit so keep an eye on him. We wouldn't want him falling down the stairs. He will have to behave himself while he's here. We do not serve alcohol on the premises, but we have no way of stopping people from bringing it in." Her lips tightened. "At least not without searching their luggage. Of course, that would mean an invasion of privacy and a possible lawsuit."

This sounded like Mrs. Roque really wanted to search Bertram Nutt's luggage to ensure he wasn't smuggling in liquor. However, from the way the housekeeper compressed her lips as she thought about it. Maisy guessed there must have been a conversation along these lines with Mr. Bryce. He no doubt had to explain about people's right to privacy. Maisy hoped the issue was now closed, because there was no way she was going to do anything like that. Time to change the subject. "So, what will we serve them at dinner if we don't do wine?" Maisy asked.

"Oh, there will be wine. We have some lovely non-alcoholic or de-alcoholised vintages brought in. Tiffany can show you where we keep them."

"Okay. Do we tell the guests about the wine, or do they already know?"

"All was explained to Ms. Dell before they booked." Mrs. Roque extracted a set of wire frame glasses from her apron pocket and perched them on her nose. She leaned forward and turned the paper to scan the list. "Ms. Nutt is in the east wing, in the Cherry Blossom room. Her brother, is in the west wing, in the Sitka room."

"Do you mind if I make a note of that on here?" Tiffany asked the housekeeper.

"Not at all, good idea. We can post it on the bulletin board by the door so we can all refer to it as needed."

The girls nodded and Tiffany extracted a pen from her left skirt pocket and wrote the details in a neat hand in the margin of the list.

"Next, we have Maxwell Lintlaw, he's a mystery novel writer. He's made his name with a cunning detective named Windsor Falcon."

"Good to know," Maisy said. She loved a good whodunit. "I might have to look him up at the library after this weekend."

"Yes, he's actually not bad, I've read one or two. We have Mr. Lintlaw in the Arbutus room, again west wing. Kent Westham is also in the west wing, the Cedar room."

Maisy was sensing a theme here. Boys on one side of the house, girls on the other. "What does Mr. Westham write?"

"Nonfiction, celebrity biographies and their self-destruction, drug overdose, relationship abuse, that sort of thing." The older woman frowned. "I'm not sure if that's an oxymoron. Celebrities are made-up people so to my mind a type of fiction. Regardless, it doesn't matter. His writing is not my cup of tea it borders on real criminal events, and I find those true crime things abhorrent."

"Not terribly literary either." Tiffany wrote the room next to his name.

"Precisely." Mrs. Roque gave a nod.

"Who's next?" Maisy prompted.

"Angela Oakla, she writes scandalously steamy romances." Mrs. Roque looked up to catch Maisy grin. "Or so I'm told." Her tone said she would not be caught dead reading anything so outrageous. "We have her in the east wing, the Geranium room." She finished her tea and move the cup and saucer aside, then stood to point to the next name on the list. "Hazel Dell, as well as being Ziola Nutt's assistant, she told me she writes contemporary romance although she hasn't published any books under her own name yet. I've put her in the Lily room, also east wing. Lily of course, is next to Cherry Blossom. I wasn't sure if Ms. Nutt would want her assistant close by but decided to err on the side of caution." Mrs. Roque frowned at the list with purse lips. "Maisy, when you go up to finish with the west wing rooms, please ensure the door through the washroom is locked from the Maple room side, leaving the Cheery

Blossom side, in the east, open. I don't want anyone taking their own unguided tours about the place."

Tiffany gave a small shiver.

"Will do. What about the office up there, it should be out of bounds too?"

"Mr. Highmere's old study is already locked. I made sure of that after I dusted in there yesterday."

Maisy gave the housekeeper a nod.

"Any sign of Mr. Highmere?" Tiffany asked in an innocent tone.

"None whatsoever." Mrs. Roque said dryly. "I'm sure our ghost will keep a low profile while we have guests."

By her tone, it was clear the housekeeper didn't actually agree with the younger women that there was some sort of spirit patrolling the second floor. However, Maisy thought, it might be she merely didn't approve of him haunting the house. "Not that Mr. Highmere knew what good manners were." This was said under her breath, but the younger women shared a smirk when they heard this.

"Oh, Tiffany, please add an asterisk beside Hazel Dell and Sylvia Highmere, to remind us they are both vegetarians."

Tiffany bent her head to comply.

"Whenever she gets here, Miss Sylvia will be staying in the carriage house. She has her own room there."

Maisy knew of Sylvia Highmere, Alicia's younger sister, by reputation. If gossip was to be believed, Sylvia was a recovering drug addict and was now interested in becoming a writer. She had tried to get involved with the film industry in Vancouver as an actress and had only ever secured small background roles once or twice.

Considering all one had to do was sign up with one of the many agencies and show up on time when called, it was easy to get background work. Maisy herself had worked as a background cast member on two films in Ladysmith and three in Vancouver. Not that she'd bring this fact up. Her grandmother and parents were not on the need-to-know list, and neither was Mrs. Roque.

"What does Sylvia write?" Maisy glanced up at the housekeeper.

"Miss Sylvia." Mrs. Roque put emphasis on the prefix, then she sighed. "Not much yet, as far as I know, but we hope for great things." Mrs. Roque gave the younger woman a tight smile.

"Sylvia doesn't have a book deal with Dunn Wolf?" Tiffany asked. "I thought..." She shook her head.

"I remember she read one of her stories at one of the open mic events we had at the café this past summer." Maisy glanced at the housekeeper.

"Did she?" Mrs. Roque sounded surprised. "Well, no, she doesn't have a contract as far as I know. Miss Sylvia will be acting as a kind of hostess for this three-day event." The older woman sounded uncertain about this statement.

Or was she worried Sylvia wouldn't show up? Maisy didn't know Mrs. Roque well enough to tell the difference.

"Now, we should get on. Our guests will be here soon." The older woman walked back to the stove.

"Yes, still lots to do before noon." Maisy picked up the tea things and moved to the sink. Tiffany took the sugar and put the milk pitcher back in the cooler.

"Probably the twelve-twenty ferry." The older woman picked up the wooden spoon and gave the soup a stir. "We will serve a late luncheon. I expect to seat them between one, and half one. Jane, or rather Gladys," Mrs. Roque looked to Maisy as her grandmother was mentioned. "Will be bringing trays of finger sandwiches and I have wild mushroom soup in the making. The garden salad is already prepared." Mrs. Roque replaced the soup pot lid and turned to her staff. "Tonight's menu is on the bulletin board. Beef Wellington is the main entrée with spinach ravioli served in sundried tomato sauce as an alternative. There is also a list of the wines we will serve. The whites are already in the chiller and the red is in the sideboard in the pantry. As I said earlier, Tiffany can show you exactly where it's kept when it's time."

"What about the veggie people?" Tiffany asked returning to the kitchen.

Mrs. Roque clicked her tongue at this term. And Tiffany's freckled cheeks flushed.

"Try and keep up, dear. Hence the spinach ravioli, that is for the vegetarians."

"Right." Tiffany nodded, shifting foot to foot, her cheeks flushed.

"We have sherry as an aperitif too. Wine comes from grapes, if Hazel does not want to partake, that's up to her. Miss Sylvia will be served water, if she does not want the non-alcoholic wine." The firmness of these words left Maisy no doubt as to Sylvia Highmere's sobriety.

Tiffany crossed to the cork board to post the guest list and their rooms with a red pushpin.

"Now, Maisy, if you could please finish making up the west wing rooms? You still have my keys?"

"I do, I'm on it." Maisy moved to the back staircase.

"Keep an ear out for Gladys, she'll be here soon with the luncheon items and may need help unloading."

"Will do." Maisy gave her a nod before heading upstairs again via the back staircase. She could just make out Mrs. Roque's words as she climbed the stone steps.

"Tiffany, when you're finished with laying the dining room table..."

The other woman's response was swallowed up by the wind howling through the trees and beating against the windows on the back side of the house, making the outer panes rattle.

Maisy shivered at the mournful tone of the wind bashing through the surrounding trees. Mounting the stairs, she grabbed a handful of black skirt to run up the treads to the second floor. The concrete steps were cushioned with rubberized material, making them less slippery.

Maisy didn't hesitate climbing the stairs from the kitchen to the floors above at her usual speed. She preferred these treads to the main foyer stairs. The plush carpeting and her smooth soled shoes made her slip if she didn't slow down.

As Maisy pushed the hallway door open, she looked first right and then left before entering the hallway.

It was silly, really, no one was up here. Too prove it to herself, she strode down the carpeted hallway to the east wing and to the rooms of the master suite. The Cherry Blossom room was on the east side which connected through a luxurious bathroom to the Maple bedroom in the west wing. That particular room was not being used this weekend and Maisy thought that was for the best.

A quick check in Cherry Blossom assured her all was ready for the book publisher /author. She passed through to the bathroom with its claw-foot bathtub, gold fixtures, and ornate six-light mirror vanity. The bathroom dated back to the 1920's with it's small black and white marble tile, graceful and opulent with its matching extras. A separate shower, its taps like the rest were all tipped with gold leaf or a close faux facsimile. Every surface had been cleaned and sparkled in readiness.

Exiting through the opposite door, Maisy came out into the Maple bedroom in the west wing, she closed the connecting access and turned the key in the lock. The mechanism gave a satisfying snick.

She turned and abruptly stopped, sensing the change in temperature. The cold spot was back.

Maisy swallowed and took one long slow breath. She eased her way around the frigid area to the door. Using Mrs. Roque's master keys, she locked the unused, though in her mind, not unoccupied room.

Now outside the 'haunted' bedroom as she thought of it, Maisy released the breath she'd held. Encountering the weird cold spots on the second floor did not exactly frighten her, though was unnerving.

There was no telling where the phenomenon would show up next. Before this occasion, Maisy had experienced the cold spots twice before. Once, just outside of the office next door to the Maple bedroom. The last person to use the study and master bedroom in life was also the former owner of the mansion, Allister Highmere. Before that, it belonged to his father and grandfather, there was no telling who the ghost might actually be, but it made sense to Maisy it was the person who'd had the most notorious death.

The other time had been by the door to the back stairs. Tiffany, the lucky duck, hadn't ever run across the places which felt icy cold one minute and back to normal room temperature the next. There had been weird goings-on in Highmere House in the past. It wasn't surprising there was a ghost haunting the second floor. Not that she spoke about it to anyone, except Jane.

Maisy moved on to the last room she had to finish, the Sitka room for Bertram Nutt. She entered the oak paneled bedroom and finished the job of making up the double sized mattress with crisp white sheets and a navy-blue down-filled duvet. The bed cover contrasted nicely with the lighter dove grey carpeting and wallpaper.

Maisy placed the last pillow on the bed, and looked around the room to ensure she hadn't missed anything. All appear to be in order, merely a last dusting was needed.

The spirit couldn't be Mrs. Olivia Frost-Highmere haunting the place, she'd only passed on a couple of years ago. Maisy took up a soft cloth from the caddy of supplies she'd left in the room before the tea break.

Jane had told her stories about all the Highmere clan, especially about Allister Highmere disappearing, allegations of murder, and then the body found on the property a couple of years ago.

When Jane mentioned seeing the shape of a ghost looking out from the second-floor study's corner window, Maisy had believed her. Even if it had been years ago, but hearing Jane tell the tale, it sounded like it had happened to her only yesterday.

As Maisy ran a soft cloth down the wood posts of the bed, she was glad she'd left the bedroom door open and could occasionally glance out to check she was actually still alone.

Chapter Three

ARLIE BIRCH, JANE'S father-in-law, and master barista, ran a clean polishing cloth over the chrome of espresso machine. Through the window, he was keeping a watchful eye on a young man around ten years old. The boy was standing outside the café, off to the right of the red-painted wood and glass café door. The kid appeared to be counting his change. He must have been a walk-on on the ten-thirty ferry.

One side of Arlie's mouth quirked up briefly. The kid's build and hair colouring reminded him of his son Jack at that age. Although this boy's auburn hair was straight, and his eyes weren't hazel. From this distance, possibly blue.

Then too, Jack had never been shy. He would have come in and bargained for whatever it was he wanted at that age if he were short of money. When his son was a boy and Ethel Crawley ran the café, she'd agreed Jack could shovel her walkway in exchange for some treat or a buck or two.

This had led to the chores list his late wife put on the refrigerator at home. One-dollar chores and five-dollar chores were written in two columns.

"That boy is always looking for money," Sara had said matter-of-factly when she explained her plan to her husband. "We have lots of money, and Jack has lots of spare time."

Arlie had grinned but shook his head. "The shed doesn't need another coat of paint."

"True, but the garage could use a tidying, lawn mowed, whatever needs doing."

"That's true. I have some vehicle maintenance coming up, he could help. Maybe it's time to show him how to change the oil, basic car care, and how to change a tire."

"Life skills are good to know."

"Always." He nodded in agreement. "That doesn't mean Jack can't learn household chores too."

"Of course, he can." Sara taught Jack how to make a meal plan, buy groceries, and stick to a budget.

Later, when Jack was older, he would clear the small café parking lot of snow too. By then, Sara had suggested their son move on to a cash transaction with Ethel. Advanced education didn't pay for itself.

Arlie sighed. He missed Sara, but the hurt of being left behind after she passed away had dulled over the years. Something to be thankful for, he supposed. And he was thankful for Gladys Wyatt's companionship.

Also, the job he had that gave him a reason to get up in the morning. It also warmed his heart to know Jane actually did truly need him at the café. She'd recognized his value and hired him long before she and Jack got together.

He made a sound halfway between a chuckle and a snort at the memory and moved on to wipe down the counter.

"What did you say?" Earl Moffatt asked glancing Arlie's way. "Do you have an opinion on this latest political intrigue?"

"Nope. Not at all. I try to stay clear of politics."

The three men sitting with Earl at his table stared at Arlie for a moment, and then all of them laughed.

Arlie had the grace to give them a head waggle nod. He actually did try to avoid politics, what with Jane's sister currently the village mayor. Although he had to admit he wasn't always successful.

The boy appeared to make a decision and slowly pulled open the door. The cool wet air rushed in behind him. He carefully closed the door and then ponderously walked up to the counter.

"What can I get for you, son?" Arlie crossed to the counter and raised his salt and pepper eyebrows at the boy. "The menu's on the blackboard." He jerked his thumb up and behind his head.

Arlie saw the kid had dark brown eyes, these he lifted to read the offerings on the board written in an array of coloured chalk.

"Tea with milk, please." The kid's voice was even, if low.

Arlie blinked. Not much surprised him lately but this order did. "You're sure that's what you want?"

"I don't exactly want tea, but I got enough money for that." The kids' eyes slid sideways toward the tray of sandwiches in the display case.

Arlie noticed. "Mm." Was the response he gave and pulled a red, one serving tea pot and matching mug off the shelf behind him. "What kind of tea would you like?"

The boy blinked. "Breakfast, please. It's what my mum usually has."

Arlie nodded and added a paper-wrapped tea bag to the tray he was putting together. "Hot water is in the far-left container on the table along the wall opposite us, along with milk and sugar. Two dollars, please."

Money changed hands and Arlie slid the tray toward the boy. "If you'd like to do a couple of chores, I could see my way to giving you a sandwich to go with the tea."

The boy's eyes widened with surprise, but he nodded. "Yeah, sure, that'd be great."

"Which one would you like?" Arlie stepped behind the display.

The boy pointed at the roast beef section. Arlie slid the refrigerated case open to grab a sandwich and put it on the tray.

"Thank you." The kid made his way around Earl's table and took a seat by the patio doors.

Arlie kept an eye on the kid as he went about other tasks.

The kid shed his coat and backpack on the opposite chair and then took the small teapot to the dispenser and carefully filled it with hot water. He took two milk and sugars with him back to his table.

While the tea steeped the boy wolfed down his lunch. With the tea, he took a bit more time, as it was hot. Still, it wasn't ten minutes later when he came back to the counter with the tray of used dishes.

"What can I do to pay for the sandwich?"

"What's your name?" Arlie took the tray and dealt with the contents.

"Miles. Miles Iverson."

"Nice to meet you, Miles. I'm Arlie Birch." The older man offered the boy his right hand. They shook awkwardly. It was probably the first time Miles had ever shaken hands with anyone let alone an adult. It was never too soon to learn proper manners in Arlie's mind.

By this time the café was empty, save for Arlie and Miles. "Put your backpack and coat by the heater to dry. Then wash your hands. You can help me clear the tables and wipe them down."

Fifteen minutes later, the task was done, and Miles looked around at his coat and bag, and then back at Arlie. "I'd sweep the floor for a muffin."

"Deal," Arlie said with a nod. "Broom is in that cupboard. Watch out for a small black cat with an orange ear."

Miles walked over to the cupboard beside the office door. "Why, what would the cat do?"

Arlie merely chuckled. "You'll see." He took the grey bin of dishes into the kitchen. When he returned, the kid was attempting to sweep the floor while the cat chased the broom's movement and randomly attacked it.

"Ruby." Arlie shook his head, crossed the room, and scooped up the wriggly animal. He opened the patio door and put her down outside.

"You didn't have to do that, she'll get wet. I could handle the cat."

"I can't handle the cat and she knows me." Arlie watched the black feline run around the building out of sight.

"It's nasty out there too." Miles sounded concerned as he moved the broom over the floor sweeping the dried sand into a neat pile.

"She'll just go home, not to worry."

"Ruby doesn't live here?"

"Not anymore. She follows us to work, but we live across the street."

The boy nodded, as though in thought. He made short work of this next task and was rewarded with his chocolate chip muffin and a refilled pot of tea.

Arlie wiped down the coffee area and check the air-pots. He could feel Miles' gaze on his back. As he tidied the sugars and stir sticks, he wondered if he should maybe get a bit more information out of the kid. Was he a runaway?

"Your last name is Birch, right?"

At these words Arlie turned around and looked at the boy. "It is."

"Are you related to Jack Birch?"

"Jack is my son."

Miles nodded. He took a breath and stood up from the table to clear up his mess. "I think Jack Birch might be my dad."

MRS. ROQUE WAS CHECKING the library when she heard the car engines proceeding up the drive. The housekeeper glanced at her wristwatch.

Yes, the twelve-twenty ferry would have berthed a few minutes ago. She exited the spacious book-lined room and walked to the front of the house to look out the foyer window.

Aggie watched three vehicles proceed up the red-brick driveway one after the other with satisfaction. The guests were on time.

Each car was a modest mode of transport in price and style. The motorcade pulled into the Highmere House circular driveway. She was pleased to see the drivers followed the new signage for parking and found spots in the gravel lot, side by each.

It would be grand to have the house full again, but this small group was a far cry from the panache of the old days, when Aggie came to this house to work as a char girl in the kitchen.

Her mother had been known as Mrs. Roque, the housekeeper, back in those days. She had merely been, Aggie, who functioned as general dog's body. From that lowly position she'd worked her way up. Earning every rung in the ladder. Her toughest critic had been her own mother, but so too, she'd been Agatha's greatest supporter.

In time, Aggie had taken over her mother's position running the household. It didn't matter she'd never married.

No young man had appealed to her enough to make her want to give up her work.

She'd also seen the worst of Olivia and Allister Highmere's catastrophic union. Even though she'd been many years their junior, younger Aggie had resolved early on in life to never put herself under the power of anyone she could not easily walk away from.

Of course, the arrival of the children, James, Alicia, and Sylvia had ensured she stayed on with the Highmere family. Someone had to protect the wee ones from the worst of their father's temper.

The whole estate had been hopping back then. Mrs. Olivia like to entertain. No doubt to keep people around and thus keep her husband under a modicum of control when he was in residence.

Aggie suspected Mr. Allister didn't want any witnesses Olivia could call upon later to attest to his abuse.

When he was away in Vancouver, Mrs. Olivia kept busy. This meant dinners, house parties, and charity luncheons, with lots to keep the staff occupied as well. There had been so many more staff, lots of people to talk to and learn from.

Still, it was good to see the house being used again after all these years. That fact alone gave the housekeeper a sense of satisfaction.

Mrs. Roque stepped to the right of the front doors. Here, a dark oak wooden counter with a satin finish offered a leather-bound ledger and pen ready for guest sign-ins. She had pictured something subtle and understated and her vision had been realized. Mrs. Roque looked around the recessed alcove to ensure all was ready. Tiffany was straightening the brochures which gave the history of the house and listed the rooms the guests were allowed to use.

They exchanged a nod. Both women were excited but suppressed the emotion to keep up a professional demeanour.

Mr. Bryce had come over to supervise the refitting of what used to be the cloak room into the conference facilities check-in area some time ago. He brought a young man with him to do the technical installations and ensured the server equipment, phone lines, and WiFi were setup with the proper security.

Behind the counter sat a desk with the merchant terminal. It was configured for credit card verification. There was also a computer and printer to issue invoices.

Over a month ago Mr. Bryce made her a surprising offer. "Would you like to be trained on the accounting software, Mrs. Roque?" he'd asked her while they shared tea in the library to discuss the Highmere House Conference staffing needs.

"Heavens, no, I doubt I'd ever retain all the information in the time you are here. Could we look for someone who can work with me, and take on the accounting duties?"

Mr. Bryce had found Tiffany Zach. The girl had hotel certifications, who knew there was such training? Tiffany was a wonder on the technology and administration side of the business. It helped that the young woman had returned to Musgrave Landing from a few years working in Victoria. She'd said city life wasn't for her and Mrs. Roque welcomed the girl who swiftly learned how to handle the bookkeeping and basics of keeping the technology running.

To the right of the desk was the remaining closet area. Mrs. Roque extracted her black raincoat. There was no sense in getting wet, but she felt she should make an effort to welcome the guests personally.

She'd had a devil of a time to convincing Alicia Highmere not to sell the main house and the estate. It took enlisting James and Sylvia, Alicia's remaining immediate family, to convince their sister not to erase their family's past. And while they made headway with their sister, those two could not close the deal.

In the end, it took Bryce Graham, Alicia's husband, and one of the few people she listened to for advice. He chimed in and then finally the CEO of Highmere Holdings agreed to use Highmere House as a conference centre. No doubt with the carrot the HHCC would create local employment and increase the economic standing of the community.

How could it not? Mrs. Roque's chin rose with pride as she thrust her arms into her coat sleeves.

Still, included in the agreement was the added stipulation Alicia would personally approve the parties who would use the facility. The housekeeper had no issues with this, it made sense, it was Mrs. Alicia's house after all. She had inherited the estate from her mother, two years ago.

Aggie hoped after a time Mrs. Alicia would let that duty fall to the housekeeper as manager of the facility. She resolved to be patient.

Tiffany was good about demonstrating how the computer worked so the housekeeper was learning to manager more aspects of the HHCC too, although slowly.

A body had to stay busy. The family didn't visit near as often as when their mother was alive.

The housekeeper buttoned her coat and then took a step forward and paused with one hand on the door pull, she turned to survey the foyer.

The front of the house was the centre piece and it showed. White marble floors gleamed and led to the ground floor rooms.

The oak wainscotting and wooden trim glowed with polish as did the huge oak staircase angled across the centre hall. A forest green runner unfolded up the steps and broke left to the east and right to the west. The matching green and cream wallpaper with flecks of gold was bright and vibrant. The cream plaster cornices, ceiling rose, and sweeping mouldings were all clean and dusted. Everything sparkled clean, including the glittering chandelier which hung from a long chain and lit the vast space of the centre foyer. Under the chandelier, rested a round cherry wood table. This held a beaten copper bowl instead of a vase of flowers.

Alicia Highmere was allergic to most flowers so Mrs. Roque ensured there would never be a vase of anything which would make her sneeze in the entrance of her home. She chose to use white silk roses in strategic locations, like the small table by the staircase.

Directly behind the table, mounted on the opposite wall, was 'Mountain Forms' by Lawren Harris, the founder of the group of seven. The Rocky Mountain subject matter on the canvas was composed of unique brush strokes of whites, greys, and contrasting green. The beautiful painting drew the eye and welcomed people to come forward and admire the work.

To the right, the most popular room, was the library. After that, a smaller drawing room. This room was locked while retreat guests were staying. The walnut floors within required maintenance.

On the left, the music room took up almost the same footprint as the library with it's grand piano. This room's door was currently standing open for the brief tour Mrs. Roque would conduct with the guests. Beyond that, there was what had in the past been Mrs. Olivia's personal sitting room which overlooked the back gardens and the waters of the Samsum Narrows. The late Mrs. Frost-Highmere used the space as her office as well. These rooms would be closed off after the guest tour was completed.

The Dunn Wolf Publishing writers retreat only requested the use of the library for meetings. Which was fine with the housekeeper, it would cut down on the amount of cleaning and upkeep for her staff.

The estate grounds were open for walks and exploring if the guests so desired. The outside areas were Seymore Willard's responsibility anyway.

Mrs. Roque smiled with satisfaction as she ran a critical eye over the entranceway. Everything was ready.

She opened one of the heavy double front doors. The wind tried its best to blast the housekeeper with rain but the sandstone porte-cochère helped prevent most of the precipitation from pelting down on her.

With a conservative blue scarf tied over her head to keep her curls in place, Mrs. Roque waded out into the weather to welcome Highmere House Conference Centre's first guests.

The wind grabbed at the fabric of her scarf, trying to rip it from her head and the black raincoat off her body as she stood on the top step. This was as far as she was going to go to welcome the six guests.

Seymore was nowhere about, and this didn't surprise her. The man was getting up there in age after all. The guests would have to handle their own luggage, but as Mr. Bryce had pointed out, it was what was expected in most hotels now a days anyway.

First to emerge from the dark green sedan driver's side door was a tall thin man in jeans and a lilac pullover. He reached inside the car and pulled out a lime-green windbreaker. The coat's fabric clashed with his strawberry-red hair and beard. He looked around him eagerly as he donned the coat against the inclement weather.

His passenger, a younger woman, got out. She wore black leggings with a colourful flowered top spilling out from under a melon-green heavy cable cardigan. She might have dark black hair under the green dye, but it was hard to tell from this distance. These Mrs. Roque knew were Max Lintlaw and Angela Oakla. She recognized the authors from their publisher's website gallery photos. Ms. Oakla had won the Saskatchewan Writer's Award for new indigenous writers, for her first book. She too, looked around her with curious dark eyes as she joined Lintlaw to remove luggage from the trunk.

Next, from the smaller metallic blue VW beetle, a woman of over six feet was disgorged from the passenger's side. Her jet-black hair was threaded with premature-grey, and she wore the mass in a long, braided queue down her back. Her cream suit was the perfect foil for her olive complexion. The suit was offset by the mid-calf sky-blue raincoat she left open which displayed her generous curves.

Almost immediately, a man possibly no more than five feet, four inches tall followed from the driver's side. His crisp charcoal-grey three-piece suit was topped with a black trench coat and black fedora.

Mrs. Roque raised her eyebrows at the head covering. It had been ages since she'd seen a man wearing such a hat. Still, the short male carried it off well, she'd give him that. The black and charcoal highlighted his blonde hair and fashionable chin stubble.

This pair had to be Kent Westham and Hazel Dell. Mrs. Roque had been curious to meet Ms. Dell. They had communicated several times over arrangements for the writer's retreat. It was always interesting to see if voices matched faces. In this case, the husky tones seem to fit the voluptuous female.

Mr. Westham stood, fists on hips, looking up at the sandstone exterior of the house and seemed pleased if his flash of white teeth was anything to go by. He turned his head and raised heavy blond eyebrows at Hazel. They shared a few words.

Mrs. Roque caught snatches of the conversation. Something about Hazel almost making them late for the ferry and it was a good thing he knew how to navigate city traffic as well as he did. His words left a sour look on the tall woman's face as he unlocked the rear of the car and extracted his bag.

He made no move to help his passenger remove her soft-sided suitcase. Which to Mrs. Roque said these two were barely friends. Any gentleman would help his lady with her bag. She felt vague disapproval for Mr. Westham from his lack of manners. Still, not her business.

"Ms. Dell?" Mrs. Roque walked down the steps and forward to greet the tall woman and introduce herself. "I am Mrs. Roque."

The tall woman turned and walked across the gravel to meet the housekeeper halfway. "Lovely to meet you." They shook hands.

"Please proceed into the house, no point in anyone getting any wetter." Mrs. Roque waved a hand for Ms. Dell to precede her into the entrance.

As she crossed the gravel parking area, the housekeeper noted the last to clamber out of their vehicle was the driver from a late model navy station wagon. He was a large, red-faced man in brown and grey tweed. He hadn't bother with an overcoat, but then his wool jacket and vest, buttoned over his protruding stomach, would no doubt afford him some protection from the wind and rain. So too, did his peaked cap, again in tweed. His bulbous nose was red and prominent. She saw no hint of hair protruding from under his matching peaked hat. From her investigation, the man looked to be Bertram Nutt.

Out of the passenger door emerged an equally round female. Her white-blonde hair fell to her shoulders in long waves. The woman wore a long flowing black dress with handkerchief hem and sleeves falling out of a fuchsia-pink raincoat which flapped around her knees. She had not fastened it against the rain mixed with snow either. Around her neck, she wore a long carrot-orange silk scarf which fell to her waist, matching her blocky heeled pumps. The colour combination was a touch jarring but fit the woman as she moved imperiously forward. In her right hand she carried either an over-sized black leather purse or briefcase.

The blonde removed dark glasses from her face to survey her surroundings. The wind chose that moment to blast them all with more wet. The woman's long hair, combined with the scarf ends, flipped across her face. She was forced to use her bejewelled fingers to claw the obstructions away from her eyes. Once the hair and scarf were tamed, her annoyed expression was turned on her driver. She gestured to the rear of the car, no doubt ordering the bald man to get her luggage.

As the female guest turned back to the doorway, Mrs. Roque could see the woman was on the hard side of sixty. The housekeeper raised her eyebrows at the black nail polish and even blacker eye makeup. The look might have been appealing on her some twenty-five years ago. Today, the heavy makeup did nothing positive for the woman's appearance. As she removed a lock of blonde hair from the corner of her mouth, she exposed her own identical bulbous nose, although it wasn't red like her brother's. This of course had to be Ziola Nutt.

Mrs. Roque allowed herself a small smile as a thought struck.

The Nutts had arrived.

Chapter Four

JACK BIRCH HANDED BACK the hunting licence booklets to the pair of men dressed in flame-orange, camouflaged patterned hunting gear.

"Thanks, and good luck." One man's first name was Jim, the other was Ted. Both had the same last name, Baird. Jack figured the pair must be related. By the look of them, the same curly strawberry-blonde hair and similar height and build, probably brothers.

Currently, the thirty-something males were on the edge of the bow hunting season. There was only a day left for any licenced hunter to harvest a black-tail deer.

"Thanks," Jim, the taller one said. "We might be done for the day, though." He tipped his touque-covered head at the horizon.

Ted grunted agreement as he replaced his licence in a clear plastic sleeve and tucked the document into his back pack.

The three men took a moment to look up and inspect the sky.

Low-pressure clouds hurled themselves across uglier black ones in the background. "You could be right," Jack said.

"The forecast did say it was going to rain." Jim swung his pack up and looped the straps over his shoulders and then shrugged the backpack to move it into a more comfortable position.

"That looks like more than just rain to me. Probably some sleet, snow, and ice too." Jack's tone was flat with distaste. He was not looking forward to the bad weather. Winter storms usually meant power outages and road accidents.

"Could be." Jim rested one hand on his bear spray holster. "We'd better get going, Ted, if we're going to get back to your truck before the weather hits." The pair nodded congenially to Jack and picked up their compound bows to make their way down the game trail.

Jack paused a moment longer to look at the threatening afternoon sky. The wind picked that moment to up its strength. Sharp cold bit at Jack's ears and face. Definitely a chance of snow.

The altitude might be a factor in the drop in temperature, but he still frowned at the odd green and black clouds boiling across the horizon. Whatever this storm turned out to be, it was not going to be good. He pulled fleece gloves out of the left trouser leg pocket of his cargo pants and put them on. Time to head back before the skies opened up.

He formed his mouth to give one short piercing whistle and a large male German shepherd exploded from a dense corpse of arbutus and spruce trees. "Come on, boy, let's get home."

Eagerly, Vimy bound across the open ground to Jack's truck and waited for him to open the driver's side door. The dog launched himself up into the cab and took his spot on the floor of the passenger's side.

Jack climbed in after his dog and rolled the engine over. The whine of the starter laboured for several seconds but finally the engine caught and rumbled to life.

He really needed to get the truck's starter changed. The problem was he couldn't do the work himself. The vehicle was government issue, the truck had to be taken into a government approved repair facility. With budget cutbacks, there would be no replacement transportation. Jack would have to wait on this one to be repaired. While he cooled his heels, his boss would expect him behind a desk in Duncan. The last place he wanted to be. Working in the woods, being in nature was where he felt most alive. Well, and when he was with Jane.

Jack looked at Vimy. "I've been procrastinating and it's coming back to bite me in the ass. Maybe I should just fix the starter myself."

Vimy dropped his chin on Jack's knee and looked up at his hero.

"Softy," Jack smiled as he scratched the dog's ears. "I'll get your lunch out once we're on the ferry."

Fifty minutes later the dark navy Conservation Services crew cab truck turned onto the highway. A downed tree delayed them as Jack had to pull a chainsaw out of the tool bin in the truck box to clear the debris. Helpfully, the massive Sitka spruce chose to fall in the ditch with only half of its lower branches blocking the road. What did not help was the wind and rain beating down on him as he worked to clear the obstruction.

There was no sign of the Bairds, so the brothers must have taken the north road.

By the time they made the dock, Jack knew both he and Vimy were both looking forward to some food when they coasted down the ramp to the ferry. It was only a quarter to one o'clock, Jack was sure he'd make the one-twenty ferry. Unfortunately, one look at the white caps roaring across Samsum Narrows told him his plan might not be possible.

Still, he hoped he was wrong when he spied Captain Gibson striding across the paved vehicle waiting area. Jack got out and cross the parking lot to intersect the captain's path.

"Hi Sherman, are the sailing's cancelled?"

"That they are, Jack." Sherman Gibson gave a nod toward the small vessel tied snuggly to the wharf. "My boat's not big enough to deal with this nonsense." He gestured to the chaotic churning grey and white waters stretching between Salt Spring Island and Vancouver Island. "I pushed it to get the last bunch across. Most were headed home early because of the storm. It's not safe and the big wigs agree with me for once. All sailings are suspended until further notice."

Jack's black Conservation Officer cap tried to escape with the wind, but he grabbed it in time. "Vesuvius has a bigger boat."

"That they do, and if you hurry, you might catch their next sailing before this storm reaches the next level and they are cancelled too."

"All right, take care." Jack turned to head back to the truck.

Gibson gave him a wave as he headed to his own vehicle.

Thirty minutes later, Jack was stopped behind a line of cars and trucks. He, along with the people in front of him, were anxiously waiting to see if there was room for them on this crossing. While they waited, he gave Vimy his lunch. A bowl of dry food and a another of water.

Satiated, the big dog was curled up on his carpet on the floor and his collapsible feeding dishes stowed.

Jack brushed crumbs from his turkey and cheddar sandwich off his black uniform coat as they got the signal from the crew member to board.

He started the engine and one-by-one the various cars and trucks rolled forward. When it was his turn, a woman well-dressed in rain gear and a hazard orange vest waved him along but stepped behind his vehicle to halt the next one.

Jack watched in the rearview mirror as the female driver of the sleek low sports car laid on the horn in protest. This driver was not impressed. Hazard orange lady ignored the reaction as she held the vehicle in place. It appeared it would take more than a horn to intimidate the ferry worker. Still, Jack kept an eye on the frustrated driver until he was sure there would be no further issues. You just never knew sometimes.

At that moment, an RCMP crew cab truck swung into the marshalling yard to his left. Jack could see the driver was

Constable Patrick Tadmore. Hazard lady waved Tadmore's vehicle in behind the Conservation truck. Now sports car woman was truly incensed. She flung up her hands and rolled her eyes, although she did stay inside her vehicle.

Jack frowned. It wasn't normal practice to allow anyone to cut in line. Odd, he hoped nothing bad had happened on the island to require the RCMP.

Usually, the Ganges Detachment handled the majority of calls, but Musgrave Landing was still considered under the Duncan Detachment, where Tadmore was posted.

This was no doubt due to the fact that for over a hundred years the village had only ever been accessible from Vancouver Island via a ferry. First owned by the Highmere family, then BC Ferries. Musgrave Landing had only just recently gained a road to Fulsome Harbour and access to the larger community of Ganges. Responsibility for the village should have been handed over from Duncan, but contracts had been signed and still had a few years to run.

A burly male ferry crewman was gesturing for him and the line of vehicles, so he quickly put his truck in gear and rolled down the ramp. He had to brake as a yellow mini cooper cautiously manoeuvred its way downward in front of him. The driver appeared inexperienced with boarding ferries, so Jack patiently waited until the small car was berthed in its slot.

He glanced in his rearview mirror.

Patrick was speaking into his radio mic. Jack knew it was early for the cop to be heading back to the village, his shift usually didn't end until six, parking in the café lot around six-thirty most nights.

THREE WEEKS AGO, THE constable had moved to Musgrave Landing. He currently lived over the bakery café. Jane decided to increase the revenue from the property by letting out the apartment above and they both agreed renting to a cop was probably not a bad idea.

He and Jane had met Tadmore last summer during the wrap up of that crazy business at the new condo building on Coast Road. The constable had helped arrest a murderer, catch more than one thief, and generally made the village a safer place. Gladys had been in the thick of that strange set of events. Maisy had been the one to snag the cop and get him to help defuse a serious situation which could have ended badly for her grandmother. Jack suspected Maisy might see Patrick Tadmore in a hero's light.

He and Jane had discussed the cop as a renter. "I'm certain Patrick will be a good tenant. I think he wants to get to know our Maisy." Jane said while they were curled up in front of the fireplace in their living room. Arlie was out at theatre practice with Gladys.

"It's hard to date someone when you live on the other side of the Narrows." Jack put his arm around Jane. "That's why I moved home." He looked down at his wife.

"True." A soft smile curved Jane's lips as she met her husband's look. Then a small frown appeared. "Did I let the fox into the hen house? I'm fairly sure Patrick is smitten with her."

"You think you're encouraging Patrick by allowing him to rent the apartment?" Jack topped up Jane's wineglass.

"Maybe, but I wouldn't rule Gladys' influence out either. I wonder what Gladys thinks."

"Dad will keep an eye on things. He's not shy about asking anyone's business."

"And not a bad thing. If Maisy's grandmother wasn't happy with Constable Tadmore, I doubt her granddaughter would be interested. Maisy pays a lot of attention to Gladys' opinion, Arlie's too."

"You could be right."

"Can I get that in writing?"

"Ha, ha."

With a pleased grin, Jane rested her head on Jack's shoulder. "Patrick will be around enough for both Maisy and Gladys to get to know him. If he's a keeper, Arlie will give him the nod too."

"You think so?"

"I discussed Patrick's rental application with him. Your dad is my second in command, you know, and Gladys thinks a lot of his opinion too."

Jack huffed a laugh. "I bet Dad loves that."

"I love that he does. Your dad is my right hand in the business and Gladys is rapidly becoming my left. Maisy is a terrific worker and great with people. I'd like to keep her happy." She lifted her head to take a sip of the red vintage. "Mrs. Roque is trying to steal Maisy for Highmere House," Jane continued after she swallowed. "She thinks the conference centre thing could really take off."

"Which is good for you."

"Yes, but I don't want to lose Maisy."

Jack said nothing, just gave his wife's shoulder an understanding squeeze.

"The first guests are coming tomorrow for the weekend. Mrs. Roque told Maisy she could use a couple of full-time people to help her run the place. She's already snapped up Tiffany Zach."

"And you want Maisy to stay to help with the catering side of your business? I'm guessing Mrs. Roque is not going to get her way."

"Not on my watch. I'll do everything I can to keep her, but it's really Maisy's decision in the end."

"I'll cross my fingers for you."

"Thanks, Love." He felt her smile. "I still have plans for the empty land next door too, and that could be something more interesting for Maisy."

"What are you thinking?"

"I have a couple of ideas for developing the area. It's got potential."

AS THE FERRY ENGINE revved up Jack wondered again what Jane was thinking with regard to the empty lot next to the café. The six-acre property was waterfront, even with the ten-foot drop down to the rocky beach.

At the signal from the male ferry worker, he rolled the truck slowly forward until he got the stop gesture and then shut off the engine.

Tadmore's white SUV was waved in opposite him on the starboard side of the ferry. Jack gave a brief wave and received one in turn from the cop.

As he set the truck's parking brake, the wind shoved at his vehicle causing its mass to rock as the force of nature tore around them. Jack looked with interest at the building white caps on the water. The power of the wind was noticeably increasing in strength.

Vimy got to his feet and moved closer to his best friend. The dog once again dropped his head on Jack's knee. Automatically Jack stroked behind the dog's soft ears.

Fat raindrops began to pelt down again, obscuring the view of the water. He looked out the side window at the dark sky instead. Black and green clouds churned across the horizon.

With the drop in temperature, once the sun went down, it wouldn't be too long before the rain changed over to snow and then ice. If they didn't have a power outage during this storm, he'd be very surprised.

He reached out and turned key to engage the truck's systems. The interior heater came on and Jack turned it up a notch. Vimy let out a contented sigh.

Jack then dug for his phone to check the weather app.

Chapter Five

ARLIE WANDERED INTO the cafe kitchen after he heard Jane return from dropping Gladys' car back at her place. "I thought Jack was coming home early. No one will be hunting in this weather."

"I think you're right, but Jack still isn't back yet." Jane hung up her coat and stepped to the sink to wash her hands. "He texted me about an hour ago. The ferry from Stoney Hill is cancelled."

Arlie grunted. "The waves are too high. There's a king tide too with the full moon. The ferries are probably canceled until after the storm is over. We can expect some flooding in the village too, I'm willing to bet."

"I wouldn't be surprised." Jane crossed to the fridge and extracted a yellow ceramic bowl of diced hard-boiled eggs. "I'm glad the café and house are on a higher elevation than some parts of the village." She also took out a red bowl which contained shredded tuna from the glass front appliance and placed them on the large wooden table. "Anyway, with Stoney Hill's ferry canceled, Jack had to take the boat from

Vesuvius and drive home the long way. It might be slow going he said. There may be trees down on the road and there will no doubt be a detour or two." As she spoke, Jane gathered the rest of the ingredients to make up the sandwiches for the conference lunch. "Can you grab me the platters, please?"

Arlie went to the cupboard and reached up to the top shelf for white oval china platters. "Great, he'll have to take the Coast Road for the last leg, that will be hell on earth with this wind." Arlie put the plates on the side of the table within Jane's reach.

The loaves of whole wheat and white bread were already sliced. He occupied himself with making rows to receive the fillings. "I wonder if Gladys' underground garage will flood."

Jane combined the ingredients of chives, green onion, spices and mayo. "Good thing she parks up top outside, then. There was standing water in her lot when I left in your truck. At the street, there was a puddle bordering on the size of a lake. Norm Gorlitz was out there in a slicker digging a trench to the culvert." She used a large wooden spoon to stir the egg salad. "Oh, I parked your truck in the garage."

"Thanks." Arlie watched Jane quickly plop a dollop of filling on every second slice of bread, he took up a spatula to spread the filling evenly. "The condo building should be fine. If the structure didn't take serious damage from the multiple times Linda Leechie flooded the place, I'm willing to bet Gladys' condo will be fine."

"Gladys did say the remediation work was completed quite well." Jane agreed with her father-in-law as she proceeded to the next step in the sandwich prep.

Arlie began cleaning up the used dishes. They made a good work team.

"I have to say it is easier to get food ready for Mrs. Roque's guests when we aren't so busy in the café." Jane handed him the last bowl.

The older man put the item in the dishwasher as he made a gruff sound of agreement. "And with Maisy otherwise engaged." He closed the machine's door and then returned to the café to check on their last remaining customer.

Jane's mouth curved into a smile. Her father-in-law was invaluable with his meticulous work ethic.

She added the egg salad sandwiches to the other platter, the tuna one was already assembled. The crusts had been trimmed off. Jane always thought that was such a waste of Gladys' lovely bread. She figured out it was better to cut the crusts off ahead of time so she could reuse the leftover bread in stuffing for a chicken or Swiss steak at home. Waste not want not was a mantra for most restaurant owners since profit margins were only three percent.

A gust of wind rattled down the old brick chimney in the kitchen. It was a lonely wintery sound. The mournful noise made Jane think of her Aunt Ethel.

"This is one of those days my aunt would say 'The wind has eyes,'" she said when Arlie wandered back over.

Arlie grunted. "It's a good thing that chimney's been capped. Keeps out some of the damp and cold." He added more items to the dishwasher and left again.

Jane moved the platters to a clean counter.

The kitchen chimney hadn't been in use since the building had been converted to electric heat over two decades ago. And yet, the unseen force found it's way into any cracks.

Jane glanced over at the structure and wondered if it were possible to have the chimney bricks removed and repurposed. Of course, if they removed the chimney the hole would need to be closed. More work to add to the future shingling job coming sooner than she'd like. It would be a lot of bother and expense merely because she didn't like the mournful sound.

"I'm glad we got that fuel tank out of the basement last year. It took up so much room and wasn't used. Still with the price of electricity rising, I'm wondering if I made a mistake." She said on Arlie's next return.

Jane opened a drawer and pulled out cellophane to wrap up the sandwich platters.

"Fuel isn't cheap either." Arlie pursed his lips as he thought. "We'd be better off with putting in an actual wood stove." Arlie paused in rinsing the utensils. He eyed the white painted brick chimney. "I bet we could put a steel liner down that thing and add a burner in the basement. Lots of room to store wood down there, the space is going to waste. We could build a holding rack or two, plus there's the old coal delivery door to move wood inside."

"What does firewood cost?"

"I'd have to ask Jack. He buys the cord wood for the house fireplace. Better yet we could make use of the dead fall from the old orchard. I just never got around to gathering any this year."

Jane frowned. "What old orchard?"

"Over behind Saint Mark's church, past the cemetery. When I last visited Winston up at the home, he told me to take as much as I wanted."

"The haunted wood?"

Arlie chuckled and folded the tea towel he'd been using to dry the utensils. "That's what you kids called it. When I was a younger man, Winston Kettlefish and his family ran a farm just outside of town, the orchard was part of it. They sold really good apples too."

"Wait, is that why there is a Stan Brothers realtor's sign posted on the Kettlefish's road?"

"Yep, Winston's kids want him to sell everything now that he's in assisted living. Of course I'd never list anything with Steady Stan Brothers, the guy's a crook and I told Winston exactly that."

She was about to ask Arlie to back that statement up with something more than gossip, but another sudden gust of wind, stronger this time, rattled all the kitchen windows.

Arlie frowned at the noise. "I'm going to check all the windows are fastened properly." He started with the laundry room off the kitchen and then the café area.

The vibrating sound made Jane look out the west window. The black sky was the backdrop for the trees whipping violently left and right in the crazy wind.

Jane frowned and felt a wave of concerned for her husband and his long journey home. Still, Jack was as competent as men came. He was more than capable and could look after himself. And yet, she worried. This storm was not the usual sort they got in early December. Good thing they'd held off with Christmas decorations and lights.

It was late in the season to get something this massive and powerful. Unfortunately, it felt like the low-pressure system was only getting started.

At that particular moment, Jane caught a glimpse of the green station wagon pulling into the loading area behind the café.

"I'm dawdling, Gladys is here." Jane immediately went back to the table and finished wrapping up the sandwiches for transport. Arlie popped back into the kitchen right after Jane said these words and helped her.

Seconds later Gladys Wyatt, the sixty-six-year-old silver-haired bundle of energy entered the café kitchen.

"Hi, Gladys." Jane called over her shoulder.

"Hey, gang." Gladys had to push the door hard to get it to close against the wind. Arlie moved across the room to help.

"I've got the Beef Wellington loaded up in the back of the car for the conference dinner tonight." She ran her fingers over her silvery hair to restore some order. "I made sure to leave room in the back for the sandwich trays though."

"Why are we supplying lunch to the House anyway?" Arlie subtly grasped Gladys' hand and gave it a quick 'hello' squeeze. She looked up to smile at him.

Jane saw the byplay and hid her own smile. Gladys' apple cheeks flushed a lovely shade of pink. Her father-in-law wasn't the type of man to put his emotions on display, so she ignored the fond gesture between the older couple. It pleased her they had each other.

She picked up two platters and crossed to the counter by the door. "Because Mrs. Roque is paying us." Jane placed the plates in the high-sided rack on the counter. "And it's a collaboration of sorts, I'm hoping for more business like this if the House hosts more conferences." She didn't say anything about the benefit of more business streams to get them through the winter months. "Plus, the sandwiches are meant to go along with the Wild Mushroom Surprise soup Mrs. Roque has chosen to serve."

"I'm making the luncheon dessert over at the House kitchen. Mrs. Roque will have all the ingredients." Gladys told Arlie.

He nodded at Gladys but latched on to Jane's first words. "Wild Mushroom Surprise, you say?" his tone was dubious. "Made by Mrs. Roque?"

"Yes, she told me she harvested the mushrooms herself." Jane turned back to the table for the last two plates. Usually, the blue racks were used to deliver the bread Gladys made for their larger customers. Like the Smuggler's Inn at Whisky Corner. Today, they would be used to supply Highmere House.

"She's been making that soup for decades." Gladys adjusted the platters in the racks. "It's a good thing these things are stackable."

"I'm not sure oval platters were the best idea." Jane tidied her work surface. "I should have bought square ones or rectangular, but we have them now." She lifted one shoulder.

Arlie wasn't done with the soup topic. "Is the 'surprise' about the kind of mushrooms Mrs. Roque uses?"

His expression had an edge, and made Jane lift an eyebrow at him.

"I hope they aren't the type that give you a religious experience." Arlie's eyes twinkled with mischief.

"Arlie!" Gladys pursed her lips and gave his hand a warning shake before handing him a tray to stack on top of the first one. "What a thing to think, let alone say. My goodness."

"Uh huh." Arlie moved to the connecting door to glance out into the café. Even though the bell had not rung. He returned after a quick glance. "If Mrs. Roque offers you some soup while you're over there, are you going to eat it?"

Gladys frowned. "I...I don't know."

Arlie returned to the counter by the door and hefted the racks for transport to the back of the station wagon. "And why would that be?" He lifted salt and pepper eyebrows at Gladys.

It was her turn to mumble some words under her breath this time.

Jane held the kitchen door open for the two, biting her lip.

"What was that, Love?" Arlie pushed the outer screen door wider with his shoulder.

"I said, Mrs. Roque's eyesight isn't as good as it used to be." Gladys bustled past him and marched to the vehicle to open the car's tailgate.

"Aha." He nodded smugly as he followed.

After Gladys drove away, Arlie returned to the kitchen. Jane could see he was still a touch smug from winning the argument.

Jane continued washing the tabletop. "No one's in the café, are they?"

"One customer, already served." Arlie glanced over his shoulder to the café interior again. "Someone who dropped by to see Jack." His tone turned serious.

"Oh?" Jane moved on to returning the cellophane wrap to its drawer. She hadn't been paying Arlie much attention until he said his son's name. "Anything I can help with?"

"I don't think so. I'll let him know Jack will be late."

The lights went out.

"Oh, no!" The dark sky lent almost no light to the kitchen. Jane turned to the counter and ran her hand along the top to find the correct drawer.

"I'll check on our customer," Arlie said in the dark. She could hear him shuffling his feet so as to not bump into anything. The light from the emergency exit in the next room was only a small help.

"Hang on a second." Her hand found the items she was looking for and grasped the heavy rubber grips. A push of her thumb and white light flooded the room. "Here, Arlie." She offered him the flashlight and switched on a second one.

"Thanks, I didn't know we had these."

"Jack put them in the drawer last week. We thought of emergency lights for the café dining area, but not the kitchen. He said we needed backup lighting of some kind in here anyway."

Arlie smiled. "He's always thinking, our Jack." He hefted the light and continued through the connecting door to the café.

Jane followed her father-in-law out of the kitchen. She was curious about this visitor who had dropped in to see Jack. Her light was superfluous, so she shut it off and tucked it into her apron pocket.

She found Arlie speaking to a boy. "Hello." She said to the young man sitting wide-eyed at the table to the left of the counter. "I'm glad it isn't as dark in here." Ambient light filtered into the room from windows on three walls. The emergency light shone from above each exit and helped some.

"Hi," the boy said. His tone was timid.

"I'm Jane." She glanced around looking for an adult. "Is your mom or dad in the restroom?"

He shook his head. Where was Jack's visitor?

At the boy's steady gaze, Jane tipped her head as she looked at him. "Are you here alone?"

The boy nodded.

"Is someone meeting you? What's your name."

"His name is Miles Iverson." Arlie chose that moment to interject. "He came over on the ten-twenty. He's here to see Jack."

Jane turned to look at her father-in-law where he stood beside the boy. "Why?"

Arlie turned to look at Miles. "Would you like to tell her, or should I?"

Miles lifted his chin in a stubborn tilt. "I need to know if Jack is my dad."

Jane knew her eyebrows were up near her hairline at the boy's answer. She blinked and moistened her lips, not sure what to say. Finally, she found her voice. "I see. Well, does you mother know where you are? This storm is pretty bad and I'm sure she's worried. Have you called her?"

"I sent my mum a text when I got here." Miles seemed oblivious to the panic he might be causing at home. He lifted both shoulders. "She'll see it when she gets off work. I should be home by then, I guess." His words trailed off.

Jane looked at Arlie. "Can I have a word?"

"Sure. Miles, can I get you anything?"

"No thanks. Is it okay if I sit in one of those chairs, my clothes are dry now." He pointed at one of two armchairs by the now cold faux fire. The heating element had died with the power outage.

"Of course." Jane gave him a smile.

Miles got up and wandered over to one burgundy tub-shaped armchair. He dragged his backpack over to him and dug around inside to extract his phone and opened a gaming app.

Jane gave Arlie a sharp tip of her head to take them behind the counter and out of earshot.

"What the heck?" Jane was incredulous.

"Heh, no worries." Arlie grinned at his daughter-in-law. "There's no way the kid could be Jack's."

"How can you be so sure? He dated other women." Jane clamped her mouth shut, took a breath, and started again. "It's possible, isn't it?"

"You know Jack, what do you think?" Arlie's confidence was unwavering.

Jane breathed in deeply through her nose, striving for calm. "Arlie, it's possible the mother never told Jack she was pregnant. Accidents happen, look at me. I was an accident.

My father never knew my mother messed around for a long time. I was lucky my dad loved me anyway."

It was Arlie's turn to blink. His mouth opened to deny the idea, but Jane noticed when doubt clouded his eyes. "Yeah, I guess that's possible."

"Not everyone is as ethical as our Jack," Jane reminded Arlie.

Chapter Six

EVEN WITH THE ROUGH waves and turbulent winds, surprisingly, the trip across the strait to Salt Spring Island took no more than the usual twenty minutes. Once off the vessel, that was when things got complicated.

Jack wasn't five minutes on the road behind a line of several other vehicles heading down the main road when the cavalcade came to an abrupt stop.

From where Jack sat in the line of vehicles, he could see a maple tree, over a meter and a half wide and had to be over a hundred feet long. The massive trunk bisected the highway. The leaves were the size of dinner plates and stuck wetly to the pavement. Jack couldn't see the roots or the crown. The outstretched limbs from the middle of the tree lay across the two-lane road as well as across both ditches.

Jack climbed out of the truck to see what he could do. The wind blew debris from the downed tree in a twister like pattern in front of him, making him raise his arms to ward off the worst of it.

Then abruptly, the force of nature dropped a couple of degrees of velocity and the heavier debris fell to the ground, which made assessing the delay a touch easier. He walked up to the obstruction along with a couple other drivers.

"What do you think?" Patrick Tadmore came to stand beside him. The cop had his fists on his hips to push back the sides of his yellow rain jacket exposing his uniform.

"I think," Jack turned slightly to the left to look at Patrick. "We are lucky the trunk is lying across the road and not the complete canopy."

A woman strode up in a rain-streaked yellow trench coat which reach below the knee of her nylon-covered legs. She wore matching yellow high-heeled pumps. Her light blonde hair was coiled up on the back of her head, dangly hoop earrings swung on either side. In her right hand she held a hatchet.

Before Jack or Patrick could say anything, she marched up to the downed tree, heels making a sharply clipped tattoo on the pavement. Right arm lifted above her head. The woman brought the hatched down with a loud thack! The tool bit deep into the bark. Wiggling the blade free, she began to repeat the movement in rapid fire.

"I think we can do better than that." Jack gave a half smile.

"You think so?" Patrick asked as both he and Jack watched the wood chips fly. "She seems motivated to get back on the road."

"Maybe not better, but faster. I've got a chainsaw."

"Ah, good. I'll ask our friend here to make room for you." Patrick moved forward as Jack returned to his truck. "Excuse me, ma'am. We have someone with a chainsaw."

Opening the truck box, Jack extracted the gas-powered chainsaw he'd already used once today to clear the road. By the time he walked back up to the tree, he'd primed the cutting tool.

"Thank you for your efforts." Patrick was saying to the female as he ushered her back the way they'd come. "Jack will have the tree cut in half in a jiffy. Let's go get some people from the other cars to help us move the logs."

"I've got a chain. We can use my truck to haul the trunk out of the way." The driver of the front vehicle said.

"Right, yes, that will be quicker. I need to get home to my kids." The woman in yellow said with considerable relief.

"Absolutely," Tadmore agreed. And as he escorted her back, he asked, "Can you tell me why you carry a hatchet in your minivan?"

"You just never know when you might need one."

"Okay." The cop drew out the word.

Jack chuckled as he tightened the saw's chain. The rest of the woman's response was lost to him as he placed noise suppressors over his ears. He pulled the cord on the saw and the tool revved to life.

After a few initial cuts to knock off several branches, Jack now had room to work in closer and could cut the massive trunk. The twenty-inch-long bar on the chainsaw allowed him to make short work of the tree barricade situation.

In this rocky terrain, most trees could not sink their roots deep enough to maintain an anchor large enough to keep them stable forever. Jack sliced into the tree and cut the wood into sections.

The cop worked with two other men to wrap a chain around a trunk of the lower segment. The chain was then attached to a winch hook on the lead vehicle and the driver used his grill mounted device to pull the timber from the road and toward the closest ditch.

The wind and freezing rain came down heavier again as the team of people worked on the rough task. Tadmore organized the people and worked shoulder to shoulder with the rest.

Jack was glad of his thick leather gloves, some of the vibrations from the saw were absorbed as sawdust flew around him. After approximately fifteen minutes he had enough of the tree cut up, all that remained was to haul the timber off the road.

As a section of trunk was unchained and rolled into the ditch, the wind chose that moment to escalate it's might and blew twigs, spruce bows, and dirt in their faces.

Undeterred, the team of people continued to work and repeated the process twice more. Shortly the road was reopened. With the chunks of downed tree dragged out of the way, the crowd began to disperse and drivers returned to get back into their vehicles.

Jack was optimistic he'd be back on the road shortly as he stowed the chainsaw in its wooden box. Making a mental note to clean and oil the saw when he got home, plus sharpen the chain. He was definitely thankful he'd had the tool with him today and closed the lid on the box as the wind grabbed at truck again, making the whole vehicle shimmy.

With the storm hammering the islands, he'd no doubt have some time during the onslaught to get the saw maintenance done along with having a look at the truck starter. Something else he really needed to deal with. No wonder Jane had taken her van to Ben's garage. He felt a bit guilty about not finding the time to deal with her distributor issue even though she waved away his concern. "Ben is a good customer, I want to return the favour, plus, I'd rather you spent your spare time on other things than vehicle maintenance." There'd been a mischievous glint in her eyes when she'd said this which made the corners of his mouth quirk upward as he stowed the gloves.

An ominous crack split the air behind Jack. He looked over his shoulder to see a giant cedar fall almost in slow motion toward the road.

The giant's roots split the ground behind it, throwing up dirt and forest detritus. The moan the tree emitted as it ponderously collapsed forward, struck everyone dumb. Spectators froze as the trunk and canopy swung toward the ground.

"Back up!" Tadmore yelled at the crowd. The commanding steel in his voice triggered the group to hurry backward and away from the tree. The fulcrum was reached and the whole thing tipped over, sending the root ball into the air and the sixty-foot monster crashing down.

Precisely on top of Constable Tadmore's truck roof.

As wind gust dropped again, an unexpected quiet spread over the group. Everyone, including Jack, all waited to see if there would be more movement from the surrounding trees. After a moment, it looked like the law enforcement vehicle was the only casualty. The trunk of the colossal giant was nicely settled in the saddle it had created in the roof of the truck.

Jack watched Patrick slowly take in a deep breath and sigh it out as he studied the situation with his truck.

The conservation office came to stand beside the cop. "We aren't going to get that tree off your truck without a crane."

"Yeah." Patrick sighed bleakly. "That's about how my day's been going." He shook his head. "I'd better make some calls." Patrick walked a few feet away and pulled out his mobile phone. "At least the road isn't blocked."

The wind rose again, pushing at Jack's back as the smell of pine sap and exposed earth blanketed the area. He tucked his hands in his coat pockets and looked over the sad state of Tadmore's vehicle. "Well, that's not going to buff out."

"Hey, buddy?" A gangly man in a set of coveralls and grimy black cap that advertised a local stone works addressed him.

Jack turned toward the man. He was one of the people who helped clear the other tree off the road.

"Should we stay, or should we head home? I got kids by themselves."

"No, that truck isn't going anywhere without the help of some heavy equipment, you people should head out. Watch for falling debris."

The height of the RCMP vehicle held the tree up on a steep angle, high enough the other vehicles could get by.

The crowd dispersed as they got back into their cars and slowly drove past Jack and the constable, taking the road to the interior of the island. It didn't take long for Jack and Patrick to be left behind.

Jack glanced at the cop. The constable was talking and pacing.

He judged it would be a moment or two before Tadmore was done, so he opened his truck door to let Vimy out for a bit. The wind had picked up and Jack again dug out his gloves. He replaced his black conservation officer cap with a black touque, still sporting the logo of his profession. As soon has he had the woolen hat on he felt better.

By the time Vimy wanted back into the truck, Tadmore was off his phone and walked over trailing the dog.

"There are no cranes available right now, probably won't be for some time." He stood beside the other man. They both took in the view of the fallen tree damage.

"Even if there was, you couldn't drive the thing."

"True, but I was thinking more of securing it at the moment."

Jack couldn't help the snort he emitted. "I'd say your truck is well and truly anchored."

Tadmore gave a resigned nod. "There are trees down all over Salt Spring and Vancouver Island. Power is out in over seventy communities too." He turned his head to look at Jack. "Including at home."

Jack nodded. "I figured. Need a ride?"

"At the very least, yeah." Tadmore rubbed his hand down his face, resignation and frustration evident.

"You know, you're the reason why we can't have nice things." Jack made a tsking noise.

Patrick grunted at Jack's bad joke. "Thanks for the offer, I appreciate it," he said and straightened to his full height, on par with Jack. "I need to unload a few things."

Jack merely nodded and followed to give the young cop a hand.

The constable was fortunate the cab took the brunt of the tree's weight. He could still gain access to the equipment and his personal belongings inside the vehicle via the rear doors.

"Can you store this for me in your truck?" Patrick handed Jack his shotgun and ammo case.

"No problem. Anything else?"

"I'll take the flares. The rest isn't a problem. I just have to put out some traffic cones."

"Traffic cones?" Jack asked lifting his eyebrows. "The wind will take them away in seconds."

"Yeah, I know, but it's policy with a vehicle out of commission."

"Your boss knows about this right?" He waved his gloved hand around to encompass the storm in general as it began to rain again. The cold sting of the falling precipitation was not fun.

Tadmore shrugged. "Even so."

Once the obligatory task was complete and the back doors locked. Tadmore rounded the hood of Jack's truck.

"Vimy, back seat." Jack said and slick as grease the dog was between the front seats and sitting on the back bench.

The door opened to a blast of wet and cold, then Tadmore was in the passenger seat. He stowed what looked like a gym bag on the floor by his feet. He dropped a closed vinyl clipboard and papers on top of the bag.

The wind now flung ice pellets and did its best to impede Tadmore from shutting the truck door, but he got it closed.

"What? No crime scene tape?" Jack buckled his seatbelt and turned the key. The engine complained for a bit but started.

"Funny." Tadmore grabbed his seatbelt too.

"Where are you going?" Jack put the truck into gear and rolled forward.

"Same as you, Musgrave Landing."

Jack started the wipers to push leaves and debris off the windshield before rolling through the gap in the first fallen tree's trunk.

"I'd have thought you'd be working late tonight, with everything that's going on." Jack waited for Patrick to offer up why he too was traveling this way, but the cop merely shrugged and turned to look out the windshield. "I have other priorities right now."

The wind shook the truck and threw more ice pellets down on them as they negotiated a curve which took them up a hill. "We'll have to take the long way, through Fulford Harbour. The road through Ganges has been closed due to flooding." The highway took them out into an open stretch between two fields.

"Whatever gets us there. I'm not picky." His tone was grim and his jaw set.

Well, Tadmore was going to be a fun passenger.

Jack squinted at the spruce branches and other detritus blowing across his path. It was getting harder to see. The heavy clouds were blocking the afternoon sun, making it seem like early evening.

Chapter Seven

IT TOOK A LOT TO RATTLE Mrs. Roque. Not after the years she'd put in working for the Highmere family. The things the housekeeper had seen and dealt with over the years had instilled a high adversity quotient in her character.

The fact the electricity was out, and she had six guests to feed and look after, not to mention a missing member of the Highmere family, it was all in a day's work. It would take much more than this to knock her off her stride.

Besides, she had to keep going forward. Her staff needed the housekeeper to be calm and collected. She would not allow the situation to make her even raise one heavy eyebrow. Mrs. Roque merely moved into contingency mode.

At least that's what she told Maisy and Tiffany. They didn't need to know her insides fluttered with anxiety about the success of this weekend. The housekeeper would not show anyone she under any stress.

Never mind that a transformer had blown, or a tree had taken out the main power cable or whatever, at the harbour? Tiffany's information was a bit sketchy.

The power company would be out to fix the damage when they could. Mrs. Roque had been told this when she phoned the emergency number. It had been a recording, so who knew when the repairs would actually be done? She compressed her lips thinking about the message, telling her to check their X account, formerly Twitter, to stay up-to-date.

"Yes, because every person in the province has a smartphone, I mean, really." Her disgust at the customer service offered by the utility evident in her tone. She scowled at her own mobile phone as she ended the call and slid the device back into her apron pocket.

The driving rain brought coldness with it. Mrs. Roque didn't think it would be long before heavier snowfall began in earnest, not just the occasional flake. Still, there were things to be thankful for. The guests and staff were safe and dry, if not exactly warm. They would also be well fed. The housekeeper had seen to that.

If she weathered this particular bit of adversity, well, it would only prove more definitively to Alicia she was able to run the big house as a conference centre.

Faint, defused light passed into the dining room from the cloud-choked sky. Without electric light, the oak panelling in the room seem to absorb the available illumination. The housekeeper debated whether to open the drapes further to allow additional light in, but then decided the white sheer curtains should stay in place. Sliding them open farther wouldn't make that much of a difference anyway.

Due to the storm-caused power outage, the housekeeper had Tiffany set up the candelabras at either end of the dining table and Maisy lit the six candles in each. The antique illumination gave the room a golden glow. The shadows cast in the dining room would add to the experience. An odd thought, but somehow, Mrs. Roque felt it appropriate.

The candles appealed more to the housekeeper for the dining room than the wind-up LED lanterns they had scattered about the house at strategic locations.

"Tiffany, can you please call Mr. Willard. He should light the fire in here and the library as soon as possible." Mrs. Roque had the extra rooms closed off too to conserve heat.

"Of course." Tiffany extracted her mobile phone from the pocket of her skirt and tapped the device.

Absently, Mrs. Roque notice the girl frown as she swiped through some screens.

The dining room door which led down the hallway and eventually to the kitchen, in the lower level, swung open. The wiry frame of the seventy-year-old man appeared in the opening. Seymore Willard had a talent for showing up just when Mrs. Roque thought she needed him. He'd been doing just that for years, like he had a sixth sense.

"Ah, Mr. Willard." Mrs. Roque greeted the groundskeeper. "Thank you for coming to make up the fires."

Willard merely grunted and crossed the room to the black marble fronted fireplace. His snow-white hair stuck out from odd angles from under his cap. The familiar ruddy face and tall spare frame had been a fixture almost as long as Mrs. Roque. He was in woolen sock feet so as not to track mud into the house. His battered work boots would no doubt be on the mat by the back door. Even so, wood chips still clung to Willard's faded green work trousers.

The housekeeper had told him yesterday she wanted a fire in the dining room for this evening's dinner. He'd already laid the wood and made the hearth ready. It was also just as well he'd filled the wood box to the left of the hearth. With the power outage, ensuring both fireplaces produced heat became a more important task.

Something else to stay on top of. Mrs. Roque made a mental note to ensure the girls stoked the fires at intervals.

The older man slowly knelt now and extracted a box of matches from inside his dark brown canvas coat. Willard struck a match head on the box. He leaned forward and carefully held the small flame under the crumpled paper, heaped wood shavings, and kindling.

Maisy stepped over to the paneled pocket doors and lit the wall sconces on either side.

"As soon as the fire is well set, I'll call our guests in, and we can serve luncheon." She directed these words to Tiffany, although the younger woman did not respond. She was reading something on her phone. "Tiffany?"

The younger woman's head snapped up to look at the housekeeper. "Yes, Mrs. Roque." She tucked her phone away.

"I'm going to see if all the guests are down. We're serving luncheon in approximately fifteen minutes." She gave her employee a steady look to ensure Tiffany was listening.

"Absolutely." Tiffany turned away to pick up a glass sconce chimney from a side table and handed it to Maisy. These were added to increase the light and shield the candle from door drafts.

Mrs. Roque shook her head as she looked over at the groundskeeper. Their eyes met for a moment in a telling glance.

The check-in process had gone...not horribly, in Mrs. Roque's mind. Tiffany had done the paperwork side of things, and Maisy had taken the guests to their rooms. There had been a tense moment when Kent Westham's credit card had failed to authorize, but he swapped it out for a different one, and it processed. One shouldn't read too much into that, computer glitches happened all the time.

"I'll go check to see if my grandma needs any help," Maisy said after the second wall sconce was lit and covered. She disappeared through the kitchen hallway door and Tiffany followed.

Willard added two split logs on the rapidly burning kindling and adjusted the set of a piece of wood. The fire was noisily creeping through the kindling and beginning to crackle nicely.

Mrs. Roque inhaled to appreciate the smell of the burning wood. Then the snapping of the dry fuel died down to a steady rumble and Willard replaced the screen in front of the fire dogs.

"Seymore, why do I have a bad feeling about this weekend?" She'd use his given name only when they were on their own.

The groundskeeper grasped the side of the marble hearth and hauled himself vertical again. "It will be fine, Aggie. Just keep your cool."

Mrs. Roque smiled at her old friend before he left the room. "That's the key, isn't it?" She gave the room a last long look and followed Mr. Willard.

In the end it took an additional half an hour to gather the six guests together. The atmosphere should have been comfortable, cozy even, with the candlelight and fire, but this wasn't the case. Not in the least.

The authors brought a kind of tension into the room with them. They all wore it like a heavy mantle, with the exception of Ziola Nutt. She had an air of distain for everyone, which included Mrs. Roque and her staff. The publisher made no attempt to hide her attitude. This realization made Mrs. Roque compress her lips in annoyance. Still, she'd been through worse, with Allister Highmere, so she ignored it.

"It doesn't matter where we sit, does it?" Ziola Nutt asked the housekeeper as she sailed around the table carrying her overlarge purse looped over one arm. She placed it on the side table by the window then she crossed over to put her hand on the back of the power seat in the middle. "I like being close to the heat." Her chair was immediately in front of the fire and would put her facing the door.

"Please seat yourself wherever you'd like." Mrs. Roque nodded.

There were three chairs on either side of the table, as the seventh guest was not in attendance and Mrs. Roque had no idea when to expect Sylvia.

Hazel Dell paused beside the housekeeper before taking a seat. She leaned toward Mrs. Roque. "Is Sylvia Highmere not joining us?" Her words were said in a low tone.

"I'm sorry, Miss Sylvia hasn't arrived yet."

Some fleeting emotion Mrs. Roque couldn't identify flashed in the taller woman's eyes. Was that relief?

"Who are you expecting, Hazel?" Ms. Nutt asked as she drew out a chair for herself before Tiffany could and plunked herself down.

"Sylvia Highmere. Her family owns this house and the estate. She was supposed to be our host this weekend. We were...acquainted at school."

"You went to St. Ursula's in Victoria?" Mrs. Roque raised her eyebrows at Hazel.

"Only very briefly. My parents had me transferred to a boarding school abroad." Hazel walked around the table to the far side. She took a seat next to her boss.

"Tiffany went to St. Ursula's too, didn't you Tiffany?" The housekeeper gestured toward the young woman.

For her part, the red-head merely nodded, but kept her eyes on Hazel.

Mrs. Roque was not one to leave well enough alone. Impulsively, she asked, "Did you know Ms. Dell at school, Tiffany?"

The younger woman blinked. "I...don't think so." She shook her head.

"She's is a few years younger than me. I was probably gone before she entered the school." Hazel, having dismissed Tiffany, shook out her linen napkin to slide it across her lap.

Ziola sniffed and shifted hard eyes to her assistant. She shook out her own serviette. "That doesn't say much for an education from St. Ursula's, does it?" She tipped her head at Hazel. "I mean, you're a secretary," then she nodded at

Tiffany. "And you are waiting tables. My, how a classical education has come down in the world." Her features turned haughty with a touch of smug amusement. "Our group is all here. Everyone, take a place, and sit down. I'm starving."

Mrs. Roque noticed the publisher missed the narrow-eyed look Tiffany sent her way. Thankfully the younger woman said nothing and moved on to pulling out a chair for Angela Oakla across from Ziola.

"I'll be an author someday." Hazel's vow was also in a low tone. She nodded thanks at Maisy as she filled the water glass.

Not low enough for her boss not to hear.

"Not if you don't work much, much harder you won't. Don't get me started on the opening chapter on your latest catastrophe of a paranormal romance." She held up a glass from her place setting and waggled it side to side. "Isn't there any wine?"

The three male authors filed into the dining room and took care of seating themselves at empty places.

"Yes." Mrs. Roque drew out the word. Things needed to be done properly, there was a logical flow to serving a meal and when the vintage would arrive in Ziola Nutt's glass. Maisy caught Mrs. Roque's eye and begrudgingly, the housekeeper gave the go ahead for wine.

The first course was a garden salad with raspberry vinaigrette dressing and fresh baked rolls which were already on the table. The diners tucked in.

The seventh guest who was expected, if Mrs. Roque counted Sylvia Highmere as such, had not made contact as yet. In a way, Sylvia's absence kept things simpler and quieter without the youngest Highmere child in attendance.

Still, the housekeeper frowned thinking about Sylvia. Why she hadn't called to say where she was, or when she'd be arriving was a bit concerning. Maybe the storm in progress was the cause, but the housekeeper doubted it. Sylvia was chronically late for life.

Mrs. Roque stifled a sigh. When Sylvia did inevitably show up, things would invariably become complicated as they always did around her. The youngest Highmere craved attention and usually made every situation about herself. Not that the housekeeper could blamed the young woman exactly. Mrs. Olivia had not been the most loving or attentive of mothers. She was sure this affected all of the Highmere offspring in some way. However, it appeared to have influenced Sylvia the most.

Vaguely Mrs. Roque wondered if Sylvia had known Hazel Dell at school as she watched Maisy collect the salad plates and put them on the sideboard. Sylvia was a couple years older than Tiffany.

Anyway, things were odd enough among the acquainted guests already in the house. What harm could one more high maintenance personality do? Still, she'd check after this course to see if Sylvia had left a message.

For now, Mrs. Roque watched with satisfaction as Tiffany began to serve the soup and Maisy filled the wine glasses. The rich smell of butter and herbs in the mushroom broth please the housekeeper. She didn't get much of a chance to stretch her skills in the kitchen these days, so it was nice to know she still had the ability.

"Ziola, I must reiterate the need to discuss what you told me earlier." Kent Westham was seated beside the publisher, on her left.

"I'll get to the subject in my own good time." She said this offhandedly as she raised her wine glass and took a healthy sip.

"Really, Ziola, I sincerely think—," Kent tried to say again.

"Enough," Ziola said sharply. "We are having lunch. Put something into your mouth and chew." She put her glass down. "I didn't come all this way to have you harangue me. Last time I checked, I own the controlling interest in this publishing house, and I'll decide when and where we discuss what subjects." She turned a steely glare at the man beside her.

The other diners exchanged curious looks but said nothing. Bertram Nutt merely ignored the whole exchange and concentrated on his soup.

Mr. Westham, his face flushed red while his lips went flat white, rolled his paper napkin into a ball between his palms. Stopped, and tried to open the crumpled mess, gave up and stuck it into his pocket.

It appeared Ms. Nutt either did not notice or did not care she had upset the author.

Mrs. Roque took a spare serviette off the sideboard and walked it over to Mr. Westham and laid it beside his plate.

He glanced up at her with a pained smile. She stepped back to take up her post by the door.

Maisy began offering the finger sandwiches to the guests on the opposite side of the table following Tiffany. Mrs.

Roque noted with approval how Tiffany continued to place each soup plate in front of the guest in the correct orientation. Both girls moved smoothly and without haste. They had taken to the training well.

Since Tiffany and Maisy appeared to have everything under control, the housekeeper deemed it acceptable for her to return to the kitchen. She needed to check on the evening meal preparations and help Gladys assemble the dessert yet to be served when this course was cleared.

Along with the sandwiches supplied by Jane's café, Gladys had prepped a beef Wellington for Mrs. Roque. She wanted to get downstairs to the kitchen to check on the roast. The recipe was a complicated process and time consuming. Still, the housekeeper wanted to offer something out of the ordinary for their first guests at the conference centre. Something which would make the place stand out over other venues.

Before leaving the dining room, Mrs. Roque changed course first and went to the sideboard to retrieve the tray with the used salad plates collected on it. She passively listened to the guests' conversation for a moment. What did they think about the food? There wasn't much conversation nor compliments. Merely silent eating or 'Can you please pass the pepper?' Of course, on the plus side, there were no complaints either.

As Mrs. Roque placed a hand on the two-way door brass push plate the conversation took another sharp turn and held her in place.

"What's your opening like for your up coming release, Bertram?" Angela looked to her right at their publisher's brother.

Bertram Nutt put his wine glass down and took a deep breath. He lifted his chin, "It was a dark and stormy afternoon..." his rich baritone voice rolled out the words and he waved his hand at the weather happening outside the window to dramatic effect.

"You are not starting your new manuscript with a version of such a tired and overused opening, are you?" Ziola Nutt's lip curled with scorn at her brother's rephrased quote. "I know you're burned out as a writer, but honestly try and make an effort."

"Of course not, Pet." There was an edge to the man's voice as he addressed his sister.

Tray in hand, Mrs. Roque turned to look at the group.

"I was merely making a joke." His hand strayed to his inside tweed jacket pocket. He stopped himself and returned to pick up his soup spoon instead.

Mrs. Roque caught the lapse, and she narrowed her eyes. She'd thought Mr. Nutt had smelt like gin when she'd greeted him and Ziola after they arrived. She'd watched from the bottom of the staircase as the men and women separated to go to their separate rooms. Bertram had been somewhat unsteady on his feet. She made a mental note to ensure at the end of the weekend, the man was sober before he drove away. With their departure scheduled for after breakfast on Monday, Mrs. Roque hoped that would not be an issue.

"You call that humour?" Ziola snorted loudly bringing Mrs. Roque back from her reverie.

"What is the agenda for this afternoon?" Angela cut in and raised her voice over Bertram's response. She looked at Hazel with lifted eyebrows.

Hazel, quick off the mark, jumped in to break the mounting tension between siblings. "After lunch, we will adjourn to the library."

Ziola gave Hazel a tight smile then took back the conversation. "I have last quarter's revenue statements to distribute."

There was a collective 'ooh', from the group. Each one of them perked up at the sound of finding out their financial situation.

Their editor waved a tuna sandwich as if she were paging through the agenda. "After that, we can begin the review of next year's new release schedule."

Hazel looked up to address Ziola again. "I think we will skip the walk in the park, since the weather is so bad, don't you?"

Ziola gave a wave of her fingers to this question as she chewed a bite of sandwich and swallowed. No one else spoke up in favour of going outside.

Touching a napkin to the corners of her mouth, Ziola lifted her head. "I have some exciting news to share with you all, too." There was a distinct smugness in the woman's tone. "I'm sure you will all be very pleased for me, and no doubt supportive."

Curious and uncertain noises were made by the group. Also, a couple of dubious glances were aimed at Ziola. Not all were fans of the woman, Mrs. Roque noted.

"As Kent intimated, there is something I'd like you all to be aware of." She gathered them all in a she looked around the table. "I'm making changes to our distribution channels."

"Again?" Max frowned.

"Zip it, Max," Ziola snapped.

The housekeeper chose to not hang about in the dining room to hear anymore. Even though this weekend had not begun as she'd planned, she was determined to make this group booking the best it could be under the circumstances. Unfortunately, there was no way to make the guests all get along.

Still, Mrs. Roque was confident she and her staff would give the writers retreat a weekend they would never forget. Storm stayed or not.

Chapter Eight

GLADYS GLANCED OVER her right shoulder as the door opened. "How's it going?"

Aggie Roque walk past the pantry and into the kitchen proper. She stopped abruptly.

When the older woman said nothing, but stared at Gladys, she returned her attention back to arranging sliced strawberries on a flan base.

"What is that on your head?" Mrs. Roque demanded.

"A headlamp, Aggie. Welcome to the twenty-first century." She smiled to soften her response. "These high-arched windows don't let in much light. And I find those windup lanterns next to useless." The headlamp actually belonged to her friend, Arlie Birch. He'd dropped by the big house kitchen briefly after the power had gone out. Partly, she suspected to check on her and partly to give her the light. His excuse had been to get her keys to check on her cat. She let him have his little fiction, it touched her the man was concerned for her. It was also cute how he'd gently adjusted the lamp so her curly grey hair was out of the way, and not caught under the strap. "All is going well?"

Mrs. Roque shook her head slightly at the sight of Gladys' head gear. "Yes, as good as I anticipated." The other woman sounded neutral if not pleased. "The lunch is going fine. Maisy and Tiffany work well together." She took the salad dishes over to the dishwashing counter and deposited the load to be dealt with later.

Gladys made agreeing noises and slid the plate of sliced kiwi closer to the dessert construction. Deftly, she arranged the green fruit to allow the red strawberries to peek through.

Aggie Roque could be a tough taskmaster, so any type of praise was a good thing. Gladys planned to share the compliment with the girls later.

Straightening from leaning over the kitchen island Gladys walked over to the washing up sink. Put in the plug and turned on the water. "Maisy is grateful for the opportunity to work with you." She nudged the lantern on the counter, to shine on to the running tap.

"I wish I could get by with just myself and one other, but it's a lot of work looking after this many people for three days."

Gladys added liquid soap to the sink. "Especially now the electricity is out. You're also not as spry as you used to be either."

"True, and Tiffany has good references and a good work ethic like Maisy. She's great with the paperwork, Tiffany got all the registrations processed before the power went out. Efficiency is important too."

"Yes, exactly." Gladys rinsed a dish.

The housekeeper sighed causing Gladys to glance her way. Mrs. Roque had begun the process of setting up the manual perk coffee pot to be ready before the dessert went out.

"Problem?" Gladys prompted. She went back to the kitchen island to begin ferrying bowls and utensils to load into the sink.

"I'd like to ask the girls to shut off their phones while they are working. Those devices are so disruptive, and they distract them from their work. We need this weekend to run smoothly."

Gladys lifted her eyebrows but didn't remark on the royal 'We' she heard in Aggie's tone. God love her, Aggie Roque liked to put on airs of importance once in a while. No doubt because she worked for 'the family' in the 'big house'.

Instead, Gladys focused on the mild criticism. "If you told them to shut off their phones, I doubt you'd get anyone to work here at all. These days most people feel they have to keep in touch at all times. It's just a fact of life now."

"Mobile phones do have an off button, you know." The housekeeper's tone was lofty. Coffee made, Mrs. Roque crossed to the gas stove and put the pot on a back burner to percolate. She then went to the island to inspect the newly assembled dessert. "But you're right about the phones, I suppose." She gave each round platter a turn. "These are lovely, Gladys."

"Thank you."

"The most I insist upon is their devices must run on quiet mode. I don't want to hear a bunch of pings and pongs while they are serving our guests."

"Mm, I understand, and I completely agree." Gladys began rinsing dishes in the first sink and then dropped them into the second with hot water and soap. "Jane has the same rule."

"Are these desserts ready now?"

Gladys returned to the work area and gave the displayed fruit selection one more final tweak and called it good. "Yes, the flans are ready to be served whenever you want them taken to the dining room."

"Good, I'll just whip the cream to put on top. The diners are still on their soup course. We have lots of time yet." The housekeeper snagged the lantern off the counter and placed it beside the commercial stand-mixer.

Gladys pursed her lips as she looked at the electric appliance but said nothing. The housekeeper wasn't planning on using the appliance, surely.

The flans, one a medley of different fruit, the other was comprised of only strawberries with dark chocolate drizzled over them. These Gladys placed on the counter by the door which led up a series of five steps and the short hall to the dining room door.

The cheesecakes were waiting to be served after each of the two evening meals. No expense had been spared. Aggie's guests might have to be rolled out the door at the end of the three days. At least the fruit would be a break from refined sugar.

Mrs. Roque went to a wall cupboard and extracted, what to Gladys looked like a medieval torture device of wire and stainless steel. She walked over to get a better look. "I haven't seen one of those mechanical wire whisks in years. Decades."

Sliding open the glass-front fridge, Mrs. Roque extracted a stainless-steel bowl of whipping cream. She placed the bowl on the counter next to a canister of icing sugar.

"Ah." Gladys realized the housekeeper's plan was. "Chantilly whipped cream, that's a nice touch."

"This hand mixer was my mother's. I never throw away anything and with a power outage like this, it will come in handy." The housekeeper dusted the liquid whipping cream with a quarter cup of the powdered sugar. "The Cuisinart is next to useless right now."

"Too true."

The two-way door opened as Maisy pushed it with her hip and came in with a tray of used soup plates and utensils. She saw her grandmother and smiled, then crossed to the dish sink.

Gladys went over to give her a hand with the chore.

"Well, it won't be a boring weekend, I don't think." Maisy's tone was understated as she began unloading her tray.

"Really?" Her grandmother began to rinse the new load of dishes. "What's happening?"

Mrs. Roque had begun turning the crank on the manual beaters to whip the cream. The noise was significant and combined with the chugging of the coffee percolator, Gladys was sure their conversation was drowned out.

Maisy shook her head as the pair worked companionably together. "I don't think any of those people like each other very much. Especially the brother and sister. Talk about snarky, nasty remarks, wow. I could put this all in a book."

They both glanced at Mrs. Roque who was concentrating on her task.

"I suppose, as long as you change the names to protect the guilty."

"Maybe." Maisy gave her grandmother a wink and then exited with a clean tray.

Gladys took a white cotton cloth from the stack by the utility room door and the sanitizer spray bottle to clean the kitchen island countertop.

Seconds later, Tiffany entered the kitchen carrying in yet more plates and glasses.

Gladys crossed to the kitchen door to help the girl. She frowned, Tiffany's pale complexion sported twin red spots, one for each cheek. "I can take that." She moved to the counter next to the oversized sink and after setting down the tray, looked back at the young woman. "Is everything all right, Tiffany?"

She blinked, shook her head and mutely moved to the pantry.

Gladys' lips twisted in puzzlement, but she said nothing as she finished dealing with the last sandwich plates. It was a good job the big house used a propane water heater. The dishwasher was no use, and heating water on the stove was fiddly.

Gladys heard Tiffany heave a shaky sigh and glanced the young woman's way.

Tiffany met Gladys' eyes as she picked up a full crystal decanter of white wine. "Everything is going well." Her tone sounded flat to Gladys' ear.

Determining the plates could soak for a moment, Gladys walked over to the pantry. She looked up at the tall redhead. "I meant with you. You seem a bit upset. Did someone say something to you?"

Dark brown eyes blinked, and Tiffany shook her head. "No, nothing like that. The power is out at home too. I was thinking about my family, my mother is on oxygen." Her voice trailed away.

Gladys scoured her memory but couldn't recall exactly what Belinda Zach's illness was. Not that it mattered. "You should give them a call, make sure everything is all right then."

Tiffany shifted her eyes sideways to where Mrs. Roque was in a whipping cream frenzy. "We aren't supposed to make personal calls during work hours."

"You never mind Mrs. Roque's rules. Sometimes she forgets we are human beings and not just employees, or in my case, contractors." Gladys sniffed. "Go call your family. I'll cover for you." Gladys put her hand out for the wine decanter.

The young woman hesitated for only a moment, then she thrust the drink into Gladys' hands and bolted for the back doorstep.

Smoothly, Gladys glided past Mrs. Roque and out the door leading to the dining room. She wasn't exactly dressed for serving guests, in her flour sack apron over her usual jeans and flowered top. Still, most people ignored the staff in her experience anyway.

As she reached for the push plate of the other two-way door into the dining room, it swung opened and she had to jump back, or the wine would have gone sailing out of her hands.

"Oh, good." Maisy took the wine from her grandmother. "Mr. Nutt has run dry again. I don't think he knows the wine is non-alcoholic," she said in a low whisper and then gave her grandmother an impish grin. "And I'm not going to tell him either."

AT THREE O'CLOCK, MAISY was directed to serve refreshments to the guests. As she approached the library, she could hear raised voices. She couldn't make out what was being said, but the volume could not be ignored. Could they still be arguing about the same topic from lunch?

Straightening her spine, Maisy quietly opened the library door wide and entered pushing the tea cart. The smell of the oiled leather, beeswax, and ancient paper greeted her. So too, the cozy aroma of the burning fire.

Briefly she wondered what it would be like to curl up with a book on the settee and absorb the heat as she closed the door. A log shifted and the wood crackled behind the massive brass firedogs in the grey slate fireplace. It was noticeably warmer in the dining room, kitchen, and here in the library, but the halls were at least five degrees colder.

Maisy rubbed her hands together to warm them up. She had been instructed to get in and get out as quickly as possible, unless she was asked to stay and serve. Otherwise, the guests could look after themselves. There was still a lot to do with regard to the evening's dinner prep.

Her grandmother had stayed and helped clean up after lunch, since washing dishes had reverted to the old school method but was now gone.

Mrs. Roque had given both her and Tiffany detailed instructions on how to comport themselves around the guests. Eyes downcast and don't speak unless spoken to.

Sure, like this was the 1900's or something.

Maisy kept this thought to herself in front of Mrs. Roque. No point in rocking the boat, as Arlie had told her. "It's important in your work life to learn how to 'play the game'. Each employer has rules and opinions you might not agree with, but you still have to follow. When you are the boss, you can change the rules." Arlie always had good advice.

Not that it mattered in front of these people. The heated conversation kept going as Maisy pushed the wheeled trolley into the room. She continued with the cart of hot and cold beverages along with plates of cookies, small cakes, and scones over to the sideboard along the windows.

Rain cascaded down the large windowpanes in a never-ending waterfall. It was brighter in here, and easy to see the storm's full strength as it bashed itself against the rocks along shore.

There was only so much light the windup LED lanterns could give out. One sat in the middle of the table between the couches and another on the mantel.

The windows had their drapes open, allowing defused light to streamed in. The dark black clouds were effectively blocking the fading December sun.

Maisy glanced across the room and found Ziola, Hazel, Angela, and Bertram clustered around the fireplace sitting on two couches or what her grandmother sometimes called davenports.

While Max Lintlaw and Kent Westham had repositioned a pair of scarlet winged-back chairs to one end of the settees to form a horseshoe around the fireplace.

Mrs. Roque would not be happy about the guests moving the antique Queen Anne chairs, let alone the drag marks across the red and gold Persian carpet. Normally, the matched set bracketed a round table and fit into the niche in front of the bay window. Not that Maisy was going to say anything to anyone. As long as nothing was ruined, why did it matter?

"What do you mean you're changing the royalty percentages?" Max was leaning forward in his chair, long fingered hands resting on his knees as he pinned the publisher in the corner of the settee with his frown. Or rather tried too. Ziola Nutt's look completely unmoved by his glower.

Ah, so a new topic. Maisy began moving teacups and saucers from the bottom shelf and placing them on the crisp white fabric runner on the sideboard.

"I just can't believe this." Angela was shaking her head. Her green-streaked and black hair swung over her shoulders. "It's too high handed, even for you, Ziola." Maisy noticed for the first time Ms. Oakla had painted her fingernails a dark green too. She decided she like the shade.

"Dunn Wolf Publishing is already taking fifty-five percent of our sales now. Increasing your cut to sixty doesn't make financial sense for most of us. We might as well go the self-publishing route." Max's distain for this business decision was evident.

"It's a good thing most writers have day jobs." Bertram's glum face perked up when he spied Maisy at the other end of the room. No doubt the prospect of further refreshments did the trick.

"Go ahead and self-publish." For her part, Ziola Nutt seemed unconcerned with the anger swirling around her. "You won't do any better than staying with me. In fact, you'll do much worse. I have the distribution contracts. I have the network platform built to leverage my relationship with each vendor. You won't be able to get into bookstores without me." If anything, she was smug. "Besides, it isn't me who is demanding the increase." Ziola Nutt waved away Lintlaw's argument. "It's the other partner in Dunn Wolf. They say we aren't covering our costs."

"Is it possible to see Dunn Wolf's financial statements?" Kent asked. "Maybe there is something I can do."

Ziola gave him a long quizzical look. "No, and no there isn't." She turned her head to look the group of authors over with a disdainful eye. "Dunn Wolf is a business, not a charity." These words were said with a patronizing tone, like none of the other authors could understand anything she was saying.

"I really think we need to stop—" Hazel interjected.

"Stop Ziola? Good luck." Bertram tucked away his silver flask as he rose to his feet. The author's face was flushed, his nose was a particularly reddish hue. The argument must have been going on for some time.

"You stop, Bertram. Your manners are insufferable," his sister snapped.

Maisy hated to interrupt the conversation, this was private business, and she could just leave them to get their own refreshments.

Bertram sent a dismissive wave toward Ziola. He turned and wandered over to Maisy and she took the opportunity to ask for direction. "I hope it's all right that I brought in the tea and coffee?" Maisy asked, looking at first Bertram and then at Ziola Nutt.

"Of course, of course, I was becoming peckish myself anyway. Your timing is very near perfect." Bertram folded his hands behind his back to peruse the offered refreshments. Maisy handed him a small plate to collect some treats.

"Anything to warm us up. This place is a refrigerator." The publisher's tone was cutting as she wiggled herself forward on the settee in preparation for rising to her feet.

Bertram slowly pivoted his bulk toward his sister. "For you, that would be impossible. Your heart is as cold as a ditch digger's well. You should be the soul of generosity. You've had every advantage." Then he shook his head, lips curled back into an unpleasant expression. Bertram walked stiffly away to the bay window to look out at the storm as he nibbled one of the cookies he'd selected.

Ziola lifted her chin in an arrogant manner and turned her head away from her brother.

Maisy swallowed but felt something had to be said. "I'm sorry if you are cold. The power outage is village wide. It's worse on Vancouver Island, there are thousands of people without electricity."

Tiffany had brought her and Mrs. Roque up to date after her call home to her father. The widespread storm had knocked power out in most major centres. The worst was the smaller areas who relied on power lines strung on poles for electricity. The massive trees the area boasted were the culprits. With the rocky soil, shallow roots had let go. Many giant cedars had fallen to block roads and pulled down the power lines.

The utility had told Mrs. Roque it could be days before electricity was restored. Crews had to get the trees out of the way first before the lines could be repaired.

Maisy was not going to mention any of this to the guests. There was enough anger in the room as it was. So, she smoothly continued to set out the tea things on the sideboard.

"It's the storm." Angela said nodding knowingly at the other writers.

"Yes, thank you Angela, we'd about figured that out." Ziola's tone was dry as she pushed her bulk out of the cushions and made her way forward to the refreshments. "Miss," Ziola addressed Maisy. "Will there be any problem with dinner tonight?" The publisher's eyes drilled into Maisy, and she froze for a moment.

Then the younger woman lifted her chin. "None at all. Our kitchen appliances are run off propane. Dinner will be served at seven. Drinks will be available in here, at six. The library has the largest fireplace, and our groundskeeper will keep the wood box well stocked."

Ziola sniffed and filled a plate to overflowing from the offered baking.

Max Lintlaw walked over to the sideboard and selected a teacup and saucer combination from the tray. "Tea for me, please." He gave Maisy a pleasant smile as she took his cup and filled it. She breathed shallowly through her mouth around the man. He used way too much cologne, and the scent made her nose itch.

Completely unaware of her reaction, she watched him take a cake plate and add selected treats, one of each, of the Victorian sponge cake and cookies before taking a serviette. Finally, he took the china cup Maisy had filled for him from the large black and white china teapot. "Thank you." He returned to his chair to enjoy his laden plate.

"Upstairs will be freezing." Hazel leaned back in her seat. "There aren't any fireplaces in the rooms."

"I am sorry, no, not anymore." Maisy poured coffee for Angela who had come up next. "All the bedrooms had been converted to electric heat some time back." Well before Maisy came to Musgrave Landing if the size and construction of the floorboard heaters were any clue. "The house was built in 1908, when coal boilers were the main method for heating."

"Gang, maybe we should just go home?" Hazel addressed the other authors. Her tone was full of concern.

"What time is the next ferry?" Kent offered Maisy his teacup for filling.

"I'm sorry, all ferries are cancelled. Probably until after the storm has passed. We were told the service will be back in operation as soon as BC Ferries can. We are all in the same boat, I'm afraid."

Everyone now had a cup of something in their hands, even Bertram, although he'd topped his tea up with the contents of his flask.

The others also held a cake plate or balanced it on the arm of a chair or on their knee. Maisy edged toward the door hoping to make her escape.

"You can stay to top us up as needed." Ziola was holding her cup out to Maisy and waved it at the large teapot. "Same again, milk, no lemon."

"Of course." Maisy so wanted to roll her eyes at the woman's attitude. She went to the trolley to pick up the teapot and began refills, offering the milk and sugar from a small tray as she went.

No wonder Mrs. Roque said to keep their eyes downcast when dealing with the guests. "Don't make eye contact, girls. It makes things easier all round."

"What did you mean, Bertram?" Kent stood and crossed the room to stand a few feet from the man. "You've intrigued me. Earlier you said Ziola should be generous. Tell us why you think that should be the case?"

Kent had abandoned his dishes on the seat of the Queen Anne chair. Maisy walked over and extracted them for placement on the bottom of the tea trolley. She looked back to see what the man had done with his napkin but realized he still held the thing. Rolling the paper into a ball between his palms as he waited for the publisher's brother to answer him.

Bertram grunted. "Not my story to tell." Although he sounded like he wanted to be prodded into it.

"If you know what's going on, you need to tell us," Angela said to Bertram.

He waggled his bald head side to side and then pivoted on his heel to take in the room.

Maisy quietly collected used plates and listened with interest. No way was she leaving now.

"Ziola has some smashing news." Distain and bitterness coated Bertram's words. "Aren't you going to tell everyone your news, Pet?" He waved the flask about has he spoke.

"I was waiting for an opportune moment." Ziola selected a third lemon filled delight from her plate, ignoring her brother's suggestion, stalling.

Bertram lifted his chin and breathed in deeply. His exhale was harsh. "Let me help you then. Everyone, pay attention."

The other four people focused on the large man. "Ziola has been approached by Aticus Blackwing of WingDing Productions." It took Bertram a second attempt to put the silver cap decorative cover back over the inner white which sealed his flask. "She is currently in negotiations to turn the Pacific Strangers books into a streaming series." He made to slip the flask into his jacket pocket and gave the group of authors an owlish slow blink.

Max was on his feet and moved forward to grab Bertram by the arm. "Are you completely serious?"

"Of course I'm completely serious." Bertram extracted his sleeve from the other man's grasp. "We are all owed a substantial amount of money from this deal in my mind."

The other three by the fireplace began to comment on this bit of news, however Bertram held up his hands for silence. "Unfortunately for us, Ziola has no plans to share the royalties with the likes of us."

"What?" Max rounded on Ziola. "We all worked on those books. We have a right to the profits too."

"I own the rights." Ziola calmly licked frosting off her index finger. She kept her eyes averted from the five authors. To Maisy it seemed as though the publisher wasn't in the least worried about the others reaction. As if she couldn't be bothered with the rest of them, the group of lesser beings were of no consequence to her.

"You can't do that. She can't do that, can she?" Angela looked to Max.

"I'll be contacting my agent." Max gave Ziola a pointed look which she waved away. "You should too, Angela. We all need to." He stepped close to the fire, putting his back to the flames.

"I'll be contacting my lawyer, for sure." Hazel took a drink from her coffee cup.

Kent strode over to stand in front of Ziola. He gave her a narrowed-eye look. "I can't believe you didn't tell us."

She gave him a bored sigh. "There is nothing you can do about it. I own the controlling interest in the company, I own the contracts, and I own the video rights to my books." She looked pointedly at Hazel. "You were all merely consultants."

In a quiet intense voice Kent stated, "Even if we weren't credited for our work, you still owe us."

"Bertram," Hazel got to her feet and slowly advanced across the carpet to stand beside Max as though they were in solidarity. "When did you find out about this deal?"

For the briefest of moments Bertram looked uncomfortable. Then he cleared his throat and continued with forward momentum. "I found out by accident. Ziola was dining with Blackwing at the Shipping News restaurant two nights ago. I was in the bar. He passed her a bunch of papers." He shrugged beefy shoulders. "I got curious."

Maisy refilled the serving plates of scones, biscuits, and cookies from the lower tray of the trolley. At the mention of the exclusive restaurant in Victoria, she picked up the larger pot and walked around to refill cups for those who had coffee and allowed her to stretch out her time in the room. Things were getting interesting.

Bertram turned his frosty gaze on his sister. "I saw you."

"So what?" Ziola snagged another frosted sugar cookie. "My deal has nothing to do with you."

"I made my way over to speak to Blackwing while you were trying to get chatty with Imogen McKnight. Why you'd want to waste your time with an internet gossip blogger is beyond me."

"Bertram, focus." Hazel snapped her fingers at him and advanced on the man to poke him in the shoulder. "What did Blackwing tell you?"

The bald man compressed his lips as he frowned at Hazel. He moved back a step from Ziola's assistant, to take command of the room again.

Apparently, Bertram liked dramatics the same as his sister. Maisy moved past them both and took up her station by the cart where she had the best view of all of the guests.

Bertram cleared his throat; he wasn't happy to have his story interrupted. "Just what I said, try and keep up." Once he had everyone's attention he continued, "As well as taking an option out on the film rights, his company has contracted Ziola to be the on-set consultant for the initial thirteen-episode season. With an option to expand the contract after the series is picked up by Netflix or Prime or some other streaming service."

After a brief shocked silence, these words caused a new wave of outrage from the rest.

"The amount of money this means is...it's huge." Angela flung up her hands.

"I know there is a copy of the contract in her immense handbag. She was reading it while we drove here." A gleam entered Bertram's eyes. He was pleased to have upstaged his sister.

Ziola was busy glaring daggers back at her brother. "This wasn't your story to tell. You are always stealing my thunder. I planned to make the announcement at dinner."

"At least I don't steal from you."

A gasp of outrage expelled from Ziola's massive chest. She gained her feet and stalked up to him and hissed in his face. "I have never stolen—"

"You did, and you know it." He shook his beefy index finger in front of her nose. "You stole my work from me!"

Hazel crossed to Ziola's former seat. The mentioned bag was on the floor, propped up against the sofa. She rummaged around inside the purse. "Ah ha!" She extracted a sheaf of papers. "Two hundred thousand dollars." Hazel shook the paperwork at Ziola.

Ziola swung around and bared her teeth at her assistant. "How dare you?" She marched back to Hazel and snatch the bag and contract out of her assistant's hands.

As bedlam erupted, Maisy made a discrete getaway.

Chapter Nine

PATRICK TADMORE WASN'T going to confide in Jack Birch, not unless he had to.

While it was true, he rented the small apartment above Jane's Eats and Treats and he knew Jack, Jane, and Arlie pretty well, this situation wasn't something he was comfortable sharing, at least not yet. He also knew Maisy Wyatt. Not as well as he'd like to, but it was early days.

For one, Patrick wasn't exactly sure of Jack's part in all this, and his sister had never said one way or another if Jack was involved. Not even when she'd called her brother during her break at the hospital, after she'd read Miles' text about his decision to take the ferry to Musgrave Landing,

Up until now, he'd always assumed his ex-brother-in-law was Miles' father. At the moment he just wanted to get to Musgrave Landing and find Miles. Some of the things the kid got up to when his mother was on shift, drove him up a wall. He had no kids of his own yet and it was like as his own dad used to say. "Patrick, you don't get to pick your family.

You just have to get along with them." Even so, sometimes Miles could be a challenge.

Thinking about family, he pulled out his mobile phone and selected Miles' number. He listened to it ring six times. The kid was not going to pick up. Miles could be stubborn that way.

Patrick switched to text. 'Miles where are you?' He waited five minutes for a response. When nothing happened, no reply or acknowledgement, Patrick shook his head.

What could the kid be playing at? He swayed to the left as Jack drove them around more tree limbs. So far, they were making decent time on the shore road even if they were going the long way home.

The next text he sent to Miles read, 'I'll be there in about an hour.'

It wasn't lost on him Jack noticed him texting. Although the older man did not ask or say anything about it, but that wasn't unusual. Most men didn't generally comment on what another guy did, so it wasn't surprising.

Unexpectedly, a warm tongue licked the side of his neck.

"Geeze." Patrick jumped then chuckled and reached back to scratch Vimy's head.

"There's a chew stick by you're feet. I think that's what he wants." Jack slowed to avoid larger tree parts on the leaf-strewn road as the windshield wipers battled the sideways rain.

The constable leaned down and found the piece of rawhide and offered it to the dog.

Vimy gently took the chew treat and lay down on the back seat with a contented sigh.

Patrick stared at the screen on his phone and came to a decision. "Jane and Arlie pay attention to every ferry arrival, don't they?"

"Pretty much. It helps them figure out if they have enough coffee and food ready to sell. Plus, my dad likes to stay informed on the comings and goings."

Arlie Birch was a busy body, everyone knew it. However, this time Arlie's powers of observation were going to be used for good. "So, if a kid got off the ferry by himself, they'd notice him?"

"Probably. Is someone missing?" Jack glanced over to Patrick. His expression was serious.

"Not officially. No Amber Alert, but I'm looking for a boy around ten years old." Should he give Jack more information?

"Call Dad. He'll tell you if a kid has been seen." Jack rattled off a number for Tadmore.

Patrick waited impatiently for Arlie Birch to pick up, although he stilled his tapping fingers on the arm rest.

"City morgue. You stab 'em, we slab 'em." Jack's dad said on speaker.

Jack merely shook his head and kept his eyes on the road.

"Mr. Birch, this is Patrick Tadmore."

"Hey Pat, what's goin' on?"

"Have you seen a young boy around ten years old get off the ferry by himself?"

"Miles Iverson?"

"That's him." Relief flooded Patrick's tone; he couldn't help it.

"He's right here, did you want to talk to him?"

Patrick did not hesitate. "Yes, thanks."

There was a brief pause followed by a tentative voice. "Hello?"

"Miles? It's Uncle Patrick." He managed to keep his voice even.

"Hi." The voice got fainter. The boy thought he was in trouble, which he was. Still, that would not help the situation.

"Hi. Your mum doesn't know where you are. Have you contacted her yet?" Patrick wanted to say a whole lot more about irresponsibility, running off without his mother's permission, and worrying her when she was caught at the hospital due to the accidents the storm was causing.

"I sent her a text. I didn't think she'd care. I was off school anyway." His tone was defensive.

"Did she answer you?"

"Yeah, she's not happy. She's worried about the storm. I'll be back before she gets home."

"No, you won't. The ferries are cancelled from Musgrave Landing and I'm fairly sure the outbound from Vesuvius is now cancelled too. Can you stay put at the café until I get there?"

"If they don't close up, I guess?"

"Let me speak to Mr. Birch." Another pause.

"Miles can hang with me as long as he needs to." Arlie Birch's voice came over the device. He's helping me around here. I've been feeding him in exchange."

"Thank you, I appreciate that and so will his mum."

"No problem."

"Jack and I are on Coast Road. We should be there inside an hour or so."

"No rush, I get that it is weather permitting. If we close up now that the power is out, I'll take Miles over to our house. I'm just waiting for Jane."

"Tell my dad to stay on the phone, please?"

"Absolutely." Patrick did as Jack asked and held the phone out to the other man.

"Dad, is Jane around?" Jack raised his voice to be heard over the engine and the wind. He steered them around part of a tree limb as he spoke. The branch was three feet thick and must have snapped off from somewhere up slope of the road.

"No, she's taken more food up to Highmere House, their writers retreat thingy is still on even with the storm. I'll tell her you are on your way home."

"If something more comes up, I'll send a text."

"Sounds good, be safe, son."

"Thanks, Dad."

Patrick ended the call. He felt better knowing Miles was with Arlie. The old guy didn't take crap from anyone and doubted Miles would get away with anything under Arlie's watchful eye.

"So." Jack glanced at him briefly before turning his eye back to the road. "What aren't you telling me?"

Tadmore had dealt with some fairly distasteful tasks in his seven years as an RCMP constable. None of it prepared him to state why Miles had gone to Musgrave Landing, at least not to Jack.

"Miles Iverson is my sister's kid."

"Yeah, I figured that out." Jack nodded. "How is Mari Ann?" He raised his eyebrows in inquiry.

Patrick stared at Jack. "What do you know about the situation?"

Jack merely smiled. "You might want to give your sister a call."

EVERYTHING WAS GOING fine until the guests' mobile phones needed to be recharged.

The group of writers trooped over to the foyer and up to the counter where Maisy was filing the processed credit card receipts. Tiffany was occupied with sorting accounts payable invoices. Earlier Jane arrived and stayed to assist Mrs. Roque in the kitchen so the pair were not needed.

"I need to make some calls, it's very important." Hazel was at the front of the line.

Maisy glanced back at Tiffany. The other young woman bent her head as she wrote a note on a delivery invoice from the butcher. This told Maisy that Tiffany was not going to engage with the group of guests, she was on her own. Plastering a pleasant smile on her face, Maisy crossed to the counter. "How can I help?"

"I'd like to know...we'd like to know, how we can charge our phones." Hazel clutched her smart device in her left hand and waved it for emphasis.

"Do you have something we can use? Like a battery inverter or some kind of generator. We simply cannot be out of touch with the outside world." Max pushed past Hazel to get to the counter.

Maisy noted the serious concern in the authors' faces. With no electricity to charge the devices, the writers were no doubt upset at being cut off. Her answer would not please them.

"I'm sorry, no, I don't think we do." It sounded like a good idea for the conference centre to have an alternative method to offer the guests. However, she doubted Mrs. Roque would have made provision for this type of situation.

Max frowned at Maisy's answer.

Kent stood back from the others. Hands in his trouser pockets, he appeared to be unconcerned about the lack of opportunity to check his social media pages or receive incoming messages. "I for one, don't mind. It's refreshing. Gives me a rest." He smiled at Maisy and then wandered away from the desk.

Ziola elbowed past Hazel and Max to gain access to Maisy. The look in the publisher's eye made Maisy decide to keep the oak countertop between herself and the aggressive woman hugging her large purse.

"Don't you have any kind of a generator?" The publisher flattened one hand on the countertop. "You must have." She persisted, slapping her palm on the wood again. Her black opal rings flashed, catching the overhead light.

"No, not as far as I know. Let me go ask Mrs. Roque, just in case."

Ziola slapped the counter for a third time in frustration. "Fine, you do that."

Maisy rounded the counter and walked briskly away from the literary crowd. Once around the corner, she hot-footed it to the back of the house. Picking up her long skirt, she took the stairs down to the kitchen two at a time.

She found the housekeeper sliding an industrial-sized roasting pan back into the propane-fueled oven.

While the tempting aroma of beef Wellington filled the warm air, it was the oven's heat Maisy appreciated most. Her fingers were going numb upstairs. Maisy stopped beside the stove and lifted her hands near the vent. "Mrs. Roque, I have a question from the guests."

"What can I do for you, dear?" Mrs. Roque placed the aqua-blue silicone oven mitts, on the left countertop beside the oversized commercial stove. Then braced a fist on one hip to give Maisy her full attention.

"The guests are asking how they can charge their devices. I don't think we have a battery generator, do we?" She plunged her warmer hands into the pockets of her black sweater and resolved to get her gloves from her coat at the first opportunity.

"No, I didn't think of it. Mr. Willard has an older model, its diesel, but it won't accommodate modern devices. It's wired in to keep the refrigeration on in the carriage house but does not extend to outlets."

"Is there a land line here or at the carriage house?"

"No, I'm sorry. The phone lines were disconnected here. Most everyone has a mobile phone now, so, we didn't think we'd need to hook them up again. The internet connection has the capability to run conference calls over something called DSL."

Maisy nodded in understanding. "And it's out, due to no electricity."

"Exactly." Mrs. Roque lifted one thick finger to rub her eye. Had the woman developed an eye twitch from this demanding group of guests? If so, Maisy could completely understand. "There is an old school land line at the carriage house. Unfortunately, I had Tiffany nip out to check if it was operational, but it wasn't."

"Probably from storm damage."

"No doubt." The housekeeper nodded. "Did none of them think to bring a car charger? They could run their vehicles and charge their phone. Not that anyone should do that for too long." The housekeeper rested her other hip against the warm stove. "Pollution is a factor."

Maisy grabbed onto the kernel of hope the older woman had given her. "I'll go back and suggest that option, thank you."

Apparently, smartphone car chargers were not a viable option either. Maisy discovered this upon her return upstairs. No one had thought to bring a cable with them.

"Even if we did, what makes you think all our phones are the same?" Hazel tried to tower over Maisy. Since the younger woman was of matching height, there could be no intimidation factor. Exasperated, Hazel shook her head. "The plug ends are all different."

All Maisy could say was, "Sorry, no one anticipated we'd have this power outage. We don't have a generator available at this time." She refrained from asking how could these people blame the conference centre staff?

Adults needed to plan their own lives and anticipate their own contingencies. Wasn't that what her grandmother was always telling her?

"I need to call my lawyer." Hazel looked down at her phone. "I've only got twenty-three percent charge left."

"Oh, go take a pill, Hazel." Ziola waved her assistant back from the counter, completely unconcerned with the other woman's plight. "It's not like you have any chance of squeezing into my deal. A lawyer won't help you."

Hazel fired off a hard look toward Ziola as she bared her teeth. "Pardon me, if I don't take your word for it. I can't believe I'm stuck here with you. You traitor."

"You are just jealous." Ziola's tone dripped with condescension. "You're crowding me, Hazel." The publisher gave her assistant an elbow, making the other woman fall back a step from her boss.

Maisy saw angry tears in Hazel's eyes.

The publisher looped her purse handle over her wrist and braced her hands on the shiny counter again. "What do you mean you don't have a generator? How can any business these days operate without some kind of backup power? And at a time like this?" Ziola used one hand to rub her mid drift absently as she spoke.

"As I said," Maisy kept her tone even. "We don't have a generator, yet. I'm sure it's one of the things Highmere House will correct in the future. We've only been open a short time." She had no idea but doubted Mrs. Roque would ever let herself be caught short like this again. The housekeeper wasn't the type to take failure lying down. Not that this was truly any type of catastrophe on her part exactly. No one could think of everything.

"That does us little good now." Max interjected even though there was no heat in his tone, merely resignation. "What about land lines? We all need to make calls to our business contacts and families."

"Again, I'm sorry. The estate had the lines in the house disconnected when the place was mothballed in the 1990's. There is a phone in the carriage house, but the line is dead. Probably storm damage somewhere." Maisy glanced at Tiffany and the girl nodded her head. "All I know is," Maisy turned back to the publisher. "Tiffany checked earlier, and there was no dial tone."

"Well, this is just wonderful." Ziola pushed her bulk away from the reception area and turned toward the staircase.

"I bet everyone all over the island is in the same boat." Angela said then stepped out of Ziola's way after she received a menacing look.

"And why don't you have some kind of elevator for goodness' sake? This is intolerable, making your guest scale these stairs every five minutes." Ziola flung her mustard-coloured scarf around her neck and put her foot on the bottom tread of the grand staircase. Her eyes lit on her assistant again and narrowed to menacing slits. "This is all your fault. If you were better at planning, things like this would not happen. You should have asked about this very type of situation."

Her assistant rolled her eyes. "Who would have thought to ask any hotel or conference facility how we'd charge our devices in the event of a power outage?" Her jaw jutted out.

"I would have." Ziola's tone was haughty. The other woman leaned on the thick banister railing and climbed the lower steps one at a time. She slowly ascended the oak staircase with her right arm braced across her stomach.

Maisy frowned, wondering if the older woman was completely all right.

For her part, Hazel breathed in deeply while gritting her teeth. Maisy noted the other woman's jaw flex with the effort to control her anger after her boss' accusations. She took a moment to glare at Ziola's back and then addressed the other three writers.

"I suggest everyone turns their phone off to conserve what little charge we have." She looked at each of them as she managed to keep her tone level. "We may be here a while." With that, Hazel turned on her heel and strode away to the library. In doing so, she passed Ziola's brother as he wandered out from the very same room.

"Where are you going, Pet?" Bertram called up after his sister.

"To have a lie down. I'm not feeling very well." This as she trudged up the remaining steps and turned down the east wing.

"Is your conscience bothering you? Is that why you're unwell?" Bertram's tone was snide.

Ziola merely lifted her lip to bare her teeth at her brother and took another step up the stairs.

"We were supposed to review our manuscript outlines for next years releases." Max had his eyes one Ziola's retreating back. There wasn't much enthusiasm in his words.

"Hazel can do it." Ziola's word drifted down to them as she'd apparently heard Max's complaint.

"Come on then, let's head back to the library. We can do an hour or so before heading upstairs to change for dinner." Kent made shooing motions.

"I'm calling my agent first, though. I want to get Ida moving on this rights thing." Max moved away from the rest.

"We can at least sit by the fire," Angela said.

Maisy was relieved Max walked away. His cologne was making her eyes water.

"We are still getting dinner, aren't we?" Angela turned to Maisy.

"Oh yes, as I said earlier, our appliances are propane. There will be plenty of hot food." Maisy said putting on a pleasant smile.

"You did? Was that in the library during tea break? I was probably preoccupied with Bertram's revelation." She looked at her cell phone. "My battery is fine, but nobody is picking up at my agent's office. I'll send them an email." Angela glanced back up at Maisy. "What's on the menu for this evening's dinner anyway?"

"There are two alternatives. Beef Wellington or vegetable ravioli in sun-dried tomato sauce."

"That will cheer Hazel up." Angela gave Maisy a smile. "Did I hear right earlier? Mrs. Roque mentioned there was going to be cheesecake for dessert."

"Absolutely, three kinds to choose from."

"Something to look forward to." Angela followed the other writers into the library, and before the door was closed, Maisy heard one last remark which made her blink.

"At least Ziola won't be able to steal anyone's ideas if she's not in the room." She identified Bertram's voice.

"Bitter much?" Angela asked as she closed one pocket door.

"Actually, yes, this isn't merely sibling rivalry you know. Ziola has been very unprofessional, karma should give her a good smack."

Angela slid the other door closed.

Chapter Ten

"AT LEAST THERE WAS hot water to shower." Max said as he offered Bertram a glass of, what he assumed, was sherry. The colour of the liquor looked right, but the aroma was off. A tray with a crystal decanter and six glasses had been waiting for them on the low table between the settee and chairs when he'd come in.

"I wouldn't say the water was exactly hot." Bertram dubiously eyed the dark red liquid in the offered glass.

Max noted that although Bertram had appeared to have changed his shirt, the rest of his clothing was the same, although his bald head seemed to shine nicely.

By the way Bertram studied the deep burgundy beverage, Max thought the older writer was going to refuse his drink. However, after a moment Bertram shrugged his large, stooped shoulders and chose one of the aperitif glasses. The delicate crystal looked tiny in his huge hands. Bertram knocked the drink back in one gulp, made a sour face, and replaced the glass on the tray with a slight shiver. "Not my thing at all."

Hazel swanned into the room with long strides and swaying hips. "I feel so much better having cleaned up for dinner." Red lips smiled at Max as she accepted her glass. Running one hand slowly down her side Hazel struck a provocative pose. The motion emphasized the fit of her long-sleeved red dress. The clingy boiled wool moulded to her body. She looked down at him from her towering height with the aid of black stiletto pumps.

Normally, Max and Hazel were close in height. He bit back a laugh as she coyly fluttered her eyelash extensions at him. "I enjoyed my shower. How about you?" Her words were a purr.

Max couldn't help but lift one eyebrow at the woman's suggestive attitude. She would figure out the lay of the land at some point during this evening. Or, maybe she wouldn't. Hazel had never impressed Max as being terribly intuitive. His decision to not disabuse her of her erroneous assumptions might be amusing too. Then a thought struck him.

"You've broken up with Kent again, haven't you?" He waved one hand at her outfit. "That's what all this is about, isn't it? Honey, I'm the last guy you want to try and make Kent jealous with."

Hazel turned sharply away from him. Max chuckled and was saved from further conversation with Hazel by Kent's arrival, accompanied by Angela.

Angela wore a sleeveless sheath of emerald green which matched the shade in her updo hair. She'd added a black woolen shawl which matched her pumps and would no doubt keep her warmer than showing off her figure. The dark shawl drew attention to her velvet brown eyes and enhanced her darker skin tone. She wore a slim gold chain around her neck with matching bracelet on her left wrist.

Kent was well turned out too, in a navy pinstripe suit and a crisp white dress shirt with a solid navy tie. Kent knew how to dress, Max had to give the horrible little man that. Freshly shaved, with his blond hair still damp from the shower, and scrupulously parted at the side, he tamed it with a bit of fragrant product.

Max also noted the gold cuff links. He wondered if Ziola had gifted Kent with the bling. It was common speculation among the group Ziola and Kent had a thing going on. Although it was more off than on. Hence Kent moving on to Hazel, however briefly.

Of course, it could be all rumour, something Ziola started, but then why was Hazel on the prowl? Was Kent back with Ziola? He shook his head. One needed a score card to keep track.

Their publisher was a demon for gossip and loved to drop clues. She enjoyed being the centre of attention. Sometime Ziola would share personal information she was party to about others in the group. Possibly to use as leverage of some kind.

How the woman had kept quiet about the lucrative streaming series deal was beyond him. Usually, Ziola shared her every waking moment with the authors, especially her successes, something she revelled rubbing in their faces.

Not that anyone of them really wanted to know so much about Ziola. At least up until now. The stakes were higher with this kind of money on the table. There had been no small amount of speculation as to how they could share in the profits of the streaming deal windfall. They all had, at one time or another, contributed to Ziola's book series.

Max was on the receiving end of a few separate conversations earlier this evening in his room. First Angela had dropped by then later, Bertram.

Bertram also let drop the fact that the initial two hundred thousand didn't include the royalties the episodes would earn from resale. Who knew how much more that could be?

After the publisher's brother had gone, Max made a call to an author friend who'd received several payments for options on his novels. One novel had been picked up three separate times although none of the deals had seen this particular book made into anything. Still, Henry had renovated his entire home and built a three-car garage with the proceeds. The deal for the historical romance book series had to be just as lucrative if one included merchandising.

He pasted on a pleasant expression and walked toward the new arrivals to meet them half-way across the vermillion carpet, tray in hand. "Sherry?" He offered them their drinks.

"Thank you." Angela took a glass. "You look spiffy, Max, love the wingtips."

Max glanced down at his black shoes. They did go well with his charcoal three-piece suit. "Thank you, Ryerson picked them out for me."

"He has great taste."

From his spot on the settee, Bertram snorted. At Max's inquiring look, he merely shook his head and glanced up at Hazel some three feet away.

Hazel was glaring narrow-eyed at Kent. Her eyes glittered, with what looked to Max like rage. Then she turned away to look down into the fire.

"At least some of us made an effort." Angela dropped her chin to look Bertram in the eye.

"We all aren't made of money like you young things." Bertram sketched an abbreviated bow from his seat. "I did my best with what I had to work with."

"Story of your life," Angela said under her breath.

Bertram frowned at Angela; he must have heard her words.

"Kent, a drink?" Max asked, moving the focus away from verbal jabs.

"No, thank you. I don't like sherry, too sweet for my taste." He walked past them all.

Angela fell into step with Max the pair moved farther into the room, following Kent to the seating by the fireside.

The robust flames licked ravenously over the three birch logs, sharing a welcomed heat with the group. It also served to add to the cozy atmosphere.

Seemingly to have forced a lightening of her mood, Hazel sauntered over to Kent and complimented him on his appearance. "That tie makes your eyes look bluer."

Kent, being several inches shorter, had to shift his eyes a considerable distance upward. "Could you sit somewhere, Hazel? Looking up at you gives me a crick in my neck."

The woman blinked dark eyes. There was a touch of hurt there, but she smoothly slid into one of the Queen Anne chairs. Although she looked away from Kent to compliment

Angela on her gold bracelet. "I love this." She ran a fingertip over the interlocking links.

"Thank you, it was a gift from my parents, along with the necklace on the sale of my first novel." Angela smiled down at the smooth gold encircling her left wrist. Max noted Angela missed the brief tightening of Hazel's jawline as she fiddled with her bracelet.

Angela shifted her gaze to the other woman again. "You look beautiful, Hazel. If this were a game of Clue, you could be Miss Scarlet."

That got a laugh out of Hazel. She flipped her long dark, grey-shot braid over her shoulder. "And you could be Mrs. Green, if there were such a character in that game."

"Wouldn't that be fun if we could play real, live Clue?" Angela's eyes danced with humour.

"I assume we are waiting upon my dear sister?" Bertram braced his hands on his knees as he looked around at them all. "Hazel, didn't you call in to her room before you came down?"

"No, why should I?"

Max watched as Hazel's good mood evaporated. It was replaced with a sour look.

Bertram heaved a sigh. "I would have thought—"

"Never fear, dear brother, I am here." Ziola sailed through the open double pocket doors. Her red pumps striking the floor confidently until she reached the carpet which muffled the sound. She was wearing a flowing black sequined dress which brushed the floor.

The others said nothing as Ziola joined their number.

Max looked their publisher over critically. The colour black and high waist concealed her bulk for the most part. The long sleeves ended at the elbow above silver bracelets with more opal stones inset in the precious metal adorning her wrists and fingers. Her white-blonde hair was upswept as well, drawing attention to the over long silver chain around her neck. The necklace dangled off her front shelf. "I see you all have a drink. Is there one for me?"

Max breathed in through his nose. It wasn't her words as much as it was her tone. It wasn't exactly what she said, but how she said it that got under his skin. By her attitude, Ziola thought all was forgiven. Two hundred grand was too much to forgive in his mind. The woman was insufferable.

Even so he reached for the tray to find the four glasses on it, empty. Someone must have gone back for seconds. Before he could offer to get another glass, Kent quickly crossed over to the sideboard which held two additional glasses.

"I'll get you a glass." He returned and picked up the crystal decanter from the low table, filled the glass, and returned to Ziola's side. She was settling herself in the other armchair, like a queen on a throne. Her bright red lips shaped in a smug smile.

"I hope you are not still angry with me for my mood at lunch, Kent." She took the offered glass.

"Of course not, Ziola." Kent flashed her a brilliant smile and rubbed her black clad shoulder suggestively as he leaned in nearer her cheek.

Ziola pursed her mouth into a kissy motion, but her lips never attempted to touch Kent's. He straightened, but kept his eyes glued to the woman while his hand rested on the back of Ziola's chair. Kent's look of adoration made Max a touch ill. The feeling reminded him of Ziola's malady earlier.

"I thought you were not feeling well." Max felt compelled to express the obvious.

"We didn't expect to see you down for dinner." Bertram pulled down one shirt cuff to expose the material more evenly in his tweed jacket sleeve. Then his right hand detoured to the inside pocket where everyone, including Max, knew he kept his gin flask.

Ziola's smile changed to merely a reveal of teeth when her gaze fell on her brother. "I did feel poorly for a time, something at lunch didn't sit right with me." She rested one wrist on the arm of her chair as she looked at him with steady eyes. "I'm feeling much better now." Her smile, real this time, stole over her lips. She took a sip of the sherry.

"You missed a spirited discussion this afternoon." Hazel nodded at her boss.

"Did I? Well, I'm sure you'll bring me up to speed before long." She turned her odd smile on her assistant. And then she lifted her chin to survey the others. "Shall we have a toast?"

Bertram fumbled with the cap to his flask.

Max wanted to say so badly to Ziola, 'You aren't fooling anyone, you know', but he bit his tongue. The others had to know how much their publisher despised them all. No doubt just as much as the group loathed her. Especially now after this afternoon's revelations about the money they were missing out on.

"To what should we drink to? Literary poverty?" Angela's tone had been low, but everyone heard her words.

She'd reminded the authors they were all about to lose even more revenue.

The lot of them were all a bunch of spineless gits. Why didn't any of them stand up to the horrid woman? Max sniffed and looked down. He knew he was as bad as the rest of them. He hated his own cowardice more than everyone else sucking up. Raising his chin, he resolved to have it out with Ziola at some point over the weekend.

"How about an end to this cursed storm?" Kent suggested.

"That's as good a toast as any." Max agreed and went to the table for the decanter. He refilled his glass and the others, except Kent and Bertram's, who lifted his gin flask instead.

Kent put his hand on Ziola's shoulder again as he said something to her alone in a low tone. His expression showed a fervent affection for the woman as he squeezed her shoulder.

And yet, Ziola wasn't smiling now.

"How about the return of the electricity." Hazel kept her head turned away from the couple as she voiced her amendment.

There was a faint murmur of agreement as those with drinks lifted their glasses and then sipped.

Awkward small talk filled the intervening minutes. Then thankfully Tiffany arrived to invite them into the dining room. The group stood and wandered out the library doors to follow their server.

Max trailed the others to stop at the tray he'd left on the sideboard. He put his half-filled glass on the silver surface of the tray. The flavour of the blended wine had not been to his taste. He doubted there was any alcohol in any of the liquor or any of the wines they were being served. Vaguely, he remembered something about no alcohol served from the website link Hazel had sent out over six weeks ago, but doubted any of the others, with the exception of Bertram would notice.

Max sighed. It was going to be a long evening.

Chapter Eleven

THE MARINA ROAD WASN'T just washed out in places, the strip of asphalt was eroded. The ditch on the mountain side of the road roared with run off. The shore side was scored by rivulets and crumbling gravel. Traversing the unstable surface didn't prove to be too much for Jack's truck, still he was glad not to have to do that twice, and not in the dark.

From the road, Jack could see the marina manager was alone. "We have to stop and give Ernie a hand. He'll never get those boats re-berthed by himself.￼

Ernest Campion was running around the docks trying to recapture the drifting sailboats.

"Of course." Tadmore zipped his jacket in preparation for meeting the weather.

Jack turned the wheel and drove them down to the marina parking lot. Sections of the paved area were flooded by a good six inches of water. "We've got king tides today too, fantastic."

"What?" Tadmore looked around at the flood conditions. "What's a king tide?" He asked as he and Jack opened their doors.

Vimy got to his feet and the dog wagged his tail hopefully at Jack. "Stay, Vimy. No point in you getting wet and cold." He'd let the dog out earlier for a bio break. Jack looked at the cop "A king tide is when the orbits and alignment of the Earth, moon, and sun combine to produce greater tidal affects than normal."

"Makes sense."

"Come on." Then Jack closed his door.

Tadmore did the same and walked around the hood of the truck. "Not a scientific term, is it?"

"No." He jogged down the rest of the hill to the concrete docks. Perforce, Tadmore followed.

They found Ernie was halfway down Alpha dock, hauling on the mid-ship mooring line of a powerboat. The craft was at least forty feet long with the fly bridge acting like a sail in the high winds. "Hey there Ernie, could you use some help?" Jack shouted down to the older man.

"All I can get!" Ernie hollered back over the noise of the wind. His weather-beaten face split in a grin for Jack and the cop. His black jacket, cap, and canvas work pants looked soaked through and yet he still grinned.

Jack grabbed a bow line and Patrick ran past Ernie to grab the rope at the back of the boat and pulled the stern in.

One powerful gust of wind caused evergreen tree boughs to explode like a bomb, raining detritus down on the three of them. The blast made the men spin around and then hunch over to cover their heads. Branches, twigs, and needles hit the docks and pelted the men.

"I think things are starting to calm down." Patrick shouted in a deadpan tone.

Jack and Ernie laughed at Patrick's attempt at humour.

The cop and the conservation officer spent the next hour helping the marina manager recapture boats which had broken their mooring cleats. Some of the metal tie-downs were broken off completely from the wooden docks, leaving chewed up screw holes. Other boats had merely snapped their lines and required refastening.

Waves, wind, and the high tide combined to thrash the marina, the vessels, and the unlucky people. Several visitor dock fingers were submerged with only half of the main dock above water. The north end dipped underwater and caused stress on the fasteners connecting the sections to the pylons. Which resulted in one section to completely break off. The twenty-foot wooden dock pulled free and floated loose with the waves pushing the long segment of wood toward the strait.

Jack saw it. "That one's trying to make a run for it."

Ernie turned to look and then ran down the wharf toward the escaped rectangular finger. "It's a navigational hazard." Ernie shouted over his shoulder. Jack pounded down the wharf behind him.

Without pausing, Ernie jumped from the wharf, cleared the open water, and landed on the errant dock. He stumbled and fell to his knees but popped back up again and turned to Jack. "Toss me a line. We need to get this lashed down again."

Shaking his head at Ernie's antics, Jack found a likely rope and tossed the end to the manager.

Ernie snatched the line out of the air and tied the end off on the only remaining cleat. "Got it, pull me back in, would ya?"

Patrick arrived as Jack and Ernie manoeuvred the dock against the wharf. The other man made it secure. Jack straightened and glanced at the black sky. It appeared the blow was going to continue for a while yet.

"Thanks for your help. I'd still be running around here like a mad man if it weren't for you guys." Ernie settled his cap back on his head.

"No problem," Patrick assured the manager.

"We've done what we can, you should get home and get some hot food." Ernie clapped a hand on the cop's shoulder.

"Call me if you need help again, yeah?" Jack said to Ernie.

"Will do. Bring the Constable with ya." Ernie grinned at the cop.

Patrick grinned. "Absolutely."

They left the marina manager to patrol his docks.

The pair waded across the flooded asphalt parking lot. With the attitude his feet couldn't get much wetter, Jack skirted the small river coming off the mountain as much as possible and led the way to the conservation truck.

The two men got into the vehicle and Jack turned the key. The engine cranked several times but would not fire. Jack exhaled in resignation, he should be happy they'd made it this close to home, but that thought didn't exactly cheer him up. He turned the key again, and then a third time. Nothing.

"We might have to walk the rest of the way." Jack reached for the truck door handle.

Ernie appeared at the driver's window and held up a set of keys. Jack lowered the window.

"Take my ride." Ernie gestured at his faded blue Ford F150 parked by the marina office and offered Jack his truck keys.

"We can't take your truck, what will you use to get home?"

The manager shook his head. "I'm not going anywhere until this thing blows over."

"What about your wife?" Patrick asked.

"Tilly knows I'll be late. She'll probably bring me supper on her quad. I'll text her in a bit."

"Thanks Ernie." Jack accepted the keys. "I'll get Dad to drive back with me. I'd feel better if you had your wheels."

Ernie gave him a head waggle in agreement. "Fine, but there's no rush."

ARLIE HEARD A VEHICLE in the driveway. He looked out of the kitchen window and saw Jack and Patrick climb out of a late model truck.

He frowned as Vimy leapt out of the driver's side. The truck looked familiar. "Heh, that's Ernie's truck."

Collars up and shoulders hunched against the wind and rain, the men walked toward the door of the Birch home with the dog leading the way.

With a grunt of satisfaction, Arlie turned away from the window to look at the kid perched on a kitchen stool. He and Arlie had been playing chess until Arlie got up to check outside. "Miles, your uncle is here."

Suddenly the boy looked a bit panicked. His expression surprised Arlie somewhat. "Jack's home." He called out to his daughter-in-law as he watched the kid.

"Oh, just in time." Jane's voice drifted in from the front room. They had a wood fire burning in there. Not only was the fireplace their form of heat at the moment it was also where they'd warmed up their supper using a pair of cast-iron Dutch ovens pushed into the coals.

"Let's put the game aside for now." Arlie picked up the board moved it to the small table by the basement door.

When this storm was all over, Arlie resolved to upgrade the kitchen's electric stove to a propane model. This being without a proper cooking surface was completely unacceptable. He couldn't believe Sara had never suggested this nor had he even thought about it. Storms happened, and power outages had to be expected.

Jane had agreed with him when he'd broached the idea. Arlie shared the house with Jack and Jane. Although he spent a fair amount of time at Gladys' place now, this old house would always be home.

As if thinking about Gladys conjured the woman, she appeared from the living room and from helping Jane. She would have heard Arlie speaking and put a hand on Miles' shoulder. "Gentlemen, supper will be ready in a few minutes, if you'd please go wash up?"

Miles slid off his wooden stool and made for the half-bath off the kitchen.

Earlier, after they'd closed up the café, Arlie called Gladys to invite her to come over for heat and food. Her condo had no such contingency plan like off grid heating. Although she declined to bring Blofeld. The cat was never good with other people, she'd told him, so she left the Persian with plenty of food, water, and a fleece blanket.

Arlie knew Ruby, Jane's cat, had also been a factor in the decision. It was never good to bring an outsider into another cat's territory. He planned to drive her over later, to check on the animal.

"Where's Albert?" he asked her. In his mind the Jack Russel terrier was more Gladys' dog than it was her neighbour's, she minded the friendly little guy a lot for Wilkes.

"Albert is with Matthew. He's got a natural gas fireplace. Matthew invited me and Blofeld too, but I'd rather be here with you." She gave Arlie a shy look but wrinkled her nose at him. "Matthew will check on my cat too."

A warm heat flooded his cheeks, and he quickly cleared his throat as the kitchen door swung open. The men entered trailed by Vimy who no doubt had just been told to shake outside first.

Constable Tadmore wiped one hand down his face to remove excess water as he stood on the dark green mat by the door. His eyes locked on Arlie. "Where's Miles?"

"Washroom." Arlie jerked a thumb over his shoulder.

Gladys walked over to the counter and picked up a stack of soup plates for the chili to be served in but paused to take in the new arrivals. "Are you really the boy's uncle?"

Vimy did a slow walk past all of them as Jack came in and closed the door. The large dog did his tongue-swipe thing as he passed the cat's food. Effectively removing the last kernels from Ruby's dish. Then he wandered to the living room, arrived at his big pillow and flopped down to curl up by the fire. Jack watched his dog preform the nightly ritual, but Arlie knew his son was listening to the conversation.

Tadmore nodded. "Yep. Mari Ann Iverson, his mom, is my oldest sister. She and Miles were the main reason I asked for Duncan when I was being posted."

It was Arlie's turn to nod. "I'm sure she's glad to have you so close."

The cop shrugged. "Probably, some of the time."

Arlie was thinking of asking why the constable lived in Musgrave Landing then, instead of the larger centre of Duncan, but Jane came out carrying one large Dutch oven by the handle with oversized oven mitts. He moved to position a steel trivet on the countertop for her. She placed the large cast-iron pot on top.

"Good timing you guys." She smiled at the new arrivals and crossed to Jack for a hello kiss.

Miles exited the washroom. He stood back from his uncle against the wall. His wide eyes were glued to Jack.

"Come on, Miles, I'll take you to my place. It's just across the road." Tadmore gestured to the boy.

Miles said nothing as he went to the coat rack to take down his jacket, still staring at Jack.

"No, don't be silly." Jane put her hand on Patrick's arm. "We've got plenty of hot food here, you may as well eat with us."

"I really think I should take—"

"Hello, Miles." Jack nodded at the boy. "I don't think you would remember me, I moved into the townhouse beside you and your parents when you were just a little guy. I babysat you once or twice when your mom had to take an extra shift at the hospital." He toed off his boots.

"Yeah." Miles said slowly. He blinked and cleared his throat. "Mum's got pictures of you holding me."

Jack walked over to the boy in his sock feet, making damp marks on the kitchen floor. "Probably your second birthday. Your dad invited me over for a barbeque." He held out his right hand.

Awkwardly, Miles shook it. His eyes kept shifting from Jack's face to the floor and back again. By turns, shy yet curious. Then he frowned up at the man. "My dad invited you?"

"That's right. I only met your dad that one time. It must have been hard for you and your mom when he left."

"I...yeah, I guess." Miles looked down, blinking rapidly to contain his disappointment. No one said it out loud, but with the tone of finality in Jack's words, it was clear he was not Miles' father.

Behind Miles, Jane folded her arms over her chest and tipped up her chin at Arlie. He raised his eyebrows and tried not to look smug, but it was difficult. Jane returned a genuine smile all the same. She turned to the cupboards and opened the silverware drawer. He'd wait till later to rub in he'd been right. Although he had to admit there were a few grains of disappointment the kid wasn't his grandson. Not that he'd wish that complication on Jane in a million years.

"Well," Arlie clasped his hands together. "Miles, can you help me grab a couple extra chairs for the dining room?"

"Sure. Where are they?"

"In the basement, come on." And Arlie lead with Miles trailing.

JANE WATCHED AS JACK lifted auburn eyebrows at the cop. "You only needed to ask, Patrick."

The younger man nodded a bit ruefully. "Yeah, I can see that. You knew what I was thinking the whole time."

"It wasn't hard to figure out, no. I'll go stoke the fire. Get more heat in here," Jack said, his eyes caught Jane's.

"Here, take these oven mitts and grab the other Dutch oven, please." She paused to give her husband a kiss on the cheek as she squeezed his bicep. "It's got Gladys' biscuits for the chili."

He took the mitts. "I will, after I get some dry socks for us." Jack's smile quirked up as his eyes twinkled with humour. "Not even once." Jack's words were for her alone. He was amused with her, but that was okay, she decided. It was good he understood her as well as she knew him. If Jack had known he had a child out there, the kid would not be abandoned.

Also, it appeared that there wasn't even a remote chance Miles was her husband's son. Life had suddenly become uncomplicated again. "Take your coat off, Patrick." Jane waved gesture to the cop and then went back to the counter to find a ladle for the chili.

Gladys put the soup plates beside the large, dark metal pot. "We can dish up here and eat in the dining room."

White ash flaked off the bottom of the black pot and onto the spotless counter. "Good plan." Jane agreed. She picked up a cloth from the sink and wiped up the ash.

The older woman grabbed a second cloth and caught Arlie by the elbow as he emerged from the basement. "You might want to give the chairs a wipe down."

"Thanks." He took the cloth.

"He might not be your grandson, but Miles can still be your friend." Gladys nodded at the boy as he carried a second county-style wooden chair through the basement door.

Arlie grunted and gave her a nod.

Gladys smiled back and gave Arlie's hand a pat.

Jane bit her lip at the older pair, pleased they seemed to understand each other perfectly well too.

During the meal Miles was quiet. He sat next to Jack and Jane noticed the boy's gaze drifted up to her husband's face every few minutes. Was the kid not completely convinced Jack wasn't his father?

Her eyes met her father-in-law's. It appeared Arlie had noticed the same thing, but he didn't comment. Instead, he gave her a shallow nod as his own eyes lit on the kid. Instantly, Jane knew Arlie would speak to the boy and clarify things for him.

Arlie turned his attention to his son and the constable as the younger men took turns explaining the day's adventures. Including how they came to be driving Ernie's truck.

Chapter Twelve

AGGIE ROQUE EXPECTED to be exhausted from the long day's preparations and serving the guests. If anything, she felt energized.

The housekeeper was grateful the beef Wellington had been an unqualified success. Gladys had done an amazing job with the main course. The results of the vegetable ravioli were fair to middling the housekeeper judged. Not her best attempt to be sure. Still, Hazel sampled the dish and told Maisy she liked it so well she wanted the recipe, so that was something.

Sylvia finally called to touch base with the housekeeper twenty minutes before Mrs. Roque was about to serve the entrée.

"I'm not going to be able to make it over there until they restart the ferries." The young woman sounded flustered and annoyed.

"Better to be late and still be, dear."

Sylvia grunted a resigned response. The sound reminded Mrs. Roque of Seymore.

"At this rate, Ziola Nutt will be long gone before I get there, and I'll miss my chance to pitch my book. I thought giving her a sample of my writing would be a sure way to get Dunn Wolf to publish my novel."

"As far as I can ascertain, Ms. Nutt and her writers have only discussed matters pertaining to the business side of Dunn Wolf Publishing. Maisy said something about only the authors discussing next years new releases, but I'll have to ask her for specifics. Hopefully by tomorrow, the storm will have passed, and you can get over here."

"I hope so too, but I'm not holding my breath. I might have to come up with a new plan." Mrs. Roque could just see Sylvia narrowing her eyes as she thought of some new strategy for getting her manuscript in front of the publisher.

The trouble was, the youngest Highmere couldn't seem to focus on anything for more than a couple of months. If Sylvia put half this effort into her academic career, she would have achieved some sort of success by now. Come January, Mrs. Roque was sure Sylvia will have moved on to some other pet project. It was a good thing she received a living allowance from her sister.

"If they do restart the ferries tomorrow morning, make sure all your devices are charged and bring a car charger. We still don't have any electricity."

"Oh, good to know. Thanks Mrs. R."

"You are welcome, dear." She'd ended the call an left the kitchen to supervise dinner service.

Hours later, the rain had turned to a snow and sleet mix. The flashlight the housekeeper carried picked out the path to the carriage house. Mrs. Roque sighed as she walked across the yard to the wrought-iron gate. She travelled the brick walk slower than normal even though Seymore had the path shovelled free of snow. One could not be too careful when it came to ice buildup.

Maybe she was getting too old to handle all the cooking for large events? Her self-doubt had been the reason she'd asked Gladys to assist with the luncheon tasks and so on. She would continue to factor in the need for extra help in the budget, Aggie decided. It made for a less frantic time in the kitchen, and everything flowed smoothly for the staff and ultimately for their guests.

Tomorrow's roast chicken was still a go, the chiller in the walk-in cooler was propane fueled so no food was spoiled. She also had an eggplant dish planned for Hazel and the evening meal. And Sylvia if she made it over.

These ferry cancellations were nothing if not inconvenient. They would have to make do with the fruit and vegetables on hand. There would be no delivery tomorrow from the market in Duncan.

Maybe she should ask Gladys to make up croissants for Monday's breakfast. She'd have to run that by Gladys and Jane in the morning but didn't think there would be any problem.

Jane's cheesecakes had been well received too. Mrs. Roque had smiled when the empty dessert dishes had returned downstairs to the kitchen, all but licked clean. They wouldn't ply the guests with intoxicants, but sugar was still available.

Mrs. Roque knew the reason behind Alicia's stipulation on no alcohol to be served on the premises. It wasn't about licencing; it was about addictions some of the family had fallen into. No matter what anyone, including herself, said publicly about what caused Olivia Frost-Highmere's death, the family knew it was from alcohol abuse. No doubt partly, a causal influence in Sylvia's addiction problem. However as far as Mrs. Roque knew, the youngest Highmere had been clean for almost two years.

Still, it was good this day was over. After dinner had been served, their guests moved back to the library. This gave the girls a chance to clean up and to prepare the breakfast room next door for tomorrow, while the housekeeper handled serving the guests coffee.

At least the gaggle of writers had behaved, and no fights broke out. The authors appeared to be on their best behaviour, even if some treated Ms. Nutt rather frostily.

Mrs. Roque had been quite shocked to hear about the behaviour Maisy had witness earlier and wondered at the thoroughness of Mr. Byrce's background check into Dunn Wolf Publishing. Something to mention at the next monthly meeting.

There had been lots of ravioli left over. The three of them had taken turns at eating dinner. Mrs. Roque had gone so far as to let the girls finish the last two pieces of chocolate cheesecake as a bit of a treat.

By eight-thirty the housekeeper was dead on her feet, and she knew it. She departed for her apartment in the carriage house half an hour later. She left Maisy collecting the used dish clothes and kitchen towels for the laundry while Tiffany collected the coffee things from the library.

Once the kitchen cleaning was complete, and the girls ensured the china, and serving dishes were put away in their proper places, then Tiffany would be on her way home. She was scheduled to be back at six in the morning to let Maisy go home and help to serve breakfast. Both breakfast and lunch tomorrow were to be buffet affairs to lessen the need for both young women to be onsite at the same time. The stainless-steel chafing dishes were already set up in the breakfast room.

The pair would clock off a lot of hours this weekend, but it was a temporary thing. Someone had to be on the premises, at all times. The original plan had been to use the small office off the adjacent reception area and cloak room. Unfortunately, with no heat available in there, the kitchen was the best second option. It held the days heat, and the stove would be useful to make a hot drink if needed. In addition, as the heart of the house, it was easy to gain access to any area via the back stairs.

Mrs. Roque planned to be back at the main house kitchen for six o'clock the next morning too, to cook the breakfast buffet. The guests would expect the meal to be ready for eight o'clock. Gladys was coming over around ten o'clock to make the lemon mousse which was the alternate dessert for dinner that evening along with the remaining cheesecake selections. Sunday would be the big finale, the guests' last meal together. There were still some details for resolve for the roasted pork tenderloin and baked salmon dishes. Monday, the group was scheduled to leave after breakfast. God willing, the ferries would be running by then.

Tomorrow, apparently there was some kind of writing workshop planned for the authors.

The gate did not squeak as she opened it. Seymore must have gotten around to oiling the thing's hinges. Sand crunched under foot here too.

At some point Mrs. Roque hoped to run the kitchen and supply all the meals herself, but if the operating budget spread to having fresh baking and desserts from Jane's café, why not? Also, why not employ the staff required when needed? In the past, the estate contributed as much as it could to the local economy of the village. And Mrs. Roque's goal was to continue the tradition.

While this power outage was annoying, she was not going to let it sink her. If anything, this little bit of adversity would test her mettle and show Alicia she could handle the running of the house as a conference and event facility. With more than a touch of pride in her step, Mrs. Roque walked around to the side door of the carriage house.

She was met with an inquiring meow and a large damp calico.

"I wondered where you'd gotten to, Missy." She let herself into her studio apartment and the cat followed. "You didn't stop by the kitchen for your treat. Well, never mind you can have it now."

Missy kept up a running commentary as Aggie led the cat into the mud room and filled her dishes with food and water. "I'm pleased you didn't steal into the main house today." A spoonful of wet cat food landed with a plop in the clean white ceramic dish. She added the small portion of roast beef shavings she'd saved for the feline too. Missy tucked into the food with no ceremony.

"It's cold in here. We'll have to turn on the gas fireplace to take the chill off."

BERTRAM NUTT DESCENDED the grand staircase with the help of the thick oak banister and a small pen light. He paused on the landing and freed up one hand so he could suck back a long swig from his silver flask.

As he swallowed the calming mouthful of gin elixir, he cast his gaze back up to the corridor which led to the east wing. Bertram had just come from that direction. He shook his head and let the light trail back down to the carpeted stairs he had yet to tackle.

He knew there would be no reasoning with Ziola, even before he'd made the final effort for a private chat in her room about her schemes. Her heart had always been too black for compromise, and nothing could change that fact now. He released a small sigh as his hand found the missive he'd taken from her bag. The streaming deal contract was tucked into his left breast pocket, next to the flask. He planned to read it over at his leisure.

Briefly, Bertram paused once more and contemplated doing something about the situation but decided against it. He didn't carry a mobile phone, never seeing the need.

There was no love lost between him and his sister, and nothing over the years changed that fact either. They weren't really family. Their relationship was that of boss and employee. He could make a fuss but decided to let everyone sleep instead.

Even now, at this point in his life, he couldn't let go of the deep resentment he harboured toward Ziola. He despised her utterly, if he were honest.

As he thought about it, Ziola had never liked him much either. He'd wanted his big sister's attention growing up, he'd idolized her for a time. However, she soon put shot to that. Any remaining attachment to her as family, dissolved when she'd stolen his first manuscript. It was funny, the incident was over twenty-five years ago, but he felt the betrayal like it was yesterday.

His sister had been the experienced writer back then. She offered to help him as his editor and beta reader rolled into one. At the time, her offer to review his documented history of Vancouver Island pleased him. His older sister was taking him seriously at last.

She was supposed to mark up the non-fiction work for edits and give him some advice on how to better frame the information to make it an interesting story. Not steal it from him.

How stupidly trusting he'd been. He'd ask her for an update every couple of weeks, and she would assure him she was slogging through the manuscript even with the constant delays she said got in the way. There was always some handy excuse as to why she wasn't finished with the manuscript. Everything from dentist visits for a bad tooth, to the internet in her area was out, or a close friend was sick. Her lists of excuses were as long as both his arms.

And then, when the first book in the Pacific Strangers series was released, she tried to argue it was a collaboration between them. Wasn't this a wonderful surprise? She adored working with him. He should be happy; they both would benefit.

Except Ziola held all the rights. He was named as a 'contributor' thus only receiving a pittance for his three years of research and painstaking documentation. And now the film rights were sold. Or video rights? He wasn't sure about the nomenclature, but he did know he was out a bushel of money.

With the flask tucked into the inside pocket of his tweed coat, he continued down the last set of steps still clutching the railing, a touch unsteady.

Even now Bertram tightened his jaw at Ziola's deception. And truthfully at his own gullibility. The streaming series option agreement, that was what it was called.

The actual full value of the agreement was over half a million dollars. He'd scanned the pages from Ziola's giant purse before tackling the stairs. Not the only event to make him mildly ill upon discovery. Even so, he'd taken the document.

The lemon enhanced gin sloshed appallingly in his stomach. Suddenly he wished he hadn't had seconds of the beef Wellington, although the meat had been superbly cooked.

Bertram wandered into the foyer. Setting his flashlight on the table beneath the mirror to shine upward, he checked the line of his jacket in the ornate antique reflection to the right of the staircase. Nothing gave away the fact he had a fifth of gin concealed about his person, nor the contract. Just as well he'd brought his own liquor supply, this place was as dry as the proverbial popcorn fart.

His own inspection of likely locations like the globe-shaped drinks cabinet in the library proved futile.

The red-head, Tiffany? He'd followed her back to the kitchen after everyone else had gone upstairs. She'd caught him in the pantry and ordered him out of the kitchen. He'd done some fast talking about trying to find the ground level washroom and was confident he'd fooled her.

Bertram tried to get into the wine cellar too, when he noticed the small brass plate above the doorway, but that room was locked. Inspired, he'd asked the formidable manager, Mrs. Roque if he could explore the lower levels of the house, as research. This idea was met with a firm, no.

Trust Hazel to find the only business conference centre which served non-alcoholic beverages. Ridiculous, in his opinion.

Of course, this place could have been Ziola's idea. She sneered at him constantly for his occasional tipple. She, who also liked to buy her Merlot by the case. He raised his chin in a defiant manner. That woman was the cause a much of his life's disappointment.

Just let her make a comment now, hah. Bertram sniffed with distain as he fluffed the yellow silk in his breast pocket and leaned forward to look at his face.

His eyes showed bloodshot lines around his irises, and his proud nose was a shade red. He could explain the eyes, reading too late. His nose was red from the cold, that was it.

Shoulders square, Bertram picked up his light. He did an about face and strolled to the library. The double doors were open, and the fireplace was still lit. At least he'd be warmer in the library. This room was more comfortable than his own in the west wing.

The grandfather clock along the north wall chimed the half-hour after nine as he crossed the room to one of the settees. He landed in the corner closest to the fireplace. Everyone had voted to turn in early so they could try to stay warmer in their rooms under the covers. Well, most of them anyway. Some of the writers had been moving around, of that he'd been certain. A door closing gave him the idea to drop in on his sister for a chat.

The help was no doubt ensconced in the kitchen. Staying warm and well fed by the propane stove which cooked that amazing roast beef. Vaguely, he wondered if there were any leftovers. His stomach released a gurgle, a warning not to even think about it. Best not to risk indigestion or worse. He glanced upward briefly.

Bertram rubbed his hands together to create some warmth. This barn of a house did not heat up much from the couple of fireplaces in operation. His fingers were numb, clumsy. He was tempted to close the pocket doors and keep what heat the fire created to himself but couldn't be bothered to get up again.

With a sigh he settled in front of the fire. With one foot, he dragged the low table over in front of his bulk and extended his legs on top. Instantly the warmth sank in.

Bertram crossed his ankles and folded his hands over his paunch. Might as well grab a snooze while he waited.

He planned to stay put until someone found the body.

Just as Bertram was drifting off into a lovely comfortable slumber, there was a noise from upstairs. Not quite a shout, but close enough.

"Ah," the man muttered to himself. "Here we go."

His lips twitched and he sat forward on the couch, but he did not move to get up.

Not yet, he decided. He pulled out his flask and removed the plastic white cap.

One for the road. He swallowed and looked at the flask. Where had the outer silver cap gone?

Chapter Thirteen

AT THE SOUND OF A SHOUT, Maisy jumped. She'd been dozing lightly in a wooden kitchen chair with her sock feet propped up on another opposite.

She blinked, a bit unfocused and unsure as to what was going on, then it occurred to her she had to go check on the guests.

As she got up, Maisy realized that for the sound to travel all the way to the kitchen, something strange must have happened up on the second floor. She thought she knew what that something was. "Mr. Highmere, I hope you aren't causing trouble."

Resolutely, Maisy grabbed the flashlight off the table and left the kitchen. Her plan was to check out the guest room hallways in both wings to confirm all was well. Hopefully, there would be no one wandering the halls. This hope included the ghost of the previous resident.

When she'd first come to work, Maisy had been told by Tiffany she was sure there was an unhappy spirit wandering the big house. No doubt because her father had found

Allister Highmere's body a couple of years ago. Albeit in a grave, but still the plot was supposed to be empty.

For her part, Maisy didn't disagree with Tiffany. She'd walked through the cold spots in the east wing of the second floor. She also swore she was being watched as she put sheets on the bed of the Cherry Blossom room. Formerly Mrs. Frost-Highmere's suite.

The powerful beam from the flashlight allowed her to see well enough to take sprinting leaps up the stairs. Sock feet helped too, but Maisy had to remember the unaccustomed long black skirt and made a grab at the handrail as she realized her mistake. She might have gone ass over tea kettle if she hadn't reacted in time in the pitch black. The phrase popped up in her mind. It was something her grandfather or more probably Arlie would say.

She shook off the abrupt shock of her downward descent and continued to climb the back stairs to reach the second level.

Maisy wished the emergency lights still worked to make finding the door easier. Moving the beam along the wall, she found the portal to the east wing and pushed open the hallway door. She'd have a look here first, then retrace her steps to check on the west wing.

Abruptly a pungent smell hit her in the nose and her sinuses closed up. "Of all the nerve." Maisy flicked the light to shine on the floor runner in front of her and strode forward. She found Angela in her night gown standing by the open door of her room. Dim light from her LED lantern spilled from the bureau in the room and into the hallway. The meagre illumination showed Angela's black and green hair was spiked up in the back. From the odour, it was readily apparent Angela had not been sleeping.

Maisy frowned at the other woman and fast walked over to the guest on soundless feet. "What do you think you are doing?"

"Ack!" Angela jumped back and grabbed the door jamb. "I'm not doing anything." She sounded breathless and her eyes were wide.

"Then you can put out your joint and open the windows in your room. Mrs. Roque will string you up for merely smoking in the house. I can't imagine what she'll do if she discovers you've been smoking pot."

"I'm not." Her mouth turned into a pout.

"Why are you lying? We can add an extra charge to your credit card for breaking the no smoking rule." Maisy shook her head scornfully at the woman.

"I didn't know."

"You signed and initialed the registration form before I gave you a key."

"I'm sorry, I'm sorry. I already put the joint out. I'll open the window." Angela did sound contrite.

"Good. What where you shouting about?"

"That noise wasn't me. I think someone should go check on Ziola."

"Why?"

Angela gestured down the hallway. "I came out of my room when I heard someone shout." Angela swallowed and looked at Maisy, she blinked concerned eyes. "I think the shout came from Ziola's room. I'm not going in there to check." She slowly shook her head and folded her arms over her middle. "That woman snarled at me once already this evening."

Maisy opened her mouth to reply but was interrupted by sounds coming from down the hall to her right. She moved the flashlight to shine the beam at the door of the Cherry Blossom room.

Ziola's bedchamber door was opening.

Hazel, wearing a loose oversized blue T-shirt over black leggings, emerged from the bedroom. She backed out in a hurry, head down with a hand over her mouth. She retreated until her back hit the opposite wall. Then she turned a shocked expression to look at the other two women. Hazel pointed with her left hand toward the open door of her boss' room. "I...I think Ziola is dead."

Maisy lifted one eyebrow at Hazel's dramatics. "You're not serious?" She stalked forward and paused at the bedroom's threshold.

Gritting her teeth, Maisy knocked lightly on the partially opened door and entered to find the evidence for herself. "Hello? Ms. Nutt?" The heavy smell of male cologne touched her nose. The scent was almost enough to drown out the stench of Angela's pot. Both smells combined would no doubt trigger a headache. Maisy pushed that thought aside for now.

The LED lantern on the night table gave off a bright glow. Still, the corners of the room were shrouded in shadow.

She gripped the flashlight tighter and fanned the light over the bed. Rapidly it became apparent to Maisy, Ziola's personal assistant could have a point.

There lay Ziola Nutt, fully clothed in her black evening gown, on the four-poster bed. Her blonde hair was down and spread on the pillow behind her. Her body rested on top of the indigo duvet and folded back white sheets. One of the woman's shoes had come off. Even Ziola's toenails were painted black to match her manicure. The red pump lay on it's side on the floor by the bed. Something shiny rested beside the shoe on the dark blue and gold carpet.

Time seemed to slow down for Maisy as she shifted her eyes upward to the bed again. She was resisting looking at the body, but knew she had to.

Oddly, she noticed the hands first. One, adorned with several opal rings was at her throat, clutching a lime-green and scarlet-red silk scarf wrapped around her neck. The other hand lay across her mid-section and appeared to be holding a gold bracelet between her thumb and fingers. A sheaf of typed pages was rolled up into a tube and rested a few inches away on the duvet as well. Like the papers had been dropped there.

Ziola's eyes were closed, and her face turned slightly away from the lamp, as though she were sleeping. Except that her upper body was propped up on two of the four pillows as if she'd been reading. An empty sherry glass rested on the night table beside her. In the reduced light, her lips appeared to be black, not the scarlet red of her lipstick earlier.

A cold feeling stole over Maisy as she moved forward. "Ms. Nutt?" She knew her voice was too soft, so she tried again. "Ms. Nutt, are you all right?"

There was no answer. Nor, Maisy noticed, did the older woman appear to be breathing. She was completely still. This was not good.

Maisy shivered but made herself step closer to the bed. There was no sign of life in Ziola Nutt, but she had to know, for sure.

Swallowing hard at the thought of what she was about to do, Maisy shone the beam of light up to the publisher's face. She placed two fingers on Ziola's carotid artery as she'd been taught in her basic first aid course.

She wanted to feel something, but there was nothing. No pulse at all. Surprisingly, Ziola was not exactly cold to the touch, but nor was her skin warm like a living person either. She frowned at the marks under her fingers. There was bruising around Ziola's throat. Maisy jerked her hand away and rolled her bottom lip over her teeth.

Digging out her phone she dialed 911. Call for support was the first thing she should do. The call hit a busy signal. As Maisy stared at Ziola's face she could see the skin had a waxy purple tinge. She ended the call. The busy signal was no help. This situation was something not covered in her course.

Maisy knew she should try CPR, but something held her back. That she was alone in the house with a killer might be it. Or it was the feel of Ziola's waxy skin along with the absolute stillness made her swallow hard. She tried 911 again. Still the fast busy signal.

Her first instinct was to think Ms. Nutt's death was from a heart attack. However, something didn't feel right about that assumption and the bruises bore that thought out. Who could have done this?

What should she do, emergency services were no doubt overwhelmed with the storm. The answer was obvious, she should call Mrs. Roque. Then try emergency services again.

Her phone still in her right hand, Maisy speed-dialed Mrs. Roque. It took several rings, but the housekeeper finally came on the line. "Yes, Maisy, what's happened?" She sounded tired but resigned.

"I'm sorry, Mrs. Roque, but Ziola Nutt is incapacitated. I think she's dead." She gave the housekeeper a succinct description of the situation, including who was in the hallway.

Stunned silence greeted this statement.

Then Maisy heard Mrs. Roque inhaled sharply. "I'll be right over. Have you called the authorities?"

"Yes, 911 just give me a busy signal."

"Ask the others to help you administer CPR."

"Will do."

"Quite right, carry on." Mrs. Roque hung up.

Taking a grip on her emotions, Maisy pocketed her phone. "Angela, Hazel come help me."

She climbed up on the bed and knelt beside the body.

Angela peaked in around the door. "What are you doing?"

"CPR. I need help."

"I can't, I don't know how." Angela shrunk back from the doorway.

Maisy struggled to get the large woman on her back to ensure the airways were open. Obviously, there was no breathing. She opened the mouth to check for obstructions as she'd been taught. There was nothing she could see or feel.

"Call 911 for me then. Hazel!"

Angela looked over her shoulder at the other woman. "I think she's having a meltdown or is in shock."

Maisy put her ear next to Ziola's mouth and listened. Nothing, she needed to start CPR.

Straightening, Maisy moved up beside the victim's chest and folded her hands one on top of the other and clasped them together. With the heel of her hands and straight elbows, she pushed hard and fast in the centre of the chest, to begin the required thirty compressions.

"All I'm getting is a busy signal." Angela complained from the hallway.

"Stay. On. The line." Maisy got the words out between compressions.

After she reached thirty, Maisy moved on to the standard two breaths. She leaned down, squeezing her eyes shut, as she squeezed the victims nose closed, she gave two puffs. The chest rose marginally, but only from the air Maisy expelled. There was a rigidity to the jaw and face that did not bode well.

"What exactly is going on here?" a baritone voice boomed down the hallway making Maisy jump. "Angela, why are you running around in your nightdress?"

"Something is wrong with Ziola." Angela's plaintive words drifted to Maisy as she started another set of thirty.

The door was pushed wider.

"What is it you think you're doing?" Bertram demanded.

"She's doing CPR, obviously." Angela supplied the information for which Maisy was too occupied to speak.

"What's the point? It looks as though Ziola has passed on." He filled the doorway.

"Help me," Maisy said weakly. She was on another round of thirty compressions and her arms had gone rubbery.

"I think not." He sniffed. "It's a lost cause I'm afraid. You should stand down."

Maisy continued on for three more rounds, but the situation did not change. She sat back on her heels. She should not stop, but had no strength left to go on. Compressing her lips she leaned forward and placed trembling fingers against Ziola's neck again seeking a pulse. There was none.

"Good Lord," Maisy whispered wiping her mouth with the back of her hand. She closed her eyes feeling miserable.

"Come away from there. Leave my sister to her rest."

Woodenly, Maisy climbed off the bed and backed away, she exited the room. With her sweater sleeve she pulled the door partly closed. She wanted to scrub her hands and face.

Bertram strode forward. He lifted his hand to push Maisy out of the way. "I need to go in there."

Anger surged through Maisy. "Don't even think of touching me or I'll lay you out on the carpet." Maisy infused her tone with steel. It was easy to promise, she was more than a bit freaked out at the moment.

Bertram took a step back and blinked at her in surprise.

No doubt never having been spoken to in this manner, but Maisy couldn't help it. Finding, let alone touching, to administer CPR to a dead body was upsetting. Not to mention it looked like the woman had been strangled.

Maisy swallowed again in an attempt to loosen her tight throat.

The smell of gin wafting to her from Bertram Nutt's laboured breathing didn't help in the least. At her steady glare, Bertram backed up another step, but continued none the less. "My sister is in there."

"I can't get through to an operator." Angela had ghosted up behind Bertram.

"Ms. Nutt is beyond help now." Maisy bit back further words.

There was evidence which told Maisy something bad had happened to Ziola Nutt. She narrowed her eyes at Bertram, Angela, and the mute Hazel.

Was one of these people responsible? What should she do if they ganged up on her? Probably not something she should think about at the moment.

Instead, Maisy stood blocking the door with her tall, but slighter frame. "I think Ms. Nutt is dead."

"Oh, my God, I thought so." Hazel spun away from the far wall. She bumped a wooden chair and ran to her room. The door was slammed behind her.

Bertram froze at the noise, but his eyes shifted back to Maisy.

Angela stared at her too. Her mouth hung open, "Was it a heart attack?"

"I don't know." That was the easiest response given the circumstances. "I need to call for some help."

"You must let me pass." Bertram persisted. "I need to get in there."

"I must do no such thing. I must call for EMS and the police." She pointed to the chair across from Ziola's door, some four feet away. "Park your butt in that seat if you want to stay."

"Why would you want to call the police?" Angela turned to Bertram. "Why does she want to do that?"

"It doesn't look like a heart attack to me." Maisy blurted the words as she took out her phone, and immediately wished she hadn't.

"What?" Bertram tried to pier over Maisy's shoulder. "It was probably that mushroom soup at lunch. You people poisoned my sister."

"We did not." Maisy all but snapped at the man. She managed to curb her tone at the last second as she pulled the door closed and pointed at the chair along the opposite wall. "We all had the same soup for lunch. Now sit down and get a grip." Maisy swallowed, trying to do exactly that herself.

Bertram shuffled across the hallway. This gave Maisy some space, but he did not sit down. Although he did lean one hand heavily on the chair back. "I can't believe this. I have a right to see my sister."

Maisy narrowed her eyes at Bertram Nutt. His tie was askew, and his clothing creased and rumpled. He moved unsteadily, he had to be drunk. She shook her head as she dialed and sent up a silent prayer. This time the call rang.

Chapter Fourteen

AFTER MRS. ROQUE GOT off the phone with Maisy, she called Seymore Willard. If anything, for moral support. However, he could help her with dealing with the guests for this current emergency too. She suddenly felt out numbered with this group of guests and Seymore had a way with people. He could make them do as he told them. Maisy needed reinforcements.

"What?" Was Seymore's response to the late-night call.

"There's been a death."

"In the main house?" It wasn't really a question.

"Yes, the publisher has passed away."

"The walking heart attack?"

"No, his sister." She and Seymore had shared a cup of tea after she'd arrived back to the carriage house. Aggie had brought the groundskeeper up to speed on what she'd seen and heard.

"That's who I meant. Her brother's the drunk."

Aggie pinned the phone between her shoulder and chin and then proceeded to pull on wool leggings. "Not surprising, that." A thought struck her. Seymore must have been keeping an eye on them all. "You haven't been using the spy holes again, have you?"

"Maybe."

"Seymour!"

"Only the one in the library. The other one in the study was sealed years ago. I did that when Mrs. Olivia was still alive."

Mrs. Roque sighed and grabbed the clean house dress she'd laid out for the morning. "Be that as it may. Maisy is all by herself up there and needs us." She pushed one arm through a sleeve and switched the phone over to her other side.

"I'll go over now."

"Thank you." She closed her eyes in relief and sniffed.

"What else is wrong?"

Aggie pursed her lips to keep the words back, but the concern in Seymore's tone made them slip out. "Alicia will never let me run the place now, not with another body popping up."

"Aggie, this is only the second one in all these years. It's fine."

"It's not fine."

"Calm down and get dressed. I'll meet you at the big house."

"What makes you think I'm not calm?" Aggie was more than a touch offended by Seymore's remark.

"You called Mrs. Alicia, just Alicia."

"Oh. You may have a point. I'll see you over there."

"Right."

MAISY'S CALL CLICKED and was transferred to a recorded message saying to ensure if this was an actual emergency, stay on the line, otherwise check the emergency agency's social media feeds. Maisy stubbornly stayed on the call. She needed a live body to speak to.

Bertram Nutt decided to sit on the wooden seat Maisy had directed him earlier. His elbows were braced on the arms of the chair.

With his head down, Maisy couldn't see his face. Was the man quietly crying? This made some sense to her. If her sister suddenly passed away, she'd be upset too.

Maisy squinted down the hallway in the other direction. Initially, when the power went out, the emergency exit signs all through the public areas had been lit. Unfortunately, the batteries on them only lasted three hours. She knew she needed to do something about that.

Maisy said to Angela, "We're going to need more light, Ms. Oakla. Can you please bring out your lantern?"

"Good idea." Angela went into her room and came out with the lantern. She placed it on the hall table outside her room. The limited glow of the lamp helped a bit.

As the recording repeated itself. Maisy was tempted to call Jane and see if Arlie and Jack were home. She was fairly sure Jack was part of the volunteer fire department. In the end, she decided to wait some more.

The nature of Ziola Nutt's death said this situation called for serious attention. Belatedly it occurred to her she was in a house full of strangers and one of them had to be a murderer.

Blinking, she forced that thought away. If she couldn't get through to someone in the next minute, she'd call her grandmother...and Jane, Jack, and Arlie, and anyone else she could think of. No way did she want to be here by herself.

The line clicked. "Emergency services, how may I direct your call?"

Maisy swallowed. "I don't know. I think I need the police and an ambulance."

"What is your emergency?"

"We've had a guest die." Maisy shifted her eyes down the hall, but Angela had gone back into her room and shut the door.

"A guest? Where are you calling from?" Maisy told the dispatcher and spent several minutes explaining the situation to emergency services.

"Is anyone preforming CPR?"

During Maisy's explanation, the wind rattled the windows on the second floor. The lack of heat was making her fingers go numb and she wrapped her black cardigan tighter around herself. "I was."

"You stopped CPR?"

"There is no pulse, no respiration, the skin is purple and stiff."

"That really isn't for you to decide."

"I'm the only one here." Maisy said weakly. "I couldn't—"

"Can you secure the room until we can get someone over there? This storm is making it impossible to cross the strait. Ganges is cut off as well."

"Too many downed trees?"

"That's what they are reporting to us, yes."

"What about the care home? Isn't there someone on staff there?"

There was a pause while Maisy heard typing and a muffled conversation. "No, not anymore apparently. They have several nurses, I can contact them if needs be, but chances are they have their hands full what with the storm and power outage. Let me talk to my supervisor. Please hold." The dispatcher went off the line for a few moments, the line clicked, and she was back.

"I can get Jack Birch, he's the fire fighter chief in Musgrave Landing. He's also on my list of EMS contacts for your area."

Relief flooded Maisy. "Jack would be great." Then a possible issue raised itself. "If he made it home. He was stuck somewhere on the road last I heard, but Constable Tadmore is supposed to be with him too. They were traveling together."

"Even better, and they would cover two aspects of the situation let me try them. Stay on the line, please." She dropped off the call again.

"Where would I go?" Maisy rolled her eyes. Her gaze drifted behind her to Ziola's closed door.

It was then the air pressure in the house changed. Someone had come in through the front doors.

Angela's appeared in the doorway of her room. "Who's that?" Her voice was high, almost a squeak. The lantern light from the hall table now showed the author was dressed in jeans and a sweater with nuclear pink fuzzy socks on her feet.

"I think it's Mrs. Roque, you better get your window open to clear out that pot smell." Maisy warned the guest. "Or you might find yourself sleeping in your car."

"Oh, I forgot." Wide-eyed at the threat, Angela abruptly disappeared.

Instantly the scent of rain penetrated the cloying smell, chased down the hallway by cold air. Maisy instantly felt more alert. Angela had opened her window, thank the Lord.

Mrs. Roque was going to be cranky about Ziola. Would she fly off the handle when she detected Angela's pot smoking?

Worse, Maisy's allergy to marijuana combined with the stench of cologne did not ease up to any degree. She needed to grab her allergy meds out of her purse stored down in the kitchen.

The stairs creaked as someone moved slowly up the treads. Maisy frowned as she got the funny feeling the new arrival wasn't Mrs. Roque? She got her answer when Seymore Willard advanced down the hallway.

Maisy lifted her eyebrows. "What are you doing here, Mr. Willard?"

"Aggie told me to come help." Willard grunted as he stopped in front of Bertram Nutt. The brother of the deceased had stood when the groundkeeper had come up the stairs. "Go back to your room, sir."

"I will not, I'm staying right here." Bertram lifted his chin indignantly and straightened his posture, if unsteadily.

He murmured something else, but Maisy couldn't make out any of it. Weirdly, Maisy was pleased to see Mr. Willard. Although she'd never had much to do with the groundskeeper, he was a familiar face. Her hand not holding the phone uncurled from the fist it had shaped itself into.

"Take a seat, then." Willard leaned forward and Bertram dropped his large bulk back onto the hall chair. The wood groaned in protest.

Bertram used his yellow pocket square like a hankie to dab at his eyes. Now Maisy felt some guilt at having been so prickly, but mostly she felt sad for him, he had lost his sister after all. Then Bertram leaned back in the wooden chair and released a belch.

Willard narrowed pale blue eyes at the other man. He pointed one long boney finger at Bertram. "Now, stop upsetting Maisy."

"I'm not."

Maisy turned away as the dispatcher came back on the line.

"We're in luck. Constable Tadmore is with Jack Birch, and they made it back to Musgrave Landing. Both will there shortly to take over the situation."

"Good, thank you so much." Maisy was so glad more people she trusted were on their way.

"No problem." Maisy noticed the dispatcher's tone sounded tired. "Would it be possible to let you off the line now?" the operator asked.

"Yes, of course. You must have tons of calls coming in."

"You have no idea." This was muttered, and probably not meant for Maisy's ear. Then in her normal professional tone she said, "Constable Tadmore has checked in, so we can leave it to him."

"Thank you." Maisy ended the call.

She moved to her right as Mr. Willard came to stand next to her. The older man folded his arms over his chest in a formidable manner. His bulky brown coat smelled like wood smoke. Strangely, it was comforting.

SEATED IN THE LIVING room after dinner and dishes were done, the five adults were happy to watch the fire and chat while Miles attempted to make friends with Ruby, Jane's cat.

Jack was about to suggest a return trip to the marina when oddly enough, both Jack and Patrick received cell phone calls one right after the other. Jack raised an eyebrow at Patrick.

The younger man moved into the kitchen to take his phone call.

Jack spoke succinctly and quickly ended the first one, to make a second call. "Joe, who's around to drive the ambulance?" He listened for a moment. "I don't know, an emergency at Highmere House, low triage."

"Oh my." Gladys covered her mouth with the fingers of her left hand.

"What's going on?" Jane was more forward. Jack noted his dad's bluntness was rubbing off on his wife.

He glanced around at his attentive audience, especially his father. He stood and took the hallway through into the bedroom he'd converted into an office for Jane.

"I bet it was the mushroom surprise soup." Arlie piped up. He gave Gladys a knowing nod.

Jack saw Gladys shoot a frowning look at his father. "Arlie, that is a terrible thing to suggest. Aggie Roque would never poison anyone."

"Probably not on purpose." Arlie grinned back. "But I bet I'm right."

Jack firmly closed the door.

THE MEAGRE LIGHT FROM Maisy's flashlight made the hallway forest green carpet looked black. So too, did the green and gold swirl patterned wallpaper.

In a move Maisy didn't think was terribly helpful, Angela had gone and woken up the other two men and told them their publisher was dead. Everyone was in the hall except Hazel, who refused to come out of her room. At this point, all guests were up and awake and in various states of dress. The problem was the motley crew were clustered around Maisy. She like this even less.

At least Mr. Willard's presence help keep them back a couple feet. He stared at them with his frozen, pale blue eyes. Still, she felt decidedly out numbered.

Her phone clutched in one hand and the flashlight in the other, she kept a watchful eye on the group cluttering up the hallway.

Maisy had asked them to go back to their rooms, but no one listened. "There is nothing you can do right now. We have emergency services people coming to help."

Kent pushed to the front of the others. This was no doubt because he couldn't see around the taller authors and possibly to intimidate Maisy. "We want to see Ziola."

She shook her head. "I can't do that. I've been instructed to secure the scene."

"Who told you to do that?" Max Lintlaw's tone was belligerent.

"The police dispatcher."

Mr. Willard shifted his feet. "The RCMP are coming."

"Where from? The ferries aren't running." Max pulled the lapels of his robe tighter and folded one over the other.

"Constable Tadmore lives in the village." Maisy had spoken to him mere minutes ago. Hearing his voice had cheered her up to no end.

"Don't let them push you around." He'd instructed her. "People will take more risks in a group. They think the others will back them up in a confrontation. If what you said is the case, one of those people might have something to do with our victim's death."

His words were not exactly reassuring, but Maisy understood their importance. She took a deep breath. "No one is to enter unless the officer on scene decides it's okay."

"She doesn't trust us." Angela pointed out.

"Can you blame her?" Bertram said from his chair across the hallway, well behind the group. "The young lady doesn't know us, nor do we know her."

Before Maisy could reply, Kent spoke up again. "It's not like we are responsible for this situation." Kent pointed a thick index finger at Maisy. "We don't trust you people, Ziola has important documents with her. We need to secure them." His swarthy face was flushed dark from anger. He was the one trying the hardest to get into the publisher's room. "One of your staff could be responsible for killing Ziola."

Maisy compressed her lips to keep them sealed and from speaking her mind. She so wanted to tell Kent Westham exactly who she thought might have strangled Ziola Nutt and it certainly wasn't anyone she knew personally. Still, she realized she shouldn't say anything.

Mr. Willard, who had stood beside her for the past ten minutes, lifted his head.

The front door must have opened judging by the change in air pressure and then thumped shut. "Someone's here," she said.

Multiple footsteps could be heard mounting the staircase and a minute later, Mrs. Roque came around the corner from the landing. The housekeeper led the way, her flashlight flickering over the collect group in the hallway followed by Patrick, Jack and Joe Aawohkitopi.

Patrick used a large metal flashlight, while the other two men wore headlamps which seemed much more sensible to Maisy than her hand light. She resolved, if this power outage went on any longer, she'd get a headlamp too.

A relieved smile curved her lips. Patrick's eyes briefly met hers. He gave her a shallow nod, then his gaze shifted as he took in the other people crowding the hallway. The guests swiveled their heads to look at the tall constable, Jack, and Joe.

"Please move aside." There was a definite command tone in his voice. "It's best if you return to your rooms for now," Constable Tadmore instructed the guests.

There was general grumbling however the onlookers didn't move.

"There's no law saying we can't witness what's going on." Kent's jaw jutted out after he spoke. Max, and Angela nodded their heads in agreement.

"You heard the officer." Mrs. Roque was having none of it. "Go back to your rooms, please. We will call you together at breakfast and give you an update then. For now, it would be best if you leave the hall. These gentlemen need room to work."

The older woman locked eyes with Kent and lowered her head like a bull about to charge. Her expression reminded Maisy of Albert, the Jack Russell terrier she walked on occasion, and his look when he found a stick he was going to bring home.

Kent backed up a step at Mrs. Roque's iron gaze and the weight of decades of responsibility. No one crossed Mrs. Roque.

"Come along, children." Bertram heaved himself to his feet and ambled off down the hallway. "We will know the outcome in good time." The rest of the group, after a brief hesitation, followed.

"That's probably the best idea." Max tightened the belt on his navy and gold paisley silk robe and followed Bertram.

Angela went to her room quickly, and quietly closed the door. The three men continued down the hall to cross the landing and headed to the west wing and their rooms. Angela's door abruptly opened, and she plucked the lantern from the hallway table and closed the door again. The light level in the corridor dropped somewhat.

Mrs. Roque sniffed and then frowned darkly in the direction the young writer had disappeared. Shaking her head, she turned to her employee. "Are you all right, dear?" Mrs. Roque placed a consoling hand on Maisy's shoulder.

"Yeah, they weren't getting past me and Mr. Willard." Maisy was dismayed to find tears in her eyes. Hold it together, you don't want to break down now.

"Thank you for your help, Maisy, Mr. Willard." Patrick's eyes were on her and his tone made her blink rapidly. "You did a great job, and I appreciate it."

"No problem." She sniffed.

"May I?" Patrick lifted his eyebrows as he gestured to the door behind her.

"Oh, yes, of course." She stepped away from the portal. Willard had already walked over to stand behind Mrs. Roque.

Tadmore paused to don disposable gloves.

"Well, now that Constable Tadmore has things in hand, I'll go down to the kitchen and make some coffee." Mrs. Roque looked at Maisy. "Did you want to come too, dear?"

"I think, Maisy should stay here for a bit, I'm guessing Tadmore will have a few questions for her," Jack said.

"Oh yes, I'm sure you are correct, Jack." Mrs. Roque gave her employee's shoulder another pat. She glanced up at the groundskeeper hovering at her shoulder.

"I'll go stoke the fires," he said and they made their way down the hallway to the door which led to the back stairs.

When Tadmore eased the bedroom door open, they were all hit with the smell of cologne. Inside the room, all was still, just as Maisy had left it. The lantern shone a yellowy pool of light on the deceased.

Jack wrinkled his nose as he too put on gloves and followed. He approached the deceased and repeated Maisy's pulse check and looked under Ziola's eyelids, then shook his head at Tadmore.

Chapter Fifteen

JACK BIRCH AND JOE Aawohkitopi waited outside in the hall for Tadmore to do his cursory check of the room.

Jane's husband looked over at a sad and deflated Maisy. "Come sit down for a minute, Maz. You look exhausted." Jack took her arm and led the girl to the wooden armchair Bertram had vacated.

"It has been a long and stressful day," Maisy admitted and lowered herself into the chair. Immediately she tucked her feet under her. In only socks, her toes were going almost as numb as her fingers. Those she stuffed into her sweater sleeves.

"I know what you mean." Jack glanced at Joe. "We should probably go get the gurney."

"That's what I was thinking. I'll go down now and start getting things set up," Joe said.

"I'll follow you in a minute." Jack tipped his head at Maisy.

Joe glanced at Maisy and nodded. He switched on his headlamp to find his way downstairs.

The two who were left in the hallway were silent as they watched Tadmore's flashlight beam move around inside the guest room.

"I had to stop CPR. No one else would help me." Maisy's hand trembled as she brushed a strand of blonde hair off her forehead. "I don't think she was alive." Tear-filled eyes looked up at him.

"You did all you could, Maisy." Jack said in a quiet firm tone.

She blinked up at Jack. "Thanks." She nodded. "How was your trip home? Jane said you had to take the long way."

Jack realized Maisy wanted to be distracted from thinking about the dead woman in the room across the hall. "We did, we had our own little adventures." Jack tipped his head in Tadmore's direction. "Patrick will have some explaining to do when he gets back to work." He added a lighter tone to his words.

"Oh? Why is that?" Maisy tipped her head.

"After he parked his truck, a tree fell on it and flattened the vehicle. I can imagine the amount of paperwork he'll have to fill out."

"Oh no." Maisy said, and covered the grin which curved her lips with the back of her hand. "I know I shouldn't find that funny, but I do."

"What was funny was the look on his face at the time. Still, no one was hurt, that's the important thing."

"True." She frowned and then she looked back up at Jack. "You found the old mayor, in the woods. After he'd been shot."

Jack nodded. "It was not something I'd ever like to repeat, I can tell you."

"I bet."

"So, if you need someone to talk to, about finding that lady. I understand what you're going through."

"Thanks, Jack. I'll keep that in mind." She allowed her sleeves to slide back and folded her hands around her phone with the flashlight in her lap. "I think Ms. Nutt was probably strangled."

"That's bad." He didn't ask how she knew, and Maisy was grateful not to have to explain the evidence.

She nodded. "The worst part of finding her like that is knowing I'm in the same house as a murderer."

Jack placed a firm hand on her shoulder. "You're not alone now."

Patrick exited the guest room. He walked across the hall to join them. "Maisy, do you happen to know who the last person in the victim's room was?"

"From the stench of cologne, I'd say it was that fellow who didn't say much. The mouthy one up front didn't smell," Jack said.

"No, it was Hazel Dell." Maisy climbed to her feet. "She was the last one in the bedroom before me. That's her room down the hall on the right.

"You okay, Maisy?" Patrick asked.

She lifted her chin. "Yeah, I'll be fine."

JACK LOOKED AT TADMORE. "I'm going to go help Joe. If it's all right with you, we'll bring up the gurney now."

"We're ready to move the victim. You should have no trouble in this wide hallway." Patrick glanced up as Angela cracked the door and peaked out of her room. He gave her a frown and she quickly closed the door. "There's no medical facilities here in the village, is there?"

"That's what I was thinking. With no ferries and the road to Fulsome Harbour now closed we have a problem."

"Is there a doctor here in Musgrave Landing?"

"Only three times a week. A locum comes out with a nurse. They have a clinic in the seniors' home. Doctor Malcolm retired to the main island last year." Maisy's blonde hair had tumbled into her eyes again and she swiped it out of the way.

"Any ideas on where we could take the body to preserve it?" Tadmore looked to Jack.

"I'll think about it. Joe might have a suggestion too."

"What about the funeral home?" Maisy looked at the cop.

Jack nodded and switch on his headlamp and pointed the beam at his feet to find his way downstairs. "That might be our best solution, for now." He nodded and then headed down the hall to the stairs.

"You'll want to call Kevin Moffatt," Maisy suggested.

"Thanks, you wouldn't happen to know his number off hand?" He raised inquiring eyebrows at her.

"Uh, no, but I'm sure you can get it." Her dry tone said she wasn't falling for his lame joke.

Patrick gave her a commiserating smile. "Maisy, you should go get warmed up. Your lips are turning blue. We can talk later."

"Are you sure?"

"Yes, you've done a great job keeping an eye on the scene, thanks so much for your help."

She ducked her head. "No problem."

"One thing, do you think Mrs. Roque has any freezer bags?" Patrick's eyes looked black in artificial light.

"Oh, yeah, I'm sure she does. I'll go get some for you." Maisy turned on her flashlight.

"Thanks." Patrick could see she was happy to leave the second-floor hallway. "No rush, get warmed up first."

PATRICK WANTED TO SHEPHERD Maisy into the kitchen where it was bound to be considerably warmer. Get her a hot drink and make sure she wasn't traumatized by the experience. However, he couldn't leave the body unattended.

Tadmore also wanted an opportunity to question his witnesses too. It was good practise to get a jump on the investigation before the sergeant showed up. Who would no doubt be arriving as soon as the storm let up a bit to allow a ferry run. In Tadmore's experience, it was always good to have something accomplished before the higher ranks arrived.

His most pressing problem was, first, he needed to find a place for the victim's body to be kept. He needed to call Kevin Moffatt and dug out his phone.

This was a murder, there was no doubt about it. The bruises around the woman's neck. That alone gave him a bit of insight into the killer. It took a lot to kill with your bare hands.

The scarf around the neck was odd. Like someone what trying to hide the obvious. Maybe they thought they could slip this by the locals, but once the coroner got a look, or anyone with homicide experience, it was evident the woman's death was suspicious.

He found the twenty-four-hour number for Moffatt's Funeral Home. This was going to be a unique conversation. So too the one he would have with the staff sergeant in Duncan.

MAISY HAD ALWAYS THOUGHT she was made of tougher stuff, but apparently not. She moved down the stairs, one hand on the railing, the other lifting her long skirt, while employing the flashlight as she went. This slowed her progress, but she felt better with every step she put between herself and the deceased Ziola Nutt.

She found Mrs. Roque, Jane, and her grandmother, in the warm kitchen. Several candles were lit and placed around the room. Maisy entered the kitchen to hear Mrs. Roque speaking. She pushed the kitchen door closed to keep the heat in and felt their eyes on her as she entered, however they kept up their flow of chatter.

"What are we going to do about the body? We can't leave it up there."

Maisy frowned. What did Mrs. Roque think Jack and Joe were here for? Her next action was to go right to the sink and wash her hands thoroughly. The odd conversation had a touch of humour to it, albeit dark. "They aren't leaving Ms. Nutt upstairs." She employed a paper towel for her face to wash away the tears and other things she didn't want to think about.

"Thank goodness for that." Mrs. Roque seemed a touch rattled now that the worse was over.

She employed a paper towel to dry her hands. The welcome aroma of coffee bubbling on the stove to the left of her grandmother, made Maisy's shoulders drop as she walked closer to the warmth. There was something everyday about the smell of coffee percolating, comforting and normal.

The housekeeper turned as Maisy crossed the kitchen. "Coffee or cocoa, dear?"

"Cocoa I would bet." Gladys smiled at her granddaughter.

"Yes, please, Grandma." She walked over to the range to warm her numb hands near the burner flame.

Gladys put an arm around her granddaughter and gave her a quick hug. "You got it, kiddo." She then filled one of the plain white mugs lined up on the back of the stove.

Maisy accepted the cocoa with a smile of thanks and wrapped her long fingers around the ceramic cup to absorb the heat. After a couple of sips of milk infused chocolate, she felt closer to normal. "So, this is where the party is." Maisy grinned at her grandmother.

"I'm always the life of the party." Gladys wrinkled her nose with a grin.

"We thought we'd come over and help where we can," Jane said with a sympathetic look and then crossed the room to touch Maisy's shoulder. "Come and sit down. How are you?" She offered the girl a sandwich from the plate she'd filled.

"I'm okay." Maisy sat at the table. She lifted one shoulder in a shrug and then took an egg salad sandwich. Before she bit into it, she remembered her other task. "Constable Tadmore asked if you have any freezer bags, Mrs. Roque."

"Yes, of course we do. Does he need some?" She sounded doubtful.

"I think he wants them for evidence gathering." Maisy put her mug on the table in front of her.

"Oh, that makes sense. Wouldn't he be carrying things like that in his car?" The housekeeper walked into the pantry and came out caring a plus-size box of the plastic bags.

"He probably does, except his truck had a tree land on it earlier and it was squashed flat?"

"Really?" Mrs. Roque blinked in surprise.

"Yep, Jack told me." She nibbled the sandwich.

"This storm has a lot to answer for. Would you mind saving my legs and take these up to the constable?" She offered Maisy the box.

"I'll do it." Jane took the bags from the housekeeper. "You stay and warm up, girl." Jane gave Maisy a firm nod.

"Thanks." Maisy gave Jane a grateful look. "I think I can feel my fingers again." She popped the last corner of her sandwich into her mouth.

"No problem. Second floor, right?"

"Yes, east wing." Mrs. Roque took the plate from Jane and placed it on the table.

"Here, take my flashlight." Maisy dug the light out of her skirt pocket and handed it to Jane. "It's completely black in the back stairwell." She dropped her voice for Jane's ears alone. "I'd suggest you walk around any cold spots."

"Yes, good point."

After Jane left, Maisy drained her mug and leaned back in the chair. In the quiet warmth of the kitchen something occurred to her. She frowned as she put her empty mug on the table.

"What is it, dear?" Her grandmother asked, pouring more cocoa into the cup. "You look to be upset still."

Mrs. Roque moved the coffee percolator off the burner so the grounds would settle then drifted over to the table too.

"Ms. Nutt's room had to be unlocked for Hazel to get in," Maisy said carefully.

"Yes, I suppose." Mrs. Roque nodded. "So? Hazel is her assistant."

Maisy sighed. She hadn't told Mrs. Roque everything when she'd phoned her boss earlier. "I think someone murdered Ms. Nutt and the last one in her room was Hazel."

The housekeepers jaw dropped open.

"What makes you say that, Maisy?" Her grandmother's tone was serious.

Maisy looked up at her grandmother. "She has bruises on her neck and a scarf was wrapped around it too."

"There's a murderer in this house?" Mrs. Roque was working her head around the situation. "I thought she probably died from a heart attack or something."

Maisy met Mrs. Roque's eye and mutely shook her head.

"No wonder you're so disturbed by finding the body." Gladys gave her granddaughter another hug.

"What does the constable think?" Mrs. Roque wanted to know.

Chapter Sixteen

ARLIE PARKED ERNIE'S smaller late model truck beside the conservation services vehicle. Jack used Arlie's truck to drive him and the cop to meet the ambulance up at the big house.

The rain had let up, but the wind was still ripping. It grabbed at the smaller Ford Ranger truck and succeeded in rocking the vehicle with its forceful gusts as he shut off the engine.

It was full dark and just after ten o'clock at night, but with what was going on up at the big house, Arlie didn't feel like twiddling his thumbs at home. Might as well get Jack's truck up and running.

Before they left his house, Arlie had put a few tools and supplies in the truck box. Who knew what was wrong with the crew cab? Still, Arlie had a feeling it was probably something simple. His son usually took good care of his things. Although in Arlie's opinion, Jack should deal with maintenance items in a timelier fashion, but hey, kids these days. What could you do?

He glanced to his right as he picked up a headlamp and put it on before adding a ball cap. Miles appeared quite happy to tag along. "You ready to give me a hand?"

"Yeah, sure." The kid unbuckled his seatbelt. "Tell me what to do."

"All right. First, we transfer my tools to Jack's truck box." Other than a second set of hands, Arlie wanted to talk to the kid. Why, after all this time, did he think he needed to find his father?

When Jack had left home for university, Arlie had been at a bit of a loose end. He missed his son. Sara had suggested he get involved with other young people as a way to keep occupied and maybe help kids with no dad.

Arlie had baulked at the idea at first. He had enough on his hands with a job, and house and yard to look after. "I don't have time for other people's kids."

"You were complaining about the teenage boys hanging out by the ferry. Round them up and get them to the Boys and Girls club. Teach them a few life skills of some kind." Sara had been sewing yet another apron for Ethel Crawley. As well as her close friend, the café owner was Sara's best customer.

"Like what?"

"I don't know, something you taught Jack to help him get on in the world. I already called Les MacDonald, the organizer. He's expecting you to be there in twenty minutes." She looked over the top of her cheaters at him.

"That was a bit high handed."

"It was." She nodded, rearranging the material to get at a difficult seam. "But you are bored and need something to do. Think of each one of those kids as a project."

Arlie had been angry at Sara for putting him in that position. He'd had a good mind not to go to the community centre to help Les. She merely looked at him with that calm expression of hers and he'd caved. "I'll go this once. I'm telling Les I'm too busy."

"You do that." She always called his bluff.

Thoughts of Sara made his mouth quirk into a sad smile. He still missed her everyday.

She'd been right, as she most often was. He'd been sucked in right away with teaching the kids. Boys and girls alike. Basic car maintenance to begin with, then welding, carpentry, and a host of other subjects the kids were interested in.

Mostly, Arlie had come to realize, they needed to have someone to talk to, about life. Years later, the kids now adults, would stop into the café to say hi to him and some thanked him for his interest in their lives back when they were teens.

Instinctively, he knew Miles was looking for something, not necessarily his father. Arlie was curious as to what that something was.

Arlie cleared his throat. "Then I'll need you to try starting the truck while I have a look under the hood."

"What will you be looking for?" Miles pulled his jacket hood over his head and opened the door.

"Trouble, I suspect."

Miles snorted and walked around to the back of Ernie's truck, meeting Arlie there.

The older man opened the tailgate and without being asked, Miles grabbed hold of the small toolbox to carry over to the other truck.

He put the box down on Jack's tailgate once Arlie had opened it. "What do you need?"

"Just leave that in there for the moment. I don't know what I need yet. It's heavy enough, the wind won't bother it."

"Oh, okay." He let go of the handle of the red metal box.

Arlie grabbed a large flashlight, and they went to the conservation truck. Using Jack's keys, he unlocked the vehicle, leaned inside the cab and popped the hood. Next, he slid the key into the ignition. "Jump in the driver's seat."

Miles complied.

"Pay close attention." Arlie shone the beam of the flashlight on the floor then looked the boy in the eye. "Gas, brake, clutch." He pointed to each in turn.

Miles nodded, following Arlie's pointing index finger as he addressed the floor pedals.

"Push the clutch in with your left foot when you turn the key. Don't give her any gas until I say. We don't want to flood the thing."

The older man reached across Miles to the floor stick shift. "We want the truck in neutral." He waggled the shifter. "Always check that first before starting up an engine."

"How do you know it's in neutral?"

Arlie blinked as he looked at the kid and then nodded. He tapped the top of the gearshift. "See the pattern on the shifter nob? First gear, second, third, reverse, neutral."

"Oh."

"Wiggling it like this shows you she's not in gear. Let's crack on."

"What will you do first?"

Arlie looked at Miles and realized the kid truly wanted to learn.

He tapped his nose. "When working on an engine I like to go with my sense of smell."

"Okay." Miles' expression said he was confused but willing to go along.

"Push the clutch in and turn the key when I say. I want to test for spark."

Arlie rolled down the window and closed the door. He leaned in under the hood. "Okay, give it a go."

Miles did as he was told. The engine turned over and tried to engage.

"Okay, stop, we have spark."

"So now what?" Miles leaned out the window.

"I want to check for leaks, fuel or air, and blowby. Let's go again."

This time, Arlie saw it. The carburetor was moving around much more than it should.

"Ha." Arlie smiled. "Stop, I need a wrench." He walked back to his toolbox.

"What kind of wrench?"

"A half-inch combination wrench." Arlie held it up as he walked by Miles. "Come and watch me. Some day you might need to know how to do this."

Miles hopped out. "Maybe I'll just go to a garage to get my truck fixed."

"You might, if you have the money to pay someone." Arlie nodded and leaned on the fender to look at the boy. "How are you going to know if they will do a good job? Stuff like this, learning to fix your vehicles, and such. These things are life skills and not something they teach in school much anymore." He turned away to lean back in under the hood.

A few minutes later, Arlie had tightened down the carburetor. "Try it again, Miles."

The boy returned to the cab and turned the key. The truck leapt to life. Arlie nodded, listened to the engine for a minute, and then closed the truck hood. He looked through the windshield at Miles. "Good job, thanks for your help."

A wide grin broke out across the boy's face.

Arlie gave him a stoic nod. He sniffed. The easy part was done.

"Yo, Arlie."

He turned to see Ernie crossing the parking lot.

Good, he could give the marina manager back his keys. Then he and Miles could head home for something hot to drink and they could deal with the hard part.

THE VILLAGE HAD A STRANGE darkness over it without the streetlights. The wind had returned in full force after the brief lull. Maybe they'd passed through the eye of the storm.

Upon Arlie and Miles' return, Vimy made a trip outside and promptly returned to evict Ruby from his bed. The sleepy cat waited exactly ten seconds before climbing back in with the German shepherd. No protest was heard from the canine.

Arlie liked having animals in the house. It made the place feel more like a home. He tossed more wood on the fire. The room was comfortably warm. He made a mental note to ensure all the bedroom doors were open to share the heat.

Back in the kitchen, Arlie and Miles washed up. They'd driven Jack's truck back home and parked the work vehicle in it's usual spot by the fence. The area closest to the house, Jack left open for Jane. Arlie's own late model Dodge truck was usually parked in the garage. It didn't see much use lately. Arlie preferred to walk most places or take the café van when it was running. He'd need to check on the repairs once the power was back on.

"The water's cold." Miles pointed out rinsing the soap from his hands under the tap.

"The water heater hasn't got any power. It'll be that way until we get the generator started up. We'll do that tomorrow morning. For now, we tough it out because we aren't wimps." Arlie handed the boy a dark grey towel they kept in the kitchen.

Next, he filled the cast-iron pot with water and took it to the living room. Arlie swung out the metal arm which was used to support the pot. This was something he'd added for Sara, years ago after they'd experienced their own first electrical outage. The fire was doing well, still he gave the logs a nudge with the poker.

Miles followed him and took a seat on the edge of the couch. Neither male said anything for a bit while Arlie got the flames higher and put the lid on the pot.

The older man glanced over his shoulder at the boy. The kid was keyed up. He probably sensed he was about to be asked some hard questions. And it was time to pay the piper.

Turning his back to the flames, Arlie folded his arms across his chest and waited.

Miles glanced up at him and then away.

Silence was broken by the crackling of the fire and the hiss of water heating up. Normally, Arlie had to admit, he wasn't the most patient of men, but it was important Miles took the initiative, so he merely studied the kid as the boy rubbed the toe of his left sock with the toe of his right.

Then the kid looked up at the older man and Arlie raised his eyebrows meaningfully.

"I got something to tell ya." Miles looked down at his feet, his toes curled into the carpet.

"Go ahead."

The boy released a breath. "I kinda knew Jack wasn't my dad."

"Is that right?"

"I was just hoping..."

"For what?"

Miles shook his head. "It's dumb. I'm dumb." He still looked at his sock feet.

Arlie noted the right sock was half-turned and the heel was on the side of his foot. "About what?" He knew he had to probe until Miles actually admitted what was really going on with him.

"I'm supposed to empty the garbage and I found a letter from my dad. It was sent from the Mission Institution."

"Ah. The prison in Mission, BC."

"Yeah."

"Your father doesn't work there, does he?"

Miles shook his head. "I'm pretty sure he doesn't. Anyway, the letter wasn't opened. It was addressed to my mum."

"You opened it anyway," Arlie guessed.

The boy nodded now, finally looking up at Arlie. "My dad wanted to know if she would visit him. If Mom would send him money."

"Did he ask about you?"

"No. When Mum got home, I asked her about where my dad was. She always told me he'd gone to Alaska. He was working in a gold mine up there and sometime he'd come back or we'd go up and visit him once we saved up enough money. I figured out she wasn't telling me the truth."

"And now?"

"She got mad I'd opened the letter, but then she told me he was really in prison. Mum said he was there for stealing and selling stuff from his work. He got in a fight with his boss, his boss was hurt bad, and died. She started to cry."

"When did she say all this happened?"

"I guess I was around three."

"Jack was still living in Duncan then."

"Yeah, Mum said it was with help from friends like Jack, that we were okay. I guess she went back to finishing her nursing course. The neighbours helped out when Mom needed a babysitter sometimes. I found the picture from my birthday. Mum doesn't have any pictures of my dad. I guess she's still mad at him."

Arlie nodded and took a guess. "You hoped this was a sort of a lie too."

Miles nodded. "I thought maybe..." He shrugged narrow shoulders.

"Hm." Arlie grunted. "There is no better man than my son, I'll give you that. If he were a father, he'd do an excellent job of raising his kid." Arlie turned back to the fire and picked up a potholder to take the cast-iron pot off the heat. "Of course, he had me to learn from."

Miles shrugged again.

"Let's make some cocoa."

"Okay." Miles popped to his feet.

"Then we will give your mum a call. You have some apologizing to do."

Miles look mulish for a moment, but under Arlie's steady gaze, lost his stubbornness. "Okay."

Arlie led the way into the kitchen. "Fix your socks."

Chapter Seventeen

JANE WAS UNENCUMBERED by long black skirts like Maisy. Her thick cable knit sweater, jeans, and runners, allowed her freedom of movement and she quickly climbed the back stairs.

She flipped her long brown braid over her shoulder and pointed the flashlight up the painted stairs ahead of her feet. It didn't take her long to find the door and exit in the hallway. What helped was the light emitting from the headlamps her husband, and Joe used to illuminate the corridor. Currently the men were occupied rolling an empty gurney past her toward the room at the end of the hall.

Jack gave her a wink as he pushed and Joe pulled the medical stretcher past.

"Hey you." She greeted him.

"Hey love," he answered. A quick smile brushed his lips. She trailed behind them bringing up the rear.

Her nose wrinkled involuntarily. "Why does it stink like pot up here?"

Jack snorted. "I'll let you have one guess."

"Mrs. Roque will have a bird when she finds out."

The men came to a halt. "Not so far. She was up here with us earlier and didn't say anything about the smell." Jack made an adjustment to the stretcher's height.

"Maybe she's been a touch distracted by something else." Jane's tone was dry.

"No doubt." Joe nodded.

Constable Patrick Tadmore emerged into the hallway. He appeared to be deep in thought although this changed when he saw the three of them standing outside the guest room.

Jane stepped forward and reached over the stretcher. "Here you go." Jane handed the freezer bags to the cop.

"These are perfect, thanks Jane."

"You might need this too." She moved around the stretcher to be on the same side as her husband. Jane then slid her hand inside his coat. They exchanged a brief telling look, then she extracted an item from her husband's shirt pocket. Jane offered the cop a felt tipped marker.

Tadmore nodded. "Yeah, I think I might." The younger man glanced over at Jack. "Before we move the deceased, can you give me a hand?"

"Yeah, sure." By Jack's expression, Jane could tell her husband was not exactly sure what the cop wanted him to do, but whatever Tadmore needed, Jack was always willing to help.

Curiosity more than anything made Jane lean on the doorframe and look through the opening to watch. Vaguely, Jane realized her father-in-law's nosiness was rubbing off on her.

Tadmore gestured to the floor.

Jack tapped the side of his headlamp above his ear and the illumination increased significantly.

As soon as Jane saw what was on the carpet she said, "Ah." Everything made sense now.

The cop tucked the box of bags under his left arm. He labeled the first one and offered it to Jack to hold open. Then with gloved hands Tadmore picked up a silver object off the floor and dropped it into the first bag. Jack sealed the bag and accepted a second one.

"What are they doing?" Joe asked from the wrong side of the gurney, he was at a bad angle to see anything.

"Gathering evidence, I would say."

The cop put the woman's shoe in the large bag and Jack pointed to the other one still hooked on the victim's foot on the bed. After a moment's hesitation, Tadmore added that one to the bag as well.

The pair continued on for several minutes. They then came out of the room with various items encased in the clear plastic. Jane offered to take the bags from Jack.

"We should move her now." Tadmore gave Jane the box of freezer bags and Jack's pen too.

"All right." Joe said. "Jack you're taking the middle? Tadmore, you get the feet, and follow my directions." They gave each other a bracing look.

In doing so, their manners changed perceptively. A seriousness passed over all three men as they coordinated in muted tones. Joe and Jack wordlessly, from long practice, angled the gurney to pass it through the bedroom door. Tadmore followed.

Jane continued to watch from beside the doorframe. The stretcher was moved up beside the bed. Joe adjusted the level to match.

First, Jack moved to the middle of the gurney and braced his hips to push it against the bed.

The cop frowned when Jack leaned across the stretcher and grasped the thin bedspread, rolling the material. As if sensing Patrick's question, he said, "I need to create a handhold."

"Hammock the feet, Constable." Joe instructed and then did the same with the head by pulling the bedspread up on either side. "Like this."

Tadmore nodded and cradled the feet inside the fabric.

"On my count, we move on three." Joe looked at Jack and the cop in turn.

Both men nodded.

"We slide the body; we do not lift. Ready?"

"Ready." They said in unison.

"One, two, three." Ziola Nutt was slid sideways to the stretcher, bedspread and all.

Jane noted the dead woman's hand didn't move from her neck. "Looks like rigor mortis must has set in." Then the hand dropped to the side.

"A bit. Rigor mortis doesn't hit all at once. It comes in stages." Jack lifted the side of the body bag to encompass the right side of the body. He grasped the left shoulder and rolled the victim on her right side.

Joe removed the bedding.

"I'll need the bedspread for forensics." Tadmore said. "Fold the topside in, to the centre, please."

Jane pulled a clear plastic bag out of the box, opened it wide, and the cop bundled the bedspread into the bag. There was too much material for it all to fit, so she left the bag open. Rested it on the hallway chair and placed a second bag over the first. To cover the exposed portion.

The gurney was rolled out into the hallway. Joe and Jack proceeded down the hallway to the stairs.

"There is coffee and sandwiches in the kitchen when you are done." Jane said, as Patrick locked the room's door.

"Thanks." He turned to her and took the accumulated evidence bags.

Thirty minutes later, Jack and Patrick entered the kitchen by the back door. Water streamed off both men's coats as they stood in the small entrance way.

"Hang your things on the hooks by the door and come in for something hot to drink. I've made coffee and Gladys has cocoa at the ready if you'd prefer." Mrs. Roque waved at the pair in.

The men complied and removed their footwear for good measure so as not to track water onto the rough kitchen tiles. They joined the group of women and Mr. Willard in the kitchen. Each took a vacant chair at the rectangular table.

"There are sandwiches on the table too." Mrs. Roque brought over another plate, these were tuna and cucumber.

"Would anyone like cocoa or coffee?" Gladys looked around the room.

"Thanks, Gladys." Jack looked at Tadmore. "I have a feeling the Constable will be needing all the caffeine he can get."

"It's looking to be a long one. I have to call in and give my inspector an update. Then, I'll have to start interviewing the guests and staff."

"Who do you start with?" Jane asked. She had returned to the kitchen after Patrick had locked the guest room.

Patrick looked at Maisy. "I'd like to start with you, if that's okay."

"Sure." She nodded. "Now?"

"Give me a minute to warm up, okay?"

"No problem." Maybe by then she wouldn't feel so emotionally numb.

Coffee was served and the sandwich plates handed around.

"What are you going to do with the body?" Gladys asked.

"What about the cooler?" Mrs. Roque took up the thread of the previous conversation.

Maisy bit her lip. She wasn't going to offer any comment but looked forward to seeing how the situation unfolded.

Gladys shook her head. "Aggie, we can't use the cooler, the food would be compromised."

"Yes, of course, what was I thinking?" Mrs. Roque tapped herself in the middle of her forehead in self-deprecation. "We'll have to use the wine cellar then. You can put the body down there, if need be."

"No one needs to be concerned—"

"Patrick, do you know when the storm will be over?" Gladys stared at the constable. Her mouth twitched.

"I—"

"Or, when the ferries will be back in operation?" Mrs. Roque backed up Gladys. "Not to mention when power will be restored? Let alone when the coroner can come out?"

"We've already—"

"You need to explore the options at hand. Besides, we've done it before." Mrs. Roque's tone told the constable to not make a fuss.

Tadmore's attempt at getting a word in edgewise crashed to a halt. He stared back at the housekeeper. "Wait, what? You've kept a body in the wine cellar before?"

"Ancient history." Gladys waved a hand at the cop. She was enjoying the back and forth, Maisy could tell.

"It was only for a short time, mind you." Mrs. Roque interjected. "The doctor had the body taken away in short order."

"Okay." Jack put his mug down and spread his hands in a calming motion. "There will be no storing of bodies on the premises. Joe has taken the deceased to the funeral home. Moffatt's have agreed to allow their facilities to be used by the RCMP for the time being. To preserve any evidence. We also have to wait until the coroner can get here to determine next steps." He looked each of the older women in the eye as he spoke. "Fair enough?"

They nodded and Jack lean back in his chair with an air of finality.

Tadmore gave Jack a nod of thanks for his support. "I found Ms. Nutt's room key on the dresser in her room." He addressed the housekeeper. "I'll keep the key until after forensics have processed the room, if you don't mind, Mrs. Roque."

"No, of course. The perfectly correct thing to do," the housekeeper said.

The kitchen clock chimed midnight.

Jack stood. "What's the plan?" He was looking at Tadmore. "You can leave Miles with us; we have plenty of room. I'm sure Dad already has him bunked down in one of the spare rooms upstairs. You are welcome to stay with us too."

"There's no source of heat in the apartment over the café, not with the electricity out." Jane interjected.

"Thanks, I appreciate this." He and Jack shared a look then his gaze shifter to Maisy.

She met his look. Neither of the males were going to mention the bruises each had seen on the victim's neck. It didn't take a pathologist to suspect strangulation. "I'm not really comfortable with staying here," Maisy said. No way did she want to be on her own.

"Of course not." Gladys piped up. "I can guarantee that." Maisy's grandmother stood and began collecting coffee cups for the sink.

"You won't be alone," Patrick said. "I need to keep an eye on the scene of death. I'll be staying."

"Absolutely," Mrs. Roque said. "We might have a killer in the house. None of us should be alone right now. I'll never sleep, I can tell you." She handed Gladys a used cup.

Jack got to his feet and made a move to put on his boots and coat.

Willard grunted agreement.

"No one said anything about this being a murder." Tadmore cautioned the group. "At the moment, it's a suspicious death."

"You can call it anything you like, officially. We know what's going on." Gladys said over her shoulder as she took away the used dishes to wash.

"Jack and I will head back to our place then. Call us if you need anything." Jane joined her husband at the back door.

"Thanks for your help." The cop addressed the couple.

With a wave, the Birches left by the back door.

Willard got to his feet. "I'll go check the fires. Fill the wood boxes." And he left the kitchen too.

TADMORE AND MAISY WERE left sitting across from each other as the housekeeper returned to her seat at the table.

"I'd like to ask you both some questions if that's all right?" Constable Tadmore said with a look at first Maisy and then Mrs. Roque.

"Yes, of course." The housekeeper glanced at her employee, and she nodded.

"First, give me a bit of background on your guests, please." The cop looked to Mrs. Roque. She told him the basics about the authors from Dunn Wolf Publishing.

"Tell me how the evening went. Were all your guests at dinner?" This question was again addressed to Mrs. Roque as he added to his notes.

"Yes, our guests were seated in the dining room at seven. After dessert, they went through to the library for coffee and brandy. I stayed to serve them. Tiffany helped Maisy clear and continued with the clean up." The housekeeper glanced at Maisy again and she nodded. "I was in the library for about fifteen minutes pouring coffee, then I came downstairs to help, probably close to eight-thirty."

"How long did that take?"

"Quarter 0f an hour at most, the girls had most of it done. Then I sent the girls upstairs to the breakfast room to prep it for tomorrow." Mrs. Roque answered.

"Then what?"

"Tiffany went home. I checked on the guests. Ziola Nutt had already gone to bed. So too, had Mr. Westham. He came back downstairs just as I was locking the front door for a wake-up call at seven. I told him we would make sure he was up. He went into the library got a glass of sherry and returned upstairs. Hazel Dell followed him."

"How did they seem?"

Mrs. Roque squinted at the folded hands in her lap as she recalled the events. "They didn't speak to one another, but that's all I recall."

"Probably still annoyed from the disagreements earlier in the day, over the royalties," Maisy commented.

"No doubt." The housekeeper pursed her lips. "I don't understand all the details, but they were all annoyed with Ziola Nutt over the issue."

"Something to ask them in the morning." Tadmore made a note. "Then what?"

"The pair of them split at the landing and each went to their own wing, and I assume, their own rooms, roughly around nine o'clock."

Tadmore nodded as he drew two separate boxes and put a list of names in each to denote who went upstairs and when. "I wonder why he didn't want to use his mobile phone as an alarm clock."

Maisy lifted her chin. "Mr. Westham told me earlier he didn't like to turn his phone on if he didn't have to. Plus, most of the guests didn't have a car charger with them and were worried they'd run their batteries dry."

Tadmore nodded although he thought Westham's excuse was a bit lame. "Then what happened?"

"I went back down to the kitchen to tell Maisy about the seven o'clock wake-up call, then I went home through the back door."

"Did you stay in the kitchen, Maisy?"

"No," Maisy took up the story. "I went around and wound up the LED lanterns. As I finished with the one on the foyer table, Mr. Nutt, Miss Oakla, and Mr. Lintlaw said good night and went upstairs to their rooms."

"What time was this?"

Maisy shrugged. "Probably around ten after nine."

"How did you know they went to their own rooms?" He looked at Maisy with raised eyebrows.

"I can't be one hundred percent certain they did, but I heard three doors close as I was checking to ensure the front door was locked."

"I thought you locked up, Mrs. Roque?"

"I did, but we do cross checks of all the doors, just to be safe."

Tadmore nodded. "It was unlikely any one had come in from the outside?"

"Yes, that's right." Mrs. Roque nodded.

"What did you do after that, Maisy?" The cop turned back to the younger woman.

"I'm on shift until six. Mrs. Roque and Tiffany would be back then." She lifted one shoulder in a shrug. "I sat here, checked my email and other stuff on my phone." Maisy slid her eyes over to Mrs. Roque. "I might have dozed off for a bit. The shout upstairs made me jump. I think the killer would have been no more than fifteen minutes ahead of me into Ziola's room, twenty tops."

Gladys returned from the sink to stand beside her granddaughter, drying her hands on a towel. She spread the towel on the oven door handle and then pick up the coffee pot.

"Why would you say that?" Tadmore centred his attention on Maisy. "How do you know?" He declined Gladys' offer of a coffee refill with a hand gesture.

Maisy's grandmother said nothing as she took the pot to the sink.

"Whoever it was in Ziola Nutt's room wound the lantern. The light was giving off the brightest level of glow it's capable of. Typically, it lasts about twenty minutes after being wound up. After that, the light drops down to its lowest level. Like a nightlight." Maisy lifted one shoulder. "Those things might be a green alternative to kerosene lamps, Mrs. Roque," she looked at her boss as she spoke. "But they are kind of useless as a decent light for doing anything, really."

Chapter Eighteen

"THAT MIGHT BE TRUE, dear, but with the battery kind it is safer. The lanterns are there to merely allow the guest to see where they are going. I have no idea if any of them would have the first clue about kerosene lamps and we can't have them accidentally burning the house down."

"That makes sense, I guess." Maisy leaned back in her chair. "So, it could be Hazel, or someone else, who wound the lantern."

Gladys slipped into her chair beside her granddaughter. "I hate to point this out my girl, but the lantern can be wound more than once."

Begrudgingly, Maisy had to agree with her grandmother. "Yes, I guess so."

The housekeeper leaned forward to Maisy, clutching her mug. "What happened before you went into the room? Start when you got to the second floor."

Tadmore gave Mrs. Roque a pointed look to quell the conversation, but the gesture was wasted.

Maisy smothered a huge yawn with her left hand. "Ms. Oakla was standing outside her room when I got to the east wing hallway. She was glassy-eyed, and it stunk to high heaven on that floor," Maisy said. "She was looking toward Cherry Blossom's door and turned around when I came up behind her."

"So, she must have been smoking up for some time, if her pupils were dilated." Gladys pointed out.

Maisy gave her grandmother a steady quizzical look. "Oh really?" She lifted one eyebrow. "How would you know, Grandma?"

Gladys looked innocently at her granddaughter. "Why because of my neighbour, Freddie Freeman. He's been a medicinal cannabis user for years." Gladys spoke of her fellow condo owner. "We all know not to knock on Freddie's door after eight o'clock at night. He's usually pie-eyed by then."

"Anyway," Tadmore drew out the word to get them back on track. "Can we continue?"

"I'll tell you one thing for free. Ms. Angela Oakla has lost her deposit." Mrs. Roque folded her hands over her middle and gave an emphatic nod.

"I'm not surprised." Maisy got up to get a glass of water, then returned to her seat.

"Was there any odour in Ziola's room?" Her grandmother asked. "Did the place smell of marijuana in there too?"

Maisy shook her head. "No, not much. Mostly, men's cologne. Like the type Max Lintlaw uses. It was colder in there than in the hallway too."

Tadmore wrote down the information in bullet point form. "Where was Bertram Nutt during all this? He was still dressed when we arrived. Did he come from the direction of his room?" Tadmore looked back up at Maisy.

She shook her head. "I don't know. I was already in Ziola's room."

"He might have been in the library. Someone was in there after the guests went up to bed," Mrs. Roque suggested.

"How do you know it was Bertram Nutt?"

"I didn't say I knew it was Mr. Nutt, only that it could have been him," Mrs. Roque said. "Someone moved the cushions and a table around like they were sleeping on one of the settees."

"I see, and when were you in the library?" he asked watching the housekeeper intently.

"I went in to check the fire while I was waiting for you, Jack, and Joe to arrive. There was no point in me going all the way up to the second floor when Seymore was there already. And someone had to let the EMS into the house and direct you all where to go."

Gladys shrugged. "Bertram might have gone downstairs after he dispatched his sister."

Tadmore took a breath to dispel the idea of murder.

"Oh, you aren't fooling any of us, Patrick." Gladys took a cookie off the plate in the centre of the table. "We know Maisy saw serious bruises on Ziola Nutt's neck. I bet Bertram was waiting for someone else to find her body before he put in an appearance." Gladys lifted her coffee cup and then used the cup to gesture to Tadmore. "He might be your killer." She dunked the cookie into the mug.

Tadmore compressed his lips but said nothing. Instead, he made a note to ask Bertram Nutt where the man had been during the latter part of the evening. And why, at almost ten at night, would he go to his sister's room in the first place?

He noticed Maisy watching him write, he was sure she was reading his notes upside down. When Patrick looked up directly at her, Maisy looked away and offered him the cookie plate instead.

Absently, he took one of the gingerbreads and gave it a healthy bite. It was delicious and he wondered if it was Maisy who'd baked them. After he swallowed, "Can we move on to Hazel Dell, please. Tell me what you saw, Maisy." He stressed her name in the hope the other women would stay silent and let her speak without interruption. Yeah, good luck with that.

"I was telling Angela to open a window and put out her joint when Ziola's door opened. And Hazel—"

"Wait. The door to the bedroom was only closed, but not locked, right?" Tadmore asked for clarification.

"Yes, that's true. I didn't even know if that's where the shout came from. I thought it was Angela. That maybe she'd seen the ghost." Maisy rubbed her forehead, brushing blonde curls out of the way of her eyes.

"Ghost? What ghost?" His forehead crinkled, the cookie in his hand forgotten.

"Allister Highmere. He's the ghost on the second floor. Or at least we think it's him." Maisy flashed a brief smile at Tadmore.

He knew his expression had evolved into one of skepticism touched with humour. These people didn't actually believe in ghosts, did they?

"Don't laugh, you haven't had a run in with him." Maisy clutched her water glass.

Mrs. Roque frowned at Maisy. "Why would Mr. Allister haunt the second floor? He died below stairs in the wine cellar."

"I don't know, do I?" The blonde shrugged both shoulders. "He's your ghost."

"Who's to say a ghost has to haunt only the place where they died?" Gladys looked at Mrs. Roque. "The second floor is where the old master's suite was, right?"

"That is true. Ziola's room has a bathroom which is shared with the master suite. We aren't using it this weekend, so that room is locked. Maisy can verify that."

"The connecting door is currently sealed. I did check it before I secured Ziola Nutt's room. No one is to go in there until forensics has processed the scene." Tadmore gave Mrs. Roque a firm look.

"Of course, Constable. Even so," the housekeeper continued. "I'm no paranormal expert but I would have thought a person's last place of life would have something to do with where they haunted." Mrs. Roque tapped a forefinger against her lips. "If indeed we do have a ghost." She offered belatedly after a quick glance at the cop.

"I doubt it. Wouldn't he be more interested in where his wife used to sleep...and other things?" Gladys pursed her lips at her friend.

The older women nodded knowingly to each other with raised eyebrows and the cop didn't even want to speculate on what they were thinking. Tadmore closed his eyes briefly, counted to five and opened them again. He wasn't sure what that sidebar was about but didn't think the details were relevant.

It had been a long day already and he still had to update his boss. There would be no sleep until he'd explained the suspicious death/possible murder to Inspector Zeffler. At least Miles was taken care of for the moment. He needed to give Mari Ann a call too.

Early tomorrow morning there would be interrogations to deal with. His calm was sadly lacking, and his next words were a bit sharp. "Let's get back to Hazel Dell."

Gladys ignored Tadmore. "Jane told me she's seen someone over the years looking out from a second-floor window. Before the house was reopened when she was a kid."

"The north corner?" Mrs. Roque asked.

"I think so."

"That's the study. Mr. Allister used it as an office, also on the second floor, in the west wing. I imagine he felt more of a connection with that room than the wine cellar."

"That makes sense." Maisy said. "The ghost has never bothered me though. I've only ever noticed a cold spot here and there on that floor. Maybe he is ignoring us."

"Oh, not at all surprising. That's how he treated all the staff, dear, back in the day." Mrs. Roque turned back to the cop. "Shouldn't we get on with this questioning, Constable Tadmore? Don't you want to solve this murder?"

Tadmore inhaled deeply through his nose and released the air. "Yep, a great idea. What happened after the door was opened? Hazel Dell came out?"

"Yes, she backed out of Ziola's room. She looked scared and shocked."

"Did she say anything?"

"Yeah, that she thought Ziola was dead. I didn't believe her, so I went in and saw Ms. Nutt was on her bed. I checked her pulse, there was nothing, no heartbeat." Maisy cleared her throat. "I tried calling 911, but the line was busy."

"You preformed CPR?" He interjected.

"Yeah, but I couldn't keep going, not by myself. It didn't seem to be doing anything either." Tadmore noted the tremble in the young woman's voice.

"You did the best you could." His tone was gentle.

Gladys put her arm around Maisy. "You did fine, my girl."

Maisy sniffed and accepted the tissue Mrs. Roque offered.

"May I ask, was the body cold to the touch?" Tadmore asked.

Maisy frowned. "Not...really. She felt kind of warm still." Absently Maisy rubbed the fingertips of her right hand against the black material of her long skirt.

He made another note. "Any idea who knew our victim left the door unlocked?"

"I'm guessing you'll have to ask the remaining guests about that." Mrs. Roque instructed Tadmore.

"Yes, thanks." His dry response was lost on Mrs. Roque, but made Maisy's lips quirk into a smile. That was something at least.

He turned to Maisy again but did not get to voice his next question.

Gladys lifted one hand. "Why would Hazel close the door after she went in to begin with?" The three women looked expectantly at the constable. "It was all females in that wing. Plus, was she checking on her boss? Or is Hazel our murderer?" They looked at him like he should have all the answers. He just wished he did.

"I don't know, but I will find out." Patrick stood and went out to the entrance way which led to the back door. He reached for his yellow high visibility coat and plunged his hand into one oversized pocket to retrieve several plastic freezer bags. He'd left the bedspread with the body. The undertaker had locked it in the storage drawer along with the deceased when he accompanied the body to the funeral home.

"Is that the evidence?" Gladys asked. The ladies all sat up a bit straighter with Gladys' words.

"It is. I gathered these items from Ziola Nutt's room. Don't open the bags please but have a look and see if you can tell me who these items might belong to." The three leaned forward as he placed them on the kitchen table.

"It's whom, dear." Mrs. Roque corrected as she spread the items out in front of them on the table.

Tadmore rolled his eyes. Maisy was the only one who noticed.

He retook his seat as the kitchen door opened and Tiffany came to an abrupt halt as she saw the group around the pine wide-board table.

"Hello, Tiffany." Mrs. Roque lifted her heavy eyebrows as she looked at her employee. "What brings you back tonight?"

"What's going on?" Tiffany was dressed in jeans, a white sweatshirt and a brown raincoat.

Mrs. Roque glanced at the cop and at his nod, she turned back to the new arrival. "Come in, dear, please close the door." Mrs. Roque turned her attention to looking over the various pieces of evidence with interest. "You are hours early, but that's not a bad thing. Constable Tadmore has some questions for us."

Tadmore figured the more the merrier. Plus, he doubted anyone had told Mrs. Roque what she could and couldn't do for some years. Allowing the other girl to join them would actually speed up the investigation.

He stood again as Tiffany carefully walked over to the group in her sock feet. She looked at the cop with round eyes.

"I sent Tiff a text about Ms. Nutt's death." Maisy looked up at him as she admitted her actions. "I'm sorry if that's not okay, but I thought she should know before she came to work in the morning."

"I don't think it's a problem." He flashed Maisy a quick smile. His tone was level when he looked at the other girl. "I'm Constable Tadmore, and you are?"

"Tiffany Zach." She took Jane's vacant chair. "I figured I should come to see if you needed any help."

"Yes, dear. We need to bring you up to speed."

Mrs. Roque thankfully allowed Tadmore to handle informing her other employee of the events from this evening. Although he was pretty sure the housekeeper wanted to interject her opinion a couple of times, she did not. No doubt Gladys' hand on the older lady's arm prevented this.

The housekeeper nodded, satisfied with his update. "We are just looking at some of the constable's evidence."

"Have a look at this stuff, Tiff," Maisy said. "You can probably help us identify some of the things. These were all found in Ms. Nutt's room."

Tadmore was too tired to argue. If this were a regular investigation, with the normal division of labour, the group would have been split up to give their statements. As it was, there was no guarantee he'd have help tomorrow either, not with the storm debris to deal with.

Resting his chin on his fist, he let the women each have a go at some of the evidence he'd collected. His notepad and pen were ready to record their opinions.

"That sherry glass is from the set in the library." Mrs. Roque frowned. "It looks like she took a drink up to her room."

"It's quite likely," Tadmore allowed.

"The silver cap belongs to Bertram's hipflask." Maisy tapped the outside of the bag with a forefinger.

Tadmore made a note.

"I agree with that." Tiffany nodded as she shrugged out of her coat. "I saw him drink from it a few times yesterday." She reached across the table and slid a bag with several long black strands in it toward her. "That's Hazel's hair, I'm fairly sure."

"I'd say you are correct." Mrs. Roque seconded Tiffany's suggestion.

The cop nodded and made a second notation. The Ident forensics team would get everything and do their thing, verifying his findings.

"I think so too," Maisy agreed with a nod. He gave her a smile.

She turned her eyes downward again. Which caused his smile to fade. Had he said something to upset her? Then realized how idiotic that thought was. She'd found a dead body, who may have been murdered. Of course she was rattled. Keep it professional.

Focusing on the next item, Maisy frowned at the bracelet. Her bottom lip caught between her teeth as she thought. "I've seen this. I know I have."

"Yes, me too." Tiffany slid the jewellery closer for them both to inspect the item. "I think that's Angela Oakla's."

"I believe you are right, Tiffany." Mrs. Roque said. "I remember this being on her left wrist as she passed me to go into the dining room for dinner last evening."

"What about this document?" The cop slid the group of pages to the middle of the table and turned it over."

"The Fourth Monkey by Sylvia Highmere." Gladys read out loud. "Well obviously this is a manuscript that belongs to Sylvia Highmere. Mrs. Roque, do you know anything about it?"

"No, I do not." The housekeeper sounded peeved. "Sylvia called me to say she couldn't make it out here until the ferries were back up and running. I have no idea how this would have arrived without Sylvia, let alone get into Ms. Nutt's room."

"Then how would Ziola Nutt gain possession of the manuscript? Could it have been left somewhere in the library, say?" Tadmore looked at each of them in turn, but stopped when he got to Tiffany, she dropped her chin.

Ah.

Maisy shook her head. "That's not likely, we cleaned this place from top to bottom before the guests arrived. If this were lying about, we'd have found it." She held the plastic wrapped sheaf of papers.

"Tiffany?" Tadmore prompted.

Her lower lip rolled over her bottom teeth as Tiffany's eyes shifted to look at her boss.

For her part, Mrs. Roque narrowed her gaze at her employee, and she held out her hand for the package. Maisy handed it over. "Tiffany, do you know something about this?" She tapped the plastic bag with her index finger.

"I...yes, I'm sorry." The younger woman squinted her eyes like she was in pain.

"Go on." Mrs. Roque's tone was carefully restrained.

"Sylvia asked me to give the first chapter of her story to the publisher because she was stuck on Vancouver Island." Tiffany's words came out in a nervous rush. "She emailed me a copy; I printed it off in the reception area."

"Why?" Mrs. Roque's voice dropped to a dangerous level.

"I agreed to help because Sylvia's my friend. I didn't think there was any problem with me leaving the manuscript for Ms. Nutt. I tried to give it to her personally, but she was always tied up with one of her authors. I thought it would be easier to put it in her room. Besides, I had work to do, I couldn't wait around for Ms. Nutt to have a free moment." Tiffany looked at the cop. "I don't want to get Sylvia or me into any trouble."

"Then please tell me when you were in Ms. Nutt's room." Tadmore kept his tone even.

"Just before they all went into dinner. They were having a drink in the library, so I ran up the back stairs and nipped in quickly. I couldn't let Sylvia down."

"Was the door locked?" The cop kept his eyes on the young woman.

"Well, yeah, I took Mrs. Roque's master key from her desk in the carriage house when I checked for dial tone on the land line." She winced and kept her eyes down. "I don't have access to the extra room keys, only Mrs. Roque does.

"Did you notice anything out of the ordinary in Ms. Nutt's room when you where in there?" Tadmore asked carefully.

"Like what?" Tiffany frowned in confusion.

"Were there things on the floor or bed which didn't belong?"

"No, I don't think so. The bed was still neatly made. The carpet was clean."

The cop nodded. "Thanks."

"Yes, thank you, Tiffany." Mrs. Roque's tone held a wealth of meaning.

The words made Tiffany lift her eyes and she sent a pleading look at both the cop and her boss as she shifted her gaze between them. "I should have told you, Mrs. Roque. I'm sorry I didn't ask permission. I relocked the door and put the keys back, I promise." Tension and regret were evident in her hunched shoulders and wobbly voice.

"Mm." Mrs. Roque said noncommittally to Tiffany's worried look.

"Ziola sure got a lot of visitors," Gladys said.

"Thank you, ladies." Tadmore closed his notebook.

"What now?" Gladys asked.

"We have a few hours before we need to start the day. Maisy, you and Tiffany go home and get some sleep." Mrs. Roque climbed to her feet. "I'll stay in the house. Tiffany, a word please, before you go." The housekeeper led her to the pantry.

Tadmore began to gather up the freezer bags of evidence.

Maisy frowned as she got to her feet and wandered to the back entrance. "I'm confused."

"About what, Love?" Gladys handed her granddaughter her raincoat and put on her own.

"See no evil, hear no evil, speak no evil. What is the fourth monkey?"

"Think no evil, dear." Gladys dug out her car keys. "Come on let's get you home to bed."

Chapter Nineteen

THE AUTHORS WERE GATHERED in the library waiting for breakfast. None of them were in a particularly good mood. Not after the night they'd all been through. Conversation had been minimal as one by one they met up in the library. Tiffany told them to wait there for a few minutes until she came for them.

Kent looked around at the group and saw dark shadows and blood-shot eyes no doubt the same as his own. It had been too cold in his room to sleep properly. The extra quilts didn't supply enough heat. He'd gotten up and added clothing. Then gone to bed again with socks and his workout clothes on. Of course, Ziola's sudden death had upset the writers and contributed to his own lack of sleep. Something he didn't want to think about. He swallowed hard.

"I wonder if it was the soup at lunch yesterday." Hazel paced to the bay window. The woman was as nervous as a cat in a roomful of rocking chairs and did not look anyone in the eye. "Ziola wasn't feeling very well after lunch."

Briefly Kent closed his eyes and rubbed his left temple. This was all such a waste of his time. He was sick of being cold, and he was even sicker of this group of dimwitted individuals. All he wanted was for the ferries to start up again so he could leave this ridiculous collection of dullards. "Don't be stupid Hazel. I had the soup, most of us did. None of us are ill or dead for that matter."

"You are correct. I don't think it was anything she ate." There was a thick derisive tone to Bertram's words. "Ziola managed to consume two helpings of beef Wellington last evening at dinner," Bertram lowered his bulk onto the red velvet settee.

Kent frowned at Ziola's brother. He watched as the bald man slid his hand furtively between the cushions. He ran his thick fingers between the back of the couch and the cushion too. "What are you looking for, Bertram?"

The large man pulled his hand back as if he were scalded. "Nothing." He slid his fingers into his inside pocket of his jacket and removed his silver flask. The decorative cap that could function as a tiny cup when telescoped open, was missing Kent noted. He watched as Bertram unscrewed the white plastic top and then took a healthy drink. Kent looked away in disgust. It wasn't even eight o'clock in the morning.

Angela flopped down in one Queen Anne chair a foot from Kent. "Well, I'm looking for my gold bracelet. The safety chain must have failed last night when I wore it for dinner. I got back to my room, and it wasn't on my wrist anymore." Her lower lip came out in a pout.

"I should ask the staff if I were you. Someone may have found your trinket and don't know who owns it," Kent suggested. "I am willing to bet they have a lost and found somewhere."

Angela beamed a smile at Kent. "Thanks, I'll do that."

"I hate this. Poor, poor Ziola." Hazel shook her head sadly and turned to walk back to the group.

"Oh, come off it." Kent muttered. "You aren't fooling anyone."

"What?" Hazel frowned as she looked down at him.

"We are all sad Ziola is dead." Angela patted Hazel's hand as the other woman leaned a hip on the empty chair beside Angela.

"Are we?" Max wasn't really asking a question but stating fact. "All I want to know is what happens to the royalties and remunerations from the shows? We all contributed to the success of those books. Ziola was the only one preventing us from getting our fair share. With her gone, I assume we can expect an equitable settlement." Max looked at the dead woman's brother. "Can't we Bertram?"

"I agree." Kent nodded siding with Max.

"I can't believe you'd bring up something like that now." Hazel sounded shocked, but surprisingly to Kent, sincere. "We shouldn't be thinking about money at a time like this."

"When should we be thinking about money?" Kent raised his eyebrows at her. "We are merely being practical. We all want our money, don't deny it, Hazel." The side of his mouth quirked up in a sly grin. "Of course, some of us want more than just what we are owed." He kept his eyes on Hazel.

She glowered at him but said nothing more.

Bertram stowed his drink flask back in its standard pocket and blinked at Max and Kent in turn. "I...really hadn't thought about it."

"I have." Angela turned wide eyes to Bertram. "What will happen to the publishing house now? Won't you keep the press open? Can't we still expect to publish through Dunn Wolf?"

"And there we have it." Kent's tone sounded bored. "It's the inconvenience you don't like, not that Ziola is gone. That and the unknown, fearing you'll have to find a new publisher."

"We all don't have a well-paid professional career to fall back on." Max tossed a hand at Kent, dismissing his statements. "You're lucky you're an accountant."

"There's nothing lucky about it." Kent's words were coated with bitterness. "I worked hard to be an accountant. I made good decisions all my life to secure my future."

"That's not what Ziola told me." Bertram rubbed a hand over his unshaven jaw. "She said you were a terrible accountant. She let you stay on because she felt sorry for you, and as soon as she got the new guy, you were gone.

Kent rounded on him. "No one gave me anything. I had to fight for everything I have. I didn't have a sister who would publish whatever I wrote. Good or bad."

"Count your lucky stars that you don't." Bertram ignored the first part of Kent's shot as he stood once again. "No one should have to put up with a sister like Ziola." He shivered and then edged closer to the burning fire.

"Who's going to run the publishing house now? Bertram, you'll take it over, won't you. You must be Ziola's heir, she doesn't have any other family." Angela leaned forward and placed a hand on Bertram's arm. It was plain all the authors wanted an answer as they all fell silent to look at him expectantly.

Bertram pivoted to look back at the others. "I don't know."

"Ziola told me she had a 'significant other'." Hazel's tone was hard.

"A what?" Angela asked.

"A lover." Max shifted his gaze to look at Kent. "Didn't she?"

"Kent? You were in a relationship with Ziola?" Hazel locked her eyes on him.

Kent inhaled deeply through his nose. "My relationship with Ziola has been going on for some time, yes." He returned Ziola's assistant's gaze with a hard look of his own.

"I didn't think you and Ziola were still a thing." Max took the other chair. "She didn't say anything to me about you lately."

"Why would she." Kent snorted. "It was private."

"What does that mean?" Bertram made an attempt at sounding indignant. "You didn't live together, not as far as I knew."

"Ziola operated purely on self-interest." Max leaned back in his chair and folded his arms over his lavender cashmere sweater. "She'd never let anyone move in with her."

"Sorry to disabuse you of that assumption," Kent said loftily. "I moved in over six months ago, we just kept the information to ourselves."

"Why?" Angela shook her head in confusion. "Gossip? Nobody cares who you sleep with."

Hazel looked away, her hand at her throat, looking like she was going to be sick.

Well, there was nothing Kent was prepared to do about that, but he didn't like where this conversation was going. He determined it was time to change the subject.

Abruptly Hazel spun around and turned her glare on the other four authors. "You are all a bunch of sheep." Her tone heavy with distaste. "You all act like you didn't know Ziola was stealing from us. No one said anything or warned anyone. Especially you, Kent. You were Dunn Wolf's accountant before any of us got involved with the company." Her lip curled as she looked at him. Then she flung a hand up as if dismissing him. "And the rest of you." She shook her head like she couldn't believe their attitudes. "Whinging and whining that you didn't get the royalties you expected. No one ever addressed the issue with Ziola."

"We did the best we could." Angela, who was the least experienced writer among them, sounded haughty. "We did all the marketing she asked of us. Allowed our books to be discounted several times a year and for what? I don't know about the rest of you, but I'm not breaking even, not even close."

"Paying your family members for reviews is never going to work, Angela. A reader can tell when the book has actually been read by the reviewer and if they've posted honest feedback." Max pointed out to Angela.

"I have never paid for a review." Outrage caused Angela to sputter.

"You did." Max nodded, hands in his trouser pockets. "You offered to put me in touch with your siblings, for a fee."

"Don't be too smug, Max," Kent's snorted distain. "You are just as bad. You have a storage unit full of your books. You buy your novels whenever sales drop below an acceptable level. You aren't fooling anyone, you know."

"I would never—"

"Yes, you would." Kent rose to his feet. "Ziola told me you had a lock-up full of books. That's why we never had to have any printed in Victoria. Once a year, I'd tell you we were running low, and you'd drop off a dozen, at half price. Cheapest way to go, Ziola said. She wished the rest of you did the same." He put his back to the fire. "I'm out money too."

"Well, yeah, you can't buy your way onto a best seller list without serious cash." Angela sniffed dismissively.

Hazel waved Angela's words away. "I bet you knew what was going on behind our backs?" Hazel jabbed an index finger at Kent. "Ziola must have included you, especially with details about the streaming deal."

Kent knew he had to keep his tone even. "I knew some of it, I did do the books for Dunn Wolf for a while." Kent walked away from the fire, tugging down his vest over his shirt in the front. "Still, I didn't know anything about the streaming."

"I think you're lying," Max said.

He shook his head. "Anyone of us could be responsible for murdering Ziola." With his back to the library doors, he watched Hazel carefully.

"What are you talking about, Kent?" Max frowned.

"Who said anything about murder?" Bertram demanded. "I thought Ziola had a heart attack. She was—"

"Think about it. Why all the secrecy if all this was merely a heart attack? Why is that cop hanging around?"

"There's still a cop here?" Angela sounded nervous.

Kent nodded. "I saw him in the hallway this morning when I came down." He pinned Angela with his gaze. "He was hanging around your door, Angela. Did you have a go at Ziola?"

"No, of course not." Outrage again evident in the youngest author's tone.

"You might not remember. Pot messes with your memory as well as your brain." Hazel tossed these words at Angela, then shifted her glare to Kent.

"What about Bertram?" Angela jumped to her feet. She stabbed a green tipped finger at the bald man. "He could have killed his sister."

"Yes, that's true." Kent leaned back on his heels and tucked one hand into his trouser pocket again as he inspected Bertram. "I'm willing to bet you have been nursing a vengeful anger toward Ziola for years." He tipped his head as he studied Bertram. "Did you do it? You weren't in your room when I went over and knocked on your door last night."

Bertram climbed to his feet. He didn't look at Kent as he walked slowly to the library doors. Then he paused and turned on his heel to look back at the group. "If you and Ziola were in a relationship, Kent, one would think you'd be more broken hearted about her death. It's one thing to claim you lived together, quite another to prove it." Bertram looked Kent up and down. "One would also ask why she travelled here with me, instead of you." He turned again on his heel and left the room.

All eyes turned back to look at Kent.

Blinking, Kent turned away from the group to look into the fire.

"What did Bertram mean?" Hazel's jaw jutted out as she grabbed the shorter man by the shoulder and spun him around. "Do you have something you want to tell me, I mean, us?"

"I will not dignify that question with a response." Kent's words came out from between clenched teeth as he extracted his arm from her grasp.

"You are probably the killer." Angela narrowed her eyes at him. "You look like a killer. Your eyes are too close together." She nodded. "Are you a psychopath?" She didn't sound scared or upset, merely curious.

"Kent also seems to know far more about the situation than the rest of us." Max ran his eyes over the other man as he spoke.

Kent got the feeling Max was sizing him up too. "I don't deserve this." He stalked out of the library and brushed past Tiffany.

She did a quick sidestep to avoid him. "Breakfast is served." She announced to the other guests.

Chapter Twenty

IN THE KITCHEN TIFFANY and the housekeeper were discussing what to do with the guests. The group of authors were hanging out in the dining room. There was no heat in the breakfast room. In a rebellious move, the guests carried their plates from there into the dining room opposite, where the fireplace was lit. Unfortunately, this meant nothing could be set up for lunch in the dining room in the way the housekeeper wanted.

The younger woman looked at Mrs. Roque. "Can we let the constable use the small office on the main floor? There is a fireplace in there. Then the authors can go back to the library."

"Grand idea, Tiffany. I'll ask Mr. Willard—"

The back door opened. Dead leaves and rain blew in through the open door along with the groundskeeper.

"Ah, there you Seymore. Could you start a fire in Mrs. Olivia's old office please?" Mrs. Roque walked over to the cupboard, to grab a coffee mug for her co-worker.

"Already done." Willard hung his coat on a hook and parked himself at the end of the table.

"Oh, thank you. You are ahead of me as usual." Mrs. Roque put the mug down in front of the man. Not in the least surprised.

He grunted a thank you as Tiffany poured him a cup of coffee. "Give the room a bit to warm up."

Tiffany filled the stainless-steel coffee carafe before putting the pot back on the stove. "I'll take this to the dining room."

"Thank you, dear." Mrs. Roque glanced over at the stairwell door as it opened. Patrick Tadmore chose that moment to enter the kitchen.

Tiffany glanced the cop's way, frowned and left the kitchen.

"Mr. Willard has a fire burning in the hearth of a ground-floor office, so it will be more comfortable for you and afford some privacy for your interviews." Mrs. Roque told him as he joined them. "It will take a few minutes to warm up the room."

"You can hang meat in there right now." Willard offered this insight and then sipped his steaming coffee.

Tadmore huffed a chuckle.

Mrs. Roque tsked at the groundskeeper, Willard didn't appear to be bothered by the housekeepers annoyed tone.

Truthfully, Tadmore found the woman a bit intimidating. Mrs. Roque reminded him of his first staff sergeant.

The cop followed Tiffany's route back upstairs.

The authors were in the dining room tucking into breakfast when Tadmore got there. The cop entered the room to hook out Bertram Nutt as his first suspect to question. The aroma of bacon quiche made his stomach growl.

"Constable, won't you have something to eat first?" Tiffany asked. "There's an empty place here." She gestured to the empty sixth chair.

He shook his head as he glanced at the spot where Ziola Nutt would have sat if she were alive.

"Just some coffee, if you please." He couldn't sit down with his suspects for the morning meal. Not unless he wanted them all to drop their guard around him. Possibly confess some potential motive. He would save that tactic for later, should he need it. For now, he wanted to get as much background on their victim as possible. Hopefully, her brother would supply the information. "Mr. Nutt, if you've finished, could you please follow me?" He smiled a thank you to Tiffany as he took the coffee.

"Take this too, you must be starved." She pressed a bacon filled croissant, wrapped in a napkin, into his hand. How could he refuse?

Bertram Nutt put his napkin on the table and stood, taking his coffee cup to follow the cop to the library.

Here, the same as in the dining room, weak light shone through the white sheer curtains. The ever-present LED lanterns were scattered about and for the moment, appeared to be giving out their maximum effort.

Tadmore advanced into the room finishing his quick breakfast. He blinked at the sheer number of books lining the walls, something he'd missed earlier when the huge room had been shrouded in darkness. If he ever got the chance, he'd like to peruse the collection, but that wasn't why they were here, so turned his attention to his first suspect.

"Please have a seat." Tadmore tucked the napkin into his pocket and closed the library pocket doors. He turned to find Nutt sitting on one of the couches in front of the fire dogs cradling his coffee cup and staring into the flames.

Tadmore removed his work coat as he crossed the room and took over one of the winged-back chairs across from the other man. There was a small table he snagged and dragged toward the armchair for their coffee cups. Then tucked his coat over the chair's arm.

He sat and met Bertram Nutt's stare. "First, let me say I'm sorry for your loss, Mr. Nutt." Tadmore held the older man's gaze as he said this. "It must be hard losing a sister." He then extracted his notepad from his pocket and fished out a pen from his grey long-sleeved shirt pocket. Tadmore knew his uniform looked creased and was beginning to develop that lived-in scent. Not something he could do anything about right this minute.

The other man placed his cup on the table and glanced down to hide his eyes for a moment. "Yes, it is." He placed his palms together in his lap, then knit them into one fist. "Ziola and I were not as close as I would have liked these past years, but it is still a blow."

"I see." Tadmore let the statement rest briefly as he opened his occurrence book and wrote down the date, time, location, and who he was about to question. "You do understand that your sister's death is suspicious?"

"Is it?" Bertram nodded. "Somehow I'm not surprised."

"There are factors which are, at the moment, unexplained. We have to wait for the coroner's service to come out and for a pathology report, but in the meantime, I have been told to treat this incident as suspicious. It could be ramped up to something more severe later." His Inspector Zeffler had been explicit. Tadmore was to ensure the suspects understood the RCMP were taking the death extremely seriously.

"When did you last see your sister?"

"After dinner. We all had coffee in here. She stayed for about half an hour. Then retired early." He cleared his throat. "I did go to her room later on, after everyone was in bed."

"Why was that?"

"I wanted to speak to her about the streaming deal she'd signed. She owes some of the profits to me and the other writers who helped with the series. I knocked on her door and there as no answer. I tried the knob and found it unlocked."

"Was she awake?"

"No, she was already dead."

"Dead? You didn't call for help?"

"Why should I, what could anyone do?" The bald man shrugged his shoulders. "I thought she'd had a heart attack or something. She'd been complaining of not being well all day."

Tadmore gave Nutt a long silent look and then continued. "You were heard saying your sister stole your work?"

"Now, that was just me flapping my gums." Bertram waved the question away. "I was annoyed. I just said things. Everyone knows I shoot my mouth off occasionally." His hand strayed inside his jacket breast pocket, but he immediately removed it and curled the offending hand in his lap.

"Please, Mr. Nutt, answer the question."

The victim's brother heaved a deep sigh. "Yes, I did say that. Or something similar."

"Is what you said true? Did your sister steal your work?"

Bertram released a long sigh. "Yes, it's true. Over twenty years ago, I wrote an in-depth history of Vancouver Island with visions of publishing the work as non-fiction. My sister, already a burgeoning author, promised to edit the manuscript for me. Be my beta read, so to speak." His hand strayed up to his inside breast pocket again.

This time Bertram compressed his lips as he stopped himself and braced his thick-fingered hands on his knees. "Ziola stole the manuscript wholesale. She rammed my history into her time period romance. In essence, combining the two works. And then got the whole thing published by a small press on the island. She signed a contract for the proceeds. Of which, I saw a small percentage. This was all done without my knowledge or permission." His chin went up.

"That must have made you angry."

"It did for a time, but the publisher wanted more of her books, so I had my agent negotiate for a larger share of the royalties. I agreed to supply settings, time periods, and basic historical facts to my sister in exchange, Ziola would write the romance part. My name was never to appear on the cover, thank the Lord."

"Something changed, though, didn't it?"

Bertram nodded. "She backed out of that deal and went with Dunn Wolf instead. Ziola decided to buy into the publishing house. Kent Westham was instrumental in that decision. He'd been the accountant back then. I believe her decision was so she would not have to split the revenue with the old publisher or me. She invited other authors in and published their first works for a third of the royalties. Then, she pursued each of the writers to contribute a novel to the series using her characters and my history research."

"Were they paid?"

"After a fashion, yes."

"What does that mean?"

"It means, Constable, that my dear sister was a cunning and devious person. She made sure any expenses were applied solely to the author. Those expenses were deducted from royalties owed to said author and not split with the business. Dunn Wolf, or Ziola, got the lion's share of the profits I can tell you."

"How long has this been going on?"

"Decades."

"Why did you put up with being ripped-off?"

"Oh, I called her on it, early on. I withheld my contributions to her books if she didn't pay me a full share."

"And did she?"

"Oh, yes."

"What about these other people, the authors who are here this weekend?"

Bertram nodded. "These people are merely a handful, there are two hundred more from all over the world."

Tadmore made a note. This case could have international implications. "Why did these other authors allow this sort of treatment to continue?" He shifted his attention back to the witness. "Why not report Ziola and have her company audited?"

"Fear of being dropped as an author and possibly blackballed, I suppose. Ziola also used intimidation to keep the authors in line, she was a bully, first and foremost. She played upon the fears most writers have. That of not being able to find another publisher. If word gets out you are a troublemaker, you might be relegated to self-publishing." He said this last statement with extreme distaste.

"So, no one else challenged your sister? None of the authors here demanded to be treated fairly?"

"No, it is frightening for natural introverts to challenge authority. To be fair, some editors act like this to a degree. Some do not, at least in my experience." He gave the constable a shrug. "Dealing with creative types can be a challenge. I've published a couple of other standalone historical volumes and my experiences with other publishing houses has been fifty-fifty. Publishing is a crazy business and causes editors a lot of stress. They tend to treat their authors like sheep."

"So why would anyone decide now was a good time to murder their publisher if this situation had been going on for some time?"

"Oh, that's an easy answer, money."

Tadmore lifted his eyebrows. "Isn't that what we're talking about?"

"Not in this quantity. You see, the book series we had all contributed to over the years has been contracted by a streaming service to make the books into a television series. We discovered this development yesterday." Bertram shrugged heavy shoulders. "No one noticed Ziola had tied up all media rights to the books. She stood to gain hundreds of thousands of dollars, and film credit as a consultant. Not to mention, as the named author on the cover, she will get credit for the whole series of books and the back list will sell like no tomorrow once the streaming service platform launches the video version of the series."

"Ah, I understand." Money and fame, were these the killer's motives? He'd worked other cases where there had been less motivations for murder. It was always sad to be faced with the consequences of human avarice. Then again, was it avarice or something else?

He had to be careful when drawing conclusions. Unfortunately, he had five people with the exact same motive. This job was never easy.

"I'm sure you do." Bertram leaned back in his seat and this time allowed his left hand to retrieve the silver drink flask from his inside pocket. He spun the white, inner cap.

Tadmore watched Nutt take a long pull from the container as he took one of the evidence bags out from his coat pocket. He laid it on the table between them.

Bertram Nutt froze as his gaze fell on the silver cap from his flask. His eyes shifted to the secondary cap, white and plastic that actually sealed the flask clutched in his left hand.

The cop knew the silver cap was merely decorative and used as a shot glass if necessary. "We found this. Didn't you notice the cap was missing?" Tadmore was working up to saying where, he merely wanted Bertram to have every chance to admit what he'd done.

"Yes, I did, last evening. When I went into the library by myself for a nightcap."

"What time was this?"

"I have no idea, possibly nine-thirty." Bertram Nutt shook his head. "It felt later than it probably was. Everyone went to bed early because of the no electricity thing. The conversation was dull anyway. People drifted off to their rooms. I was the second to leave after Ziola. I thought I'd go to bed, but it was so damnable cold in my room I returned downstairs and decided to sleep on the sofa."

"Were you woken up at some point?"

"Yes, I heard a shout from upstairs. I waited to see if there was something more, but all was quiet so I thought I should go up and check on the ladies." Bertram gave the cop a vague smile.

"The cap to your drinking flask was found on the floor of your sister's room. How do you explain that?"

Bertram closed his eyes tight as he squeezed the flask with white fingers. "I already told you that bit."

Tadmore merely waited.

The older man inhaled deeply through his nose and let it out in a rush. "All right." He nodded. "I went to Ziola's room before I came downstairs. I thought I could try and reason with her. Get her to include the other writers in the largess she was set to receive. Authors don't make a lot of money.

Don't believe the movies you've seen. Most have to keep their daytime jobs and we all have to work on promotion, advertising, organizing signings, and interviews." The large man heaved a gigantic sigh.

"Unless you are a celebrity of some kind, publishers don't do much for us, except print and distribute the books to online platforms and stores." He snorted. "None of them have proof readers anymore."

"I feel for you, Mr. Nutt, but when did you go to see your sister?"

"When I left my room before coming down here."

"Tell me about it."

"I entered the east wing and found Ziola's room. She told me she was in the Cherry Blossom room. I knocked, but there was no answer."

"And then?"

"I tried the handle after a third knock. It was unlocked, I called out to her I was coming in to chat. I opened the door and went in. She was propped up on her pillows, like she was reading. It was hard to see. I grabbed the lamp off her night table and wound it up." Bertram swallowed as he stared at his hands. "She was still dressed for the day, and I didn't touch her. I thought it would startle her too much if she were sleeping. With more light, I could see she wasn't breathing. Ziola hadn't moved even though I spoke to her while I was tending to the lantern." Bertram dropped his chin to his chest and shook his head. "By then I could see she was dead."

"What did you do?"

"I was in shock. I just stood there staring at her. I must have taken a drink from my flask. I never noticed I dropped the cap."

"What did the room smell like when you entered?"

Bertram frowned as he flicked a tear away from his left eye. He looked directly at Tadmore. "It smelled like Max's cologne."

The cop made a note then looked back up at the older man. "You said she was still dressed, how?"

He lifted one hand. "In the black dress she'd had on for dinner, shoes too, although one was off, lying on the carpet."

"Anything else?"

"No, I don't think so."

"Where was her scarf?"

"On the night table beside the lamp."

Chapter Twenty-One

"WHY ON EARTH WOULD I be in Ziola's room? What possible reason could I have?" Max Lintlaw was now in the hot seat. He watched Tadmore pace in front of the fireplace.

"That's exactly my question, Mr. Lintlaw." Tadmore couldn't help his pacing. He needed to move. It was vital he stay alert. The coffee Mrs. Roque had brought him after he'd finished with Bertram Nutt was wearing off. Being on his feet helped.

Somewhere along the line, a cat had entered the room and was now curled up in front of the hearth. As he walked past the fireplace, the animal gave him a dirty look, so he changed course to walk behind Lintlaw's seat on the couch. The author was forced to swivel his head to keep the cop in his sights.

"I did not go into Ziola's room, at all. Ever."

Tadmore circled the couch and came to stand in front of Lintlaw. "Are you sure?"

"Positive. I didn't even know where her room was until Angela hammered on my door to wake me up last night and tell me Ziola was dead."

"Then why is the scent of your cologne so readily apparent in that room?"

"Again, I have no idea." His fervent words sounded convincing.

"Mr. Lintlaw—"

The author held up one hand to halt Tadmore's words. "That isn't to say that I didn't notice my things had been rummaged through. I saw my bottle of cologne was noticeably depleted when I returned to my room after dinner."

"Didn't you lock your door?"

"Yes, I did."

"Were you angry with your publisher for not sharing the profits of the streaming series contract with you?"

"Of course I was. That's why I plan on adding those facts to my civil suit. I've drafted an email already to my lawyer, Tommi Case. We will go ahead with the suit no matter what. I'll sue the estate if I have to."

Tadmore sat and made a note in his book. "When did you begin your case against Dunn Wolf Publishing?" He watched his second suspect closely.

The other man sat looking into the crackling fire then returned his gaze to the cop.

"October 1st of this year I contacted Tommi's law firm. Right after we received the statements from the second quarter. Dunn Wolf Publishing financial reports are always a quarter behind, or more. Ziola would sometimes not send one out at all. She would merely send us each a few dollars and say that was all we'd made from our books without any documentation to back up her email. Things were looking better this year, at least for a while. Dunn Wolf had a new accountant. I've never met him, David something." He shrugged lean shoulders. "Still, I know I've made more sales than Ziola ever admitted to."

The cop wrote down the details. "How do you know that?"

"Because on Amazon we all have author profiles, and they are linked to our book titles. We can see when sales spike or drop. I think Ziola forgot about this. We can see our book rankings on the other platforms too, but not in as much detail. I track when mine go up or down with spreadsheets."

"Why do you do that?"

"To know if an advertising campaign I've paid for is working or not."

"Can you see any stats on the historical romance series Ms. Nutt sold the rights to?"

"No, I'm not a named author. None of us are."

The cop noticed Lintlaw gritted his teeth and looked away. "The streaming deal is a lot of money."

"It is. I want my cut, and I want credit for the work I did. It would help the sales of my other books. Maybe then I could stop working for Victoria Waste Disposal and write full time."

Tadmore decided to ask one last time. "Were you in Ziola Nutt's room for any reason? Any reason at all? Did you have some kind of personal relationship with your publisher?"

"Are you asking if I slept with Ziola?" Max shook his head with a dry laugh. "Absolutely not, Constable. You see, I'm gay and in a committed relationship."

The cop nodded. "Thank you, Mr. Lintlaw, for clearing that up. I'll let you go for now." He gave the other man a nod. "If I have more questions for you, of course you will be around." It wasn't a question.

"Of course." The author got to his feet and exited the library closing the door behind him.

Alone, except for the snoozing feline, Tadmore got to his feet again and moved toward the fire to drop another log on the flames. He paused to scratch the cat between the ears and received a rumbling purr for his troubles.

He grasped the fire screen and moved it to one side to expose the fire and frowned as he noticed something odd in the fireplace to the far-left side of the burning wood. It was a small fragment, not melted in the heat. Tadmore reached for the tongs of the wrought iron fire tools displayed to the right of the fireplace.

Dropping into a squat, he carefully reached out with the tool to trap the object in question between the jaws of the tongs. It was a plastic bag, only part of a corner was left. The plastic was discoloured, a dark yellow.

The cop dropped the item on the bricks of the front of the hearth and away from the flames. He used one of the spare freezer bags he'd kept from the box Mrs. Roque had kindly given him. Scooped up the item into the clean bag, then ran his fingers over the seal and wrote on the white label when and where he found the item.

He would need forensics to tell him what the bag had been used for. And yet, he had a guess as to what caused the yellow residue. This remnant of plastic would be high on his list of items to hand over to Winchester's Ident team when forensics finally made it out to Musgrave Landing.

AT FIFTEEN MINUTES to eleven o'clock, Mrs. Roque looked up at Maisy coming in the kitchen door. She wore a fresh black and white uniform. And from the look of the girl, she was rested, and the spring was back in her step.

"What are you doing here, dear?" The housekeeper lifted a large quiche pan into the oven. "You're early." She straightened and closed the oven.

Maisy hung up her raincoat on a hook by the door. "I got some sleep and a hot shower. I'm ready to go again." She smiled and her blonde ponytail bounced as she walked into the kitchen proper.

"In that case, please go check on the ground floor office and see if it's warmed up enough to move Constable Tadmore into it for his suspect questioning. I want those people out of my dining room, ASAP. We need to arrange it for luncheon." Mrs. Roque shook her head and flexed her jaw to suppress her next thoughts. It was disrespectful to comment on any guest, but it was difficult not to, with that lot. "We can't set the room up for lunch if that bunch are loitering about."

"Will do. Would you like me to call Jane, or my grandma? You could get some rest. I doubt the café will be opened today anyway. Everyone will be hunkering down until the last of the storm has passed."

"Thank you, dear. Actually, I napped a bit after you left this morning, but I did call Jane. She'll drop by to give me a hand after she takes Arlie and some food up to the community centre. Some people need to shelter there. One or two homes were damaged by fallen trees and more with flooding." Mrs. Roque handed Maisy a tray with coffee, and fresh cups and saucers. "The constable would no doubt need a cup of something by now too."

"Did Patrick get any sleep?"

"Possibly," she said and added a freshly baked scone. "He kept an eye on the fire in the library overnight."

Maisy left the kitchen and tried not to think about Patrick as she crossed the foyer to the back of the house. She'd been intrigued by the man last year when they'd first met. Her grandmother's condo building had been the centre of a crazy robbery and murder. Patrick had been on the investigation team. Even then she'd thought his easy manner and deep brown eyes were attractive. They'd barely exchanged a dozen words back then. Since he'd come to rent Jane's apartment above the café, she'd gotten know him a bit more, but hardly enough to be considered more than acquaintances.

Usually, Maisy thought of herself as confident and outgoing. She had never thought twice about asking a boy out before, but then, that was the thing. There was nothing about Patrick that said boy, he was definitely all man. How could he possibly be interested in a twenty-year-old girl? She did not want to look like a ninny in his eyes, so she kept her distance. He was friendly and they shared a laugh once or twice when he came in for breakfast some days in the few weeks he'd been living in the village. Saturdays she knew he went hiking or went into town to visit his sister in Duncan.

Since he'd been at Highmere House, this was the most they'd ever interacted. She'd come to realize it wasn't enough. This awareness warred with her ambitions for her own future. Something more to think about later when things calmed down.

Maisy passed the open library doors as she crossed the foyer but didn't see Patrick. She continued on to the office door which was closed. Resting the tray on her hip, she turned the brass doorknob and swung the door inward.

A pleasant view of the back gardens and the waters of a small bay were visible from two windows. The scene was much more serene now that the wind had dropped somewhat. A watery sun was making an attempt to come out and melt the accumulated snow from the previous night.

The wood paneling here was lighter, white oak, The desk and credenza were also white oak. A pair of rich brown leather club chairs sat facing each other by the fire. This room had a cozier feel than the library, probably because it was half the size.

At one point, Mrs. Roque had told Maisy, this had been Mrs. Frost-Highmere's office. The comfortable furniture and other décor didn't have many feminine attributes. Although the wall art was all of flowers done in gentle water colours.

The temperature was comfortable with the fire crackling. It was warmer than anywhere else in the house with the exception of the kitchen. No doubt due to the southern exposure of the windows.

Maisy put the coffee tray down on the table between the club chairs. After tossing on a couple more lengths of wood onto the fire, she closed the door again and headed over to the library. With the pocket doors now open, she surmised Patrick wasn't questioning anyone.

Maisy saw him straighten from petting the calico cat as she entered. "How's it going?" Maisy stopped at the first settee and rested her nervous hands on the back.

Patrick gave her that dangerous half-smile of his. "It's going. What's happening now?"

"I'm to move you to the office so we can remove the crowd in the dining room. Let them come in here instead, if that's okay." She lifted her eyebrows at him. "There's coffee waiting for you there too."

"Sold!" He grinned at her. "I doubt there are any more bits of evidence in here anyway. He held up the plastic bag in his right hand.

Maisy swallowed her reaction to his grin. Instead, she put on a look of inquiry. "Find something good?"

"Part of a sandwich bag, I think. It was in the fireplace someone tried to burn it."

"That would not be me or Mrs. Roque, and probably not Tiff. We know better than to do something like that. Mrs. Roque would have kittens if she knew someone was burning rubbish in the fireplace." Curiosity made Maisy get over her shyness and walk over to look at the evidence. "That's a funny yellow colour."

"It is. Smells funny too."

"Oh?" She shifted her eyes up to his.

He blinked, cleared his throat, and then opened the sealed bag. "Tell me what you think."

Maisy leaned in to take a sniff. She wrinkled her nose. "That reminds me of Max's cologne."

"It does, doesn't it? He was just in here."

Maisy frowned. "Why would anyone keep cologne in a plastic bag?"

"That's a good question." Patrick resealed the bag. "I have a feeling some of Max's cologne was placed in here." He put the item in his coat. "Let's go to the office, then I can go get Hazel Dell for questioning." The cop folded his coat over his arm.

Maisy led the way. "It's through that door. The fire has taken the chill out of the room."

"Thank you." Patrick made no move toward the office.

"Do you want to leave your coat?" Maisy asked.

"I have evidence in my pockets, I don't want it to be out of my care."

"I see." Maisy retraced her steps.

The pair entered the dining room, Maisy spotted Kent and Hazel off by the window. They appeared to be having an intense, yet whispered conversation.

Bertram, Angela, and Max were seated at the far end of the table closer to the door. Each was nursing a cup of coffee. All three looked uncomfortable and did not look toward the couple across the room.

"That looks interesting." Patrick commented in a low voice. Kent was saying something quite emphatic which resulted in Hazel jutting out her bottom jaw in a stubborn way. "Ms. Dell, could I have a word?"

Hazel swivelled her head in the cop's direction, she blinked, looking distracted for a moment. "Yes, no problem. Do you mind if I run upstairs for my sweater first?"

"No, I'll meet you in the office kitty-corner from the bottom of the stairs on the right."

With a nod, Hazel walked briskly out of the room with her bare arms tight to her body.

Kent released a sound halfway between a growl and a snort and marched right after the tall woman. "Excuse me," He curtly strode between Maisy and Patrick.

Maisy's lips pursed as she watched the short man catch up to Hazel on the lower stairs. The temperature of the house was not comfortable, she wondered how Hazel could stand it with bare arms in the first place.

Patrick gave her a wink as he left the dining room.

Maisy turned to the other three still sitting at the table. "We need to prepare the dining room for lunch." She told them. "If you could move to the library, it would be much appreciated, thank you."

At the promise of being fed again, the three willingly moved out. Tiffany returned with a resupplied tea trolley and made to follow the guests. "Library?"

"Yep." Maisy snagged one of the plates with a selection of baking and took it back to the office for Patrick. No way was one scone going to cut it.

She knocked tentatively and Patrick opened the door. His look of gratitude as she carried in some refreshment for him made coming into work early worth it. He really did have the best smile.

Hazel appeared and closed the door behind her.

Maisy stepped over to the tray she'd left on the table between the chairs and added the plate by the coffee pot. The other woman lowered herself into the seat closest to the cop. Covertly, Maisy looked the other woman over as she offered her the pastry plate, but Hazel declined.

"I'm so glad you moved the body." She gestured for Maisy to pour her a cup of coffee. "I was not looking forward to sleeping next door to a dead person." Hazel was vibrating with some kind of nervous energy.

Maisy couldn't determine the cause as she filled Hazel's cup. The other woman took the coffee Maisy offered her and leaned back in her chair, crossing one long leg over the other. The split in her skirt exposed a long section of shapely leg clad in black hose. The black skirt contrasted well with her red silk blouse and grey sweater. Both of which clung to her curves.

"No, I can understand that." Patrick's tone was neutral. He offered the agitated woman an empathetic smile.

Picking up the other cup, Maisy shifted her eyes to Patrick, he was now looking a her. She felt an irrational wave of pleasure. "Coffee?"

"Yes, please."

Hazel shook her head, and clutched the cup in both hands like it was a lifeline. "Where...what did you do with her body?"

"That's really none of your concern at the moment. A postmortem will be required as this is a suspicious death." Patrick's eyes caught Maisy's for a moment, and she remembered she should not say anything about murder.

"Maisy, you were there when Ms. Dell came out of Ms. Nutt's room, weren't you?"

"Yes, Ms. Dell told us her boss had passed away." Maisy held the empty tray flat in front of her. She had been sure Patrick would make her leave now that the coffee was delivered.

He turned to Hazel. "How did you know Ms. Nutt was dead?"

Hazel rolled her eyes. "She wasn't breathing, I could see that."

"And it was you who screamed?" the cop asked her.

"Yeah, that was me. I thought Ziola was sleeping. I touched her shoulder, and that was when I realized she was dead. It's shocked me." She hid her mouth behind her cup.

"The door wasn't locked?"

"No. I knocked first and there was no answer, so I tried the knob."

"It didn't surprise you Ms. Nutt's door wasn't locked? Did you expected the door to be unlocked?"

Hazel shrugged. "You have to know her to understand Ziola. She did things her way, always."

"Why did you go to your boss' room?" Tadmore picked up his cup of coffee and sat on the edge of the desk watching Hazel.

"I...I wanted to talk to her about getting my name on the new novel I helped her write for her series. To be recognized as a co-author, at least. I didn't care about the royalties. She could take a hundred percent, as long as I could leverage my involvement."

"Why would you give your labour away for free?"

"I'm not an accredited author like the others. They all received some kind of payment for their contributions. I can't expect that."

"Because you worked with her, knew her, you thought Ms. Nutt would agree?"

"I did. Or at least, I hoped she'd be fair with me. This particular novel is expected to sell even better than the rest of the series if the pre-sales campaign is anything to go by." She put her cup down on the small side table and clasped her hands tightly in her lap. "The responses back from the beta readers for the ARCs has been very favourable."

"What's a beta reader and what is an ark?" Tadmore frowned.

The brunette gave him a slow smile as she pulled her long dark braid over her shoulder to fuss with the end. "We have people who will give us their opinion of a novel before it's published. An ARC is an advance reader copy of the manuscript."

"Is that why you closed the room's door?" Maisy asked. "You expected an argument from Ms. Nutt?" Maisy shifted her eyes to Patrick. Belatedly she realized she was interrupting.

"That's a good question." The cop looked back at Hazel.

"I don't know why I closed the door. I guess I wanted privacy for our talk." Hazel coyly lifted one shoulder. The boat neck of her blouse slid off one pale shoulder.

With this action it occurred to Maisy she had to stay in the room with Patrick while he questioned Hazel. The woman was dangerous.

He nodded. "Did you see anyone else in the hallway before you went into Ms. Nutt's room?"

Hazel shook her head. "I knew Angela was awake. I could smell her joint in the hallway, but I didn't see anyone."

"Did you hear anyone else?"

"No." Hazel leaned forward and selected a ginger cookie from the plate, she slowly nibbled the edge as she looked wide-eyed at the cop.

Maisy narrowed her eyes at the other woman, she had the feeling Hazel was up to something or maybe lying.

"Tell me what the room looked like when you went in." The constable put his empty cup down.

"The lantern was going, that's how I saw Ziola was still dressed for the evening. She had her jewellery on, her scarf too. Her shoe was off. She must have been removing them when she passed."

"What was on the night table?"

"An empty glass of sherry. The lantern, of course, and that was it, I think."

"Did you notice anything else laying about?"

Again, Hazel shook her head. "I don't think so. I was, am, so upset by Ziola's death. I wasn't thinking straight. After I touched her, I backed out of the room."

Tadmore's cell phone rang. He looked back at Hazel. "You can go, Ms. Dell. Thank you. If I have more questions, I'll speak to you again."

He didn't have to tell Hazel twice; Maisy raised her eyebrows at how quickly the other woman dropped her half-eaten cookie on her saucer and left the room.

The cop quickly dealt with his call.

Maisy put her tray down on the desk and took the opportunity to refill his cup.

After Patrick hung up, Maisy gave him a nod. "Is there anything else I can do?" She knew she should get her butt back downstairs and give Mrs. Roque a hand.

"Do you think Hazel was upset Ziola had stolen, in her mind, Kent's affections?"

"And that was why they were arguing in the dining room just now? It's possible I guess."

"You sound skeptical. You don't think Hazel would be angry with Ziola, jealous, enough to strangle her?"

Maisy passed Patrick the plate and he selected a sugar cookie. "I have a problem thinking anyone who is in love, is capable of murder."

"Interesting, why?"

"When someone is in love, well, love is a positive open emotion, isn't it? There's no evil in it. That's what murder is, it's evil."

Patrick bit into his biscuit and gestured for her to go on.

"I think if someone does strangle the person they are infatuated with, fixated on, or whatever, it's not love they are angry over, it's lack of control over the other person."

She handed him a serviette.

He wiped his fingers. "You may have a valid point." He finished his coffee and put his cup on the tray. "Things are about to get interesting."

"Is that so?" Maisy began gathering the used coffee things onto the tray.

"The coroner is on the ferry from Stoney Hill."

Chapter Twenty-Two

IT WASN'T ONLY THE coroner who made the trip across the Samsum Narrows from Stoney Hill to Musgrave Landing. Tadmore got a text from his sergeant the Ident forensics team would make the trek as well.

This was great news. He didn't want the investigation to stall due to lack of factual evidence to counter his suspects claims. It was evident some of them were lying. And while he was certain he knew who was covering up their actions, he needed to be sure before taking the interrogations to the next level.

Tadmore called Jack as he walked down to the harbour and asked him to meet at the ferry.

His plan was for Jack to take the coroner to the funeral home while Tadmore conducted Winchester and his forensic team back to the Highmere mansion.

As he proceeded down the driveway from the estate, he caught a glimpse of the groundskeeper at work. Mr. Willard was running a tractor with a set of forks on the bucket. The groundskeeper was clearing debris from the driveway.

Tree limbs, mostly, from the surrounding maples, spruce, and arbutus. The wind was still high, although not as destructive as yesterday. Not close to hurricane levels, but still cold with leaves and moisture flung about. Tadmore was glad of his heavy work coat.

The groundskeeper dropped the machine's bucket to the earth and waved at Tadmore. Wanting to be friendly, Patrick strolled over to say hello.

Twenty minutes later Constable Tadmore reached the ferry berth. Across the churning grey waters, he could see the outline of the white and blue ferry making its way across the Narrows. Turning to the parking lot, he found the conservation vehicle, the only one present.

"Nice to see you got your truck running." He came to a stop at the driver's window. Jack had powered down the glass when he'd seen Patrick approach.

"Dad did, actually. Apparently, my carb was loose. He and Miles fixed it while we were up at the big house last night."

"Miles helped Arlie?"

"He did." Jack nodded. "I'm glad it wasn't the starter. I really didn't want to have to get into that right now."

From his expression, Patrick could see Jack had more to say on the subject of Miles but left it for the moment.

"Thanks, Jack. I appreciate you and Jane allowing my nephew to stay with you during this situation."

"No problem." Jack leaned his forearm on the windowsill. "I'll take the coroner up to the funeral home and stay with the crew until they are ready to return to the morgue on Vancouver Island. If something comes up, I'll call you."

"Or Inspector Zeffler will. He's coming too."

"Ah." Jack nodded.

"It should be my sergeant, but everyone is working flat out right now. There's a lot of storm damage and the power outage is widespread."

"Yeah, Musgrave's volunteer firefighters are spread out all over too. Clearing detritus from the roads. A couple of houses had trees fall on them. The rooves are compromised. The village has activated the emergency shelter at the community centre. Jane and Dad are over there serving food. Miles is helping too."

Tadmore was impressed. It didn't matter who had motivated his nephew to volunteer to help others, as long as it happened. "Everyone has to earn their keep. That's what my parents taught us."

"Mine too." Jack agreed.

The ferry pushed a swell of water against the stone wharf as it nosed its way into the vessel berth.

Minutes later, the white coroner services van followed Jack's truck up the hill on High Street. After a brief conversation, Inspector Zeffler followed the van in his SUV.

The constable waited for the forensic vehicle to pull to the side of the road, and he climbed in the sliding door. "Winchester, nice you could make it out." He took the empty seat behind the driver and passenger.

"Thanks for giving us something else to do beside traffic control. Canterbury was getting bored with imitating a human stop light." Winchester waited for him to buckle in, then put the van into gear. "Highmere house, again, huh?"

"Yep, the family are not implicated this time though."

"We read the call report." Canterbury said from her seat on the passenger side. "Sounds like something from a movie script."

"That just might be, it's a house full of writers, so your description might be right on the nose."

"What's the plan?" Winchester made the left turn to take them down Coast Road.

"At some point the staff and guests need to be fingerprinted."

"I'll take care of that," Canterbury said.

Tadmore nodded. "I have a stack of bags with items found in the victim's room. None of which should have been there."

"Did you leave us anything to do?" Canterbury turned her head to look over her shoulder at him on the back bench seat.

"Lots. I only picked up the obvious stuff and the bedspread the victim was lying on. I locked up the guest room last night after we moved the body to the funeral home."

"I guess you couldn't preserve the evidence if the body were left in situ?" Winchester signaled and they turned into the estate driveway and rolled through the wrought-iron gate.

"Where are you keeping the evidence? Locked in your SUV?" Canterbury asked in a leading way.

Tadmore got a sinking feeling. "Um, no." He kept his eyes glued to the windshield. "My vehicle was damaged in the storm. I had to leave it until it can be towed." He patted the large pocket of his high vis raincoat. "I've kept the evidence with me."

There was a snicker from the passenger seat. Tadmore briefly closed his eyes. Canterbury obviously knew something about his flattened vehicle. His sergeant was right, two people couldn't keep a secret unless one of them was dead. Someone in Zeffler's office was a blabbermouth.

"You've got a new nick name back at the Detachment, Tadmore."

"I'm sure I do," he said, containing a sigh.

"Lumberjack."

"Great."

Winchester began to whistle the tune. Monty Python's *The Lumberjack Song* as the cop parked next to a green Volkswagen beetle.

"I'M CERTAIN THE HYOID bone is broken." The pathologist, Dr. Teng, said as he stripped off his disposable gloves.

"Meaning strangulation." Inspector Zeffler watched Teng put the gloves carefully into the large disposal bag he'd lined a receptacle with earlier.

"Yes." The doctor nodded. "The bruises caused by the scarf appear to be postmortem. The fibres of the scarf are embedded somewhat."

Zeffler knew the techs would take everything back with the body and incinerate the used coverings at their facility. Nothing that could be used as evidence or to support evidence would be left behind. "You'll have to confirm that fact with an autopsy?"

"I will, yes." The pathologist confirmed. At no more than five-feet-five inches tall the white disposal coveralls made Dr. Teng look like he was wearing a bulky snowsuit a couple of sizes too large. He gestured to his assistant. "You can prepare the deceased for transport now, Belinda."

Teng walked to the sink in the basement room of the funeral home. Normally used to prepare the deceased for burial or cremation, the place was uncluttered and spotless.

Upon inspection of the room, the pathologist had agreed to give Inspector Zeffler a cursory examination of Ziola Nutt. For that he was thankful. This preliminary opinion would move things forward quickly.

Kevin Moffatt, the mortician, and business operator shifted from foot to foot by the door. "So not a natural death, then?" He looked at Teng a touch wide-eyed.

The pathologist glanced over his shoulder at the younger man. Teng inspected Moffatt over the rims of his gold wire-frame glasses. "Anything I say must remain confidential, Mr. Moffatt. This is preliminary and my opinions are merely that as well. A high-level analysis only for the edification of the Inspector."

"Oh, I completely understand." Moffatt folded his hands behind his back, making his brown suit jacket strain at the middle button. "Is there anything else I can do for you, Dr. Teng? Anything you need?"

"Hot coffee would be a blessing."

"Absolutely, I'll have some made right away. Please join me in the counselling room to the left of the stairs when you're ready."

"Thank you." Teng soaped his hands and turned on the tap with his elbow.

Kevin opened the stairwell door and disappeared.

Zeffler waited for Moffatt foot steps to fade, and then crossed the concrete floor to the doctor.

The coroner, Gerald Bishoff, had been waiting with Zeffler and followed him across the windowless concrete room.

The three men watched as Belinda efficiently enclosed the body once again in the black plastic fabric. The odour of stale cologne, among others, was much reduced.

"Is there anything else you can tell me?" Zeffler asked. "Other than our victim was strangled." His hands were buried in the side pockets of his high visibility raincoat. He'd left his hat in the car. The floor was damp with the number of rain-drenched visitors, but the convenient central drain helped remove the water.

"Maybe." Teng finished washing his hands and tossed paper towel also into the same receptacle. He unzipped his white suit in preparation for removal. "First, where is our EMS tech?"

"Jack Birch is upstairs," Zeffler said.

Teng shucked his white fabric suit, disposed if it, and put on his jacket over his T-shirt and jeans. "Belinda, I'm going upstairs to talk to the EMS tech. I'll be back in a minute to help."

"I'll give Belinda a hand." Bischoff stepped forward.

"Thanks, Gerald. I'll meet you back at our van then, Belinda."

"Sounds good." The tech nodded but didn't look up from her task. The coroner stepped to the opposite side to help her move the body onto a gurney.

Zeffler and Teng made their way up to the first floor and found Jack in the reception area. The man they sought sat propped up in a waiting room chair. Head back and eyes closed. His hands were interlocked over his chest. By the frown Birch wore, Zeffler didn't think the man was sleeping.

As they approached him, Jack opened his eyes and stood. The man was younger, and an inch taller than Zeffler. They both towered over the shorter doctor.

Teng stopped in front of him and looked up at Jack. "What time did you transport the body?"

"At eleven-thirty-five by my watch."

Teng's eyebrows came up at this proposed accuracy.

Zeffler snorted. "Mr. Birch has ample experience with handling situations like this. He's SAR, Search and Rescue. We've worked together before."

He and Jack exchanged commiserating nods.

"Mm. Well, was there any stiffness, any sign of rigor mortis when you transported the body?"

"Some in the face and jaw. The rest was warmish and flaccid, the victim hadn't been dead long. I'd say under three hours."

"I agree that fits. The victim was found probably no more than an hour, hour and a half after death."

"Which puts my time of death between nine to eleven o'clock last night." Zeffler nodded.

"Potentially. I'll know for certain once we get back to the lab. Is this enough for you, Inspector, for now?"

Zeffler nodded. "It gives me something to start with, thanks. I have to go catch up with my team at Highmere House." Zeffler thanked Jack and Teng and then headed to his own vehicle.

Chapter Twenty-Three

UPON ARRIVING AT HIGHMERE house, Zeffler updated his constables with the new information from the pathologist. The Inspector was no stranger to Musgrave Landing, Tadmore knew. His boss had history in the village with a couple of previous cases. As their inspector said at the end of the briefing in the office on the first floor, this community was never dull.

Now on the second floor at the crime scene, Tadmore patiently waited while his boss stood at the bedroom doorway and took a moment to study the room. Zeffler had a reputation for resolving cases quickly and being instrumental in supplying what it took to ensure a good arrest and subsequent conviction.

Due to the fallout from the storm, all detachments were stretched pretty thin. All officers were working overtime shifts as it was to meet the increased call volume. Everything from the regular, run of the mill infractions, to traffic control in busy areas where the traffic lights were nonfunctional. The result was the detachment could only spare one senior officer for the murder of Ziola Nutt.

"What did you make of this scene, when you opened the door, Constable?" the senior cop tossed the question over his shoulder to Tadmore. His boss was charged with the overall suspicious death investigation. Tadmore had been responding officer, so was drafted to be Zeffler's sidekick for the investigation. Something Tadmore was grateful for, the experience would be invaluable.

"My first feeling when I walked into this room last night was that the victim's death might have been a heart attack. When we examined the body before we moved it, I determined there might have been a suspicious reason for the death."

"How many murder investigations have you participated in?"

"Two, sir. One as crowd control and one as a secondary officer assisting with house-to-house information gathering."

Zeffler nodded but said nothing. He gestured for the constable to continue.

Tadmore knew what was coming. Zeffler had that 'teaching' tone in his voice.

"I noticed some items on the floor and the bed and as I didn't want them to be impacted by moving the body, I took photos and collected the items." He'd done what he thought was right at the time. Even though it wasn't until he'd sorted through the evidence when he began to think the whole thing looked staged. At least the coroner confirmed the deceased was murdered.

"What would you have done differently?"

"I'd have started questioning the guests right away." He looked down at the carpet where the lady's shoe and the cap for the drink flask had been found. "I think the delay has allowed the killer to fabricate a story."

"You agree the killer is no doubt known to the deceased?"

"I'd say that's a firm bet."

Zeffler walked slowly into the room. "I've never seen this many clue-like items found in one murder scene, ever. We had a wealth of evidence."

Tadmore stayed two steps behind the senior officer.

Forensics finished their work in the Cherry Blossom room that morning. They left behind yellow numbered markers from Tadmore's photographs where the evidence had been found. As well as fingerprint dustings about the room which dotted the furniture, woodwork, and bed. Both doors, and in some areas on the floor, which Tadmore lifted an eyebrow at.

The team has also carried away the bedclothes, and the rest of Ziola Nutt's belongings. The room had a cold, abandoned feel to it.

"It is odd." The tall dark-haired inspector had sorted through the constable's collection of clear plastic bags when they'd returned to Highmere House. Zeffler made Canterbury pause in cataloguing the findings to allow this. She'd been halfway through carefully transferring the evidence to numbered and officially labeled evidence bags at the time.

"What does Ident's report say so far?"

Tadmore dug out his phone and scrolled until he found the preliminary results email. "First items addressed were the fingerprints. It appears there are six different sets of prints in this room besides the victim's"

"Any initial identities established yet?"

"Agatha Roque."

"Yes, she would be on file from that business two or three years ago." Zeffler paced the length of the room. "Anyone else?"

Tadmore blinked, wanting to ask why the housekeeper's prints were on file, but merely answered, "Canterbury has fingerprinted the staff and guests, she'll do a comparison check."

Zeffler frowned as he crossed to the bathroom and looked in. "Two of the sets of prints no doubt belong to the other two staff. That leaves us with three guests."

"That's what I'm thinking. Bertram Nutt, the victim's brother admitted he was in here last night. He actually found the body first, but assumed she'd died from natural causes."

"It's rather strange the brother didn't call for help. Or report it."

"I agree. Hazel Dell was observed by the staff member Maisy Wyatt coming from this room."

"She's the reporting party, yes." Zeffler kept his hands locked behind his back as he moved around the room. "If we exclude the three staff, Bertram Nutt and Hazel Dell, that leaves us with one more guest not accounted for."

"Yes sir, or the perpetrator wore gloves." Tadmore glanced up from his phone.

Zeffer gave him a nod of agreement. "The coroner did say the fibres embedded in the deceased's skin match the scarf found around her neck."

"Is that our murder weapon?"

"Possible, but not likely. He thought the scarf bruising was postmortem. In addition to the marks, there is bruising from where hands were placed around the throat." The senior cop looked toward the four-poster bed. "Does that tell us whoever killed the publisher had the strength to hold her in place while they tightened the material or used bare-handed strangulation?"

"Do you think the killer tried to use their bare hands first, then switched to the scarf, or vise versa?" Patrick asked.

"Either is possible, I don't know yet. Any indication if the bare-handed method was male or female?"

"No, sorry. Ident heard from Teng, the scarf marks are postmortem."

"Two sets of marks then?" The inspector narrowed his eyes as he pondered this piece of information. "Anything from the toxicology yet?"

"Not yet." Tadmore slipped his phone into his right trouser pocket. "Do you think she was drugged or drunk before death?"

"Again, it's possible. No one heard anything. At the least I would have expected a struggle. A shout for help, something. That tells me the victim was probably incapacitated in some way. Maybe drugged."

Tadmore mimicked his boss as they looked around the room at the large print rose wallpaper, walnut wood furniture and the discoloured part of the floor where the area carpet had been. Ident had been thorough.

Zeffler abruptly moved forward to look at the large water colour print above the headboard. He used one gloved finger to push the picture to the side. It did not move easily.

"Find something?"

"How far up this wall was the victim's head?"

Tadmore studied the area. "I'd say her head was just below the picture from Maisy Wyatt's description. She had to move the body to preform CPR."

"Ziola Nutt was a tall woman. Flailing about would have moved this print. Ask Winchester if there was anything found on or around the artwork."

"Will do." Tadmore could tell his boss was thinking things through. He had that detached, studying the middle-distance look.

"The cologne was no doubt sprinkled around the victim to make investigators think Max Lintlaw had been in Ziola Nutt's room." Zeffler paced the room again, this time moving north-south. "You found that partially melted bag in the fireplace in the library." Zeffler tipped an index finger at the constable.

"I did."

"The flask lid dropped on the floor, here." The inspector pointed downward at yellow marker number two. "To make it seem as though Bertram Nutt was in the room."

"Which he admitted. I have a witness, that heard the arguments over money concerning the guests and the deceased. Each of them had a motive."

Zeffler nodded. "A bracelet from Angela Oakla, lost after dinner." His eyes went squinty. "The piece of jewelry could have been lifted and dumped here as well."

"With everyone downstairs, getting into Hazel Dell's room to extract a sample of hair wouldn't have been difficult if they could also get by the lock on this door."

"True. Or the connecting bathroom door." Zeffler gestured in the opposite direction. "A shared bathroom between the master bedroom and this one."

"The other room is unused at the moment. The door was locked."

"Where is the hallway access to the master suite?"

"Down the corridor, in the west wing. There is also another which leads from that bedroom to a short hallway which connects to the back stairs."

"Does it now?"

"I found the other room connections and checked to see if any door had been unlocked or tampered with." Tadmore had gone exploring after Maisy and her grandmother left last night. He'd also wanted to see where the other guests were housed. "There is one additional item."

Zeffler looked at him.

"Sylvia Highmere's manuscript. Tiffany Zach dropped it off in this room earlier, just before dinner. She explained her actions when I questioned her last night."

"Did she notice anything unusual in this room at the time?"

"She said there was nothing out of the ordinary, no staged evidence when she put the manuscript on the victim's night table."

"Mm." Zeffler slid his hands into his trouser pockets as he looked over the room. "Still all the evidence is circumstantial. How do we prove which guest is the killer? For all we know, it could be your friend, Maisy Wyatt. She was left alone with the guests that evening."

Tadmore suppressed the urge to defend Maisy, he could feel his ears getting hot.

Zeffler was talking again. "We have background checks being done on everyone?"

"Yes, sir. Criminal and juvenile records as well."

"Good. Whoever is responsible for putting the staged evidence in this room knows how to pick locks." Zeffler turned to look at his constable.

"It wouldn't take much to penetrate these old mechanisms." Tadmore grasped the handle of the hallway door to examine the lock.

"That's because we know how it's done. Most people don't, only those who have B and E experience would know. We need to ensure all the keys are accounted for."

"I'll follow up with the staff."

"Do that."

THE INSPECTOR FOUND Constable Tadmore in the first-floor office of Highmere House half an hour later.

"Has Winchester found anything else for us yet?" The Ident van was still parked in front of the house.

"Nothing new so far, but Winchester is reviewing the additional evidence from the crime scene. The personal items and so on," Tadmore reported. "Although the victims purse seems to be missing."

The inspector removed his wet coat and hung it from the rack by the office door. "Do you have any working theories?"

Tadmore nodded. "Yeah, I'm working on the angle the room our victim died in was staged. Since there's something from each guest found in the room."

"Not all of the guests," Maisy said as she entered carrying a tray of coffee and a plate of pizza buns, the kind with a meat filling. "It's like a game of clue."

By the aroma, the baking had to be fresh from the oven, and made Tadmore's stomach growl. He'd never eaten so well at a crime scene before.

Both men's head swivelled to watch her as she placed the tray down on the table between the two club chairs.

"Excuse me, who might you be?" Zeffler shot Tadmore a pointed look.

"This is Maisy Wyatt, sir. She found the victim." Tadmore gestured for Maisy to come forward. "This is my boss, Inspector Zeffler."

"Nice to meet you." She shook the inspector's hand.

Zeffler ran an eye down her uniform. "I'm going to go out on a limb and guess that you work here, right?"

Maisy snorted a laugh and nodded. "The tray and apron are a dead giveaway."

Zeffler chuckled. "You weren't here, when I worked the previous case. When we found the body in the cemetery," Zeffler said.

"No, but don't you usually find bodies in cemeteries?" Maisy looked up at the inspector innocently.

"Not like this one." Zeffler gave her a disarming smile.

The result of the inspector's lame joke and conversation made Maisy's shoulders drop as some of the tension went out of her posture. Zeffler was good at defusing tension. Tadmore made a mental note to employ that tactic in future.

"What did you mean by a game of clue?" Zeffler's full focus was on their witness.

"The fact there was an item from each guest in the room, except one."

"Mm, well spotted. A red herring so to speak, to deflect attention?"

Maisy nodded again. "Except for Kent Westham. Patrick didn't find anything from him."

Zeffler raised one black eyebrow at his constable when Maisy used Tadmore's first name.

The younger cop could feel the tips of his ears redden again, he struggled to ignore the sensation and merely returned Zeffler's look as blandly as he could.

The office door was pushed wider, and Constable Canterbury walked in. "We found this." She held up an evidence bag with a paper napkin rolled up into a ball, inside. "Winchester said to bring it right in. We're pretty sure there will be useable DNA on the serviette."

Tadmore took the evidence bag and held it up to frown at the find. "Where was this found?"

"Rolled inside the carpet," Canterbury said, she sniffed the air and locked eyes on the large platter of pizza buns.

"Okay, I stand corrected." Maisy placed napkins beside a stack of plates and cutlery, along side cream and sugar for the coffee. "Mr. Westham does that with paper napkins, rolls them into a ball. I've found a couple, one under his chair in the dining room and another beside his coffee cup in the library." She poured coffee into the two cups on the table and placed the tray and coffee pot on the desk for easy access.

"That accounts for all the guests, then?" Zeffler glanced at Tadmore.

"Thanks." Tadmore handed the evidence bag back to Canterbury and she left the room. "Unless one of these things is actually a double red herring," Tadmore suggested as he took his cup and gave Maisy a quick smile.

"Who does the cologne belong to?" Zeffler took the coffee Maisy offered him and one of the club chairs. He stretched out his long legs. Tadmore frowned slightly at Zeffler's amused expression. He was testing Maisy.

"Max Lintlaw, he was wearing that scent yesterday when he arrived." Maisy stepped back from the table holding her tray in front of her. "The flask top is Bertram Nutt's, and the bracelet belongs to Angela Oakla."

"What is the other woman's name?" Zeffler looked at his constable, innocently.

"Hazel Dell, sir. We believe the long strands of dark hair are hers, but again DNA may need to be employed to prove it."

Zeffler grunted agreement as he shifted his gaze to stare at his feet for a moment.

"Yes, I think we can all agree the crime scene was staged, constable." Zeffler got up and added a dollop of cream to his coffee and slowly stirred it as he thought out loud. "Someone obtained access to all the guest rooms." He took a sip.

"There was also the manuscript," Tadmore added.

"No, I'm not forgetting that item." Zeffler said and looked at the other cop over the top of his coffee cup.

"Tiffany would never hurt anyone." Maisy's tone was shocked as the implication revealed itself to her.

"Are you sure?" The inspector shifted his gaze to watch Maisy. "How did Tiffany gain access to Ms. Nutt's room?" Zeffler put his cup down and reached for a plate, then placed a warm bun on it.

"She used Mrs. Roque's master key." Tadmore sipped his black coffee.

"Tiffany took her boss' keys without permission?"

"Yes, but—" Maisy spoke up for her friend.

Zeffler held up one hand to forestall her. "She was only thinking about gaining access to the room, not the consequences. We only have her word that she put the manuscript in Ziola Nutt's room before dinner."

Maisy frowned as she thought about it.

"Have you ever used the housekeeper's keys?" Zeffler balanced his plate on his lap as he cut off a chunk. He forked the bite to his mouth and chewed with pleasure.

"Yes, but she gave them to me, to lock up the connecting room. I gave the keys back to Mrs. Roque when I was done making up the last room in the west wing yesterday."

Zeffler turned to Tadmore. "Anything to add?"

"Mrs. Roque showed me all the duplicate keys, they're all accounted for. She's moved them to the carriage house safe."

"Good, we can tick that box." The inspector turned to Maisy. "My complements to Mrs. Roque on these buns, delicious."

"I'll be sure to pass on your words." Maisy exited the office.

"I've received the background checks information," Tadmore was saying to his boss as she closed the door behind her.

AFTER MAKING A RUN out to the forensics van with hot food and coffee, where it was well received by the other two cops, Maisy circled back to the office. She had her excuse ready when she approached but found it wasn't necessary.

Maisy found the office door open and only Tadmore sitting at the desk writing in his notebook. Zeffler was nowhere to be seen.

"Is it all right if I come in?"

Tadmore's dark head came up. "Sure," he said and flashed a quick smile.

Maisy went to the pile of used dishes on the table between the club chairs. She began to load her tray. "Interrogations all done?"

"One left."

"Oh." Maisy took a cloth from her pocket and wiped table crumbs on to one plate. She tried to think of a way to ask who was left and if the cop had found out anything new.

"Angela identified the bracelet, so we can confirm it's hers," Patrick volunteered. "Other than that, she wasn't much help."

"You've left Kent Westham until last?"

"Yep, hopefully he'll be sweating by the time we talk. I'm sure the other writers have spoken to each other about what I've asked them." He closed his notebook and leaned back in the chair.

"I see." Maisy stacked the empty coffee cups and saucers together.

"It's handy you dropped by; I have a couple more questions for you."

"Sure," she said, looking up again with the tray in her hands.

Tadmore got up and took the tray from Maisy and placed it on the desk. "Have a seat and relax."

Maisy took a chair and folded her hands in her lap. It felt odd to be formally questioned. Last night around the kitchen table hadn't been stressful at all. This was completely different.

"Did any of the guests leave the dining room during dinner?"

"Maybe, I don't remember." She shook her head.

"Please think about it."

Maisy took in a deep breath and thought through the meal. Again, she shook her head. "We were so busy getting the food delivered, clearing the previous course dishes and serving useless wine I can't say for certain, but I don't think anyone left after they sat down."

Patrick opened his mouth to ask a follow up question but paused. "What is useless wine?"

"De-alcoholised wine. It's all we serve."

Tadmore frowned. "Why? Why not real wine?"

"Because no alcoholic beverages are served here. It's a rule Alicia Highmere-Graham put in place. Her mother had an issue with alcohol and Sylvia Highmere is a recovering addict. That translates into no mood-altering substances are allowed to be served." Maisy lifted one shoulder. "Although, as Mrs. Roque pointed out; we can't stop people from bringing it in with their luggage. Or in a hipflask." Maisy wrinkled her nose. "I doubt Bertram Nutt has been sober for a moment since he arrived."

The cop nodded at this information and added it to his notes. Tadmore opened his mouth to ask another question when a scream split the air.

Chapter Twenty-Four

MAISY WAS A HAIR FASTER through the door with Tadmore right behind. The pair dashed out just as the scream was cut off by the sound of thumping. A crash greeted them as they rounded the corner. Maisy slid across the marble floor into the foyer as the cop pounded after her.

There was a body at the foot of the oak staircase. The small table beside the stairs was toppled over, a vase smashed and white silk carnations strewn on the floor.

"Oh, my God!" Angela cried as she emerged from the library with Bertram and Max right behind her. "She's fallen down the stairs." Angela rushed to the crumpled heap lying on the floor. It was Hazel Dell.

Maisy moved to help Angela assess her fellow author. She placed a hand on Angela's arm. "Don't move her yet, she might have broken something."

The prone woman let out a moan of pain.

On the midway landing, where the stairs divided in two for each wing, stood Kent Westham. Tadmore frowned up at him. An odd expression, like shock, was evident on the other man's face.

"What on earth is happening out here?" Mrs. Roque strode briskly from the dining room followed by Tiffany. They came to a stop beside the male authors.

Maisy knelt down by Angela to speak to Hazel. "Are you hurt?" She gently moved dark hair out of Hazel's tear-filled eyes. "Go slow." She eased Hazel's arm down to her side from where it had been flung over her head.

"I don't know." The injured woman attempted to untangle her legs. "It was suddenly so cold. I felt—"

"As Maisy said take it slow." Tadmore too now squatted down beside the dishevelled woman.

Hazel's usual tight braid had loose strands of hair falling every which way. Two gel fingernails were broken, and one shoe had come off.

"I think I hurt my ribs. My left side is burning." Hazel hissed air between her teeth and an ugly look formed on her features. She lifted her head and glared up the stairway at Kent. "You pushed me." The accusation was shoved through clenched teeth with pure enmity. "I felt your hand on my back, you shoved me down the stairs."

"I did no such thing." Kent sounded outraged. His eyes darted to the cop and then to the other authors who moved forward to look up at him.

Various expressions of disbelief and confusion registered with Tadmore.

"I didn't push her." Now panic coloured his tone. "I never touched her." The accused voice ratcheted up several notches.

"Kent, how could you?" Angela shot a menacing look up at the man.

"A better question is why," Maisy said, and turned a frown up at Westham.

"I did not push Hazel down the stairs." Spittle was pooling at the corners of his mouth as he clutched the railing and vehemently denied any involvement in Hazel's accident.

"So, what did happen, then?" Tadmore straighten to his full height.

"I didn't...Hazel, she threw herself down the stairs." He stabbed an index finger at the prone woman. "She's trying to frame me." He shook his head, his tone sounded desperate and indignant to Tadmore's ears. "She wants you to think I'm capable of monstrous things so you'll charge me with Ziola's murder."

"Heh, this isn't the first time she's used that strategy." Tiffany's voice was muted, and Tadmore doubted the rest of those assembled in the foyer heard her words, but they were clear enough to him.

The cop narrowed his eyes at the other young woman as she in turn, glared at Hazel with loathing. Tiffany cocked one hip and folded her arms over her middle as she looked at the fallen woman with distaste, Tadmore was sure Tiffany meant what she said.

"Should I call for an ambulance?" Maisy asked the housekeeper.

"Not yet. I have experience dealing with injuries. I am first aid certified," Mrs. Roque said as she came forward inserted herself between her employee and the guest lying on the marble floor.

Maisy grasped Mrs. Roque's arm to steady the housekeeper as the older woman ponderously lowered herself down.

Once on the same level, Mrs. Roque began to examine the fallen woman's arms and legs. "Nothing appears to be broken, unless you've fractured a rib." She winced as she sat back on her heels with a frown of concern aimed at Hazel.

Tadmore nodded and turned to give Kent a steady look. "Mr. Westham, please come downstairs. We need to have a discussion."

"I didn't do anything." Kent flung up his hands in exasperation.

"Why are you saying Ms. Dell is trying to frame you?" Tadmore lifted his eyebrows, hoping the author on the stairs would relax and calmly submit.

Kent shook his head, no doubt wishing he'd never opened his mouth to accuse Hazel. Tadmore didn't want to have to chase the other man through the house, so he kept his voice level. "I have a couple of questions about Ms. Nutt." He looked down at Hazel. "And what you know about Dunn Wolf's finances."

"Oh." Kent nodded and slowly made his way down the staircase, keeping to the extreme right-hand side of the treads to avoid the fallen victim.

Mrs. Roque and Maisy helped the fall victim to sit up.

"Come along, gentlemen." Mrs. Roque addressed Max and Bertram. "Help us get Ms. Dell moved to a more comfortable location." She gestured for the men to come and help.

Maisy picked up Hazel's fallen shoe. She leaned over to put the shoe in front of the injured woman so Hazel could slip it on as Bertram and Max helped her gain her feet. Maisy then stood and assisted her boss to clamber to her feet.

"We could call EMS and see if someone there is available."

"I'll call Jack." Tadmore gestured for Kent to go ahead of him into the office.

"Where do you want us to take her?" Max asked.

"Into the library, please." Mrs. Roque instructed the men. "Each of you put a shoulder under Ms. Dell's."

Tadmore's phone pinged as he escorted Kent into the office. He glanced at the device and scrolled for a couple of seconds as he read. "Have a seat, Mr. Westham, while I make this call."

Although Kent did as he was instructed, he kept his eyes down and leaned forward in his chair as he tugged down the navy vest of his suit. Tadmore kept his eyes on the man as the device rang on the other end of the call.

"Hey, Jack. Can I ask you for a favour?"

"Of course."

The cop explained the situation with Hazel Dell and Jack agreed to come to Highmere House as soon as possible and assess the woman's injuries.

After the call ended, Tadmore gave his interrogation subject a pensive look. "On second thought, let's join everyone else in the library. Then I will be there when Jack arrives."

Kent popped to his feet. "And you can keep your eye on that woman, good move."

When the pair arrived at the library, Max and Bertram were getting Hazel settled in one of the Queen Anne chairs as Tadmore brought up the rear.

He grasped the matching armchair and moved it several feet away, but opposite from the first and offered Kent the seat. "Sit here, please."

"Is Jack on his way?" The housekeeper asked as she supervised Hazel's placement in the chair.

"He is." Tadmore nodded.

"Good, I'll ask Maisy to bring us a fresh pot of coffee." Mrs. Roque turned to the other young woman to give the order. "Maybe some tea too."

"Actually, Mrs. Roque," Tadmore interjected. "I'd like everyone to just take a seat in here, please, for the moment."

His eyes found Maisy's and registered her grateful expression. The way their amber depts sparkled, he knew she didn't want to be left out of the final stages of his investigation.

Still, this wasn't the reason he wanted all the principals in the same room. Tadmore shifted his eyes away from her. He needed to make sure everyone was accounted for and under his supervision. If that meant Maisy thought he was doing this to include her, that was a side benefit.

"All right, Constable, if you think this is strictly necessary." The housekeeper didn't sound like she agreed with him but would go along for now.

The actual reason was his boss would expect this since Tadmore was the only cop on the scene. It shouldn't be too long now until Inspector Zeffler wrapped up his conversation with their last witness and joined them. His boss had texted him just before he called Jack.

Tadmore slid the right pocket door closed, as the rest of the group took a seat or found a perch in the large book-lined room. He parked himself in front of the remaining open door. Things were about to get dicey.

The cop turned to study Kent while waiting for the group to settle before he spoke. Westham kept his gaze on his folded hands resting in his lap. The diminutive man had to sit forward to keep his feet flat on the vermillion carpet, one of the reasons Tadmore had chosen the winged-back chair.

Angela had parked herself on the settee next to Hazel's chair and patted her shoulder, in a comforting manner.

"Now, first things first. Let's deal with the fall down the stairs Ms. Dell." He waited until Hazel looked at him. "Why did you fling yourself down the staircase?"

"I didn't...I—"

"Of course you did." Kent Westham snapped at her. "You've always been a drama queen. You think you can pin this whole debacle on me if you play the victim?" His words sounded less like a question, and more like a statement in fact.

Tadmore held up one hand, effectively stifling any further words from Westham. He pivoted to look at Tiffany leaning on the sideboard, arms still folded across her stomach. "Tiffany, what did you mean about Hazel using the same 'strategy?"

Tiffany compressed her lips and then lifted her head. She appeared to make a decision and dropped her defensive pose, arms to her sides. Although her hands curled into fists.

The cop watched the young woman carefully. "You've seen Hazel do something like this before, haven't you?" Tadmore shifted to first names, confident Tiffany and Hazel shared a history.

The young woman's eyes shifted around the room, finally they locked on Mrs. Roque.

"Tiffany?" Mrs. Roque tipped her head at her employee. "Do you know something? It's all right, please tell the Constable."

The maid nodded at the housekeeper and stood up straighter. "I did know Hazel from St. Ursula's. She was a couple years ahead of me. Back then, everyone knew who to steer clear of. If Hazel got into trouble, she would pretend she was the victim of some attack. She was a master at pointing the finger at someone else."

As one, the others turned to look at Hazel. Angela stopped rubbing Hazel's shoulder and blinked, shocked at the ugly expression on her friend's face.

"How was Ms. Dell capable of getting away with this?" He kept his tone level and avoided inflection.

"Hazel would hurt herself." Tiffany swallowed and her voice gained strength. "I saw her once when I was putting field hockey equipment away. I don't think she knew I was in the storage room. She broke her own finger with a lacrosse stick. Betty Westbrook was blamed and was expelled, even though it was Hazel who gave Betty the fat lip first."

"You're lying." Hazel grated the words out as she held her hand against her side, breathing shallowly. "You always were a liar."

Tiffany slowly shook her head with her eyes locked on Hazel. An intense gleam appeared. "No, we all knew what you did. After Betty was gone, things began to go missing. Students blamed each other. Fights were common. Nobody knew who was getting into students' rooms and lockers. Then you were caught leaving a dorm you had no business being in." She nodded her head at Hazel. "Miss Mahon was taking you to see the head mistress. You flung yourself down the staircase and later said Miss Mahon pushed you because you were going to report her for inappropriate behaviour."

"I never went to school at saint whatever. You can check. This is all lies."

"You did. Your last name wasn't Dell then, it was Linstrom. I remember you. You bullied me. Just like you tried to bully Betty and tried it on Miss Mahon. She was the best maths teacher at St. Ursula's, and you drove her away." Tiffany lifted her chin. "Betty didn't have a friend like Sylvia to help her. I was lucky, unlike Miss Mahon and Betty. Hazel is the stone-cold liar. By the time the investigation was over, Miss Mahon had to resign and leave the school. It's hard to prove something, when it never happened, but the thefts stopped." She swallowed again. "I guess you decided not to press your luck. Sylvia always wondered how you learned to pick locks. She figured it had to be something you learned before you came to St. Ursula's School for Young Ladies."

"It was, probably from the company she kept at the juvenile offender's detention facility," Tadmore interjected, he'd watched Hazel through all of Tiffany's story. Now he returned his phone to his pocket. "We have your background, Ms. Dell. You changed your name when you turned eighteen. You were Hazel Lindstrom before that, and you did attend St. Ursula's school on an endowment for troubled youth."

"I was on my own, I had problems, but I turned my life around. At least I'm not a murderer, not like Kent." Hazel was beginning to sound desperate to Tadmore. "I stole, yes, but from strangers. At least I didn't steal from my friends." Her eyes cut back to Kent.

Max sat up straighter from his seat beside Angela, staring at Kent. "Wait, what?"

No one acknowledge his question as Hazel rambled on. "You were a criminal right from the start, I should have seen it." Hazel's eyes were red-rimmed and moist with tears. Real or manufactured, remained to be seen. "You told me you loved me." The words sounded like a curse.

Kent turned his face away from Hazel.

"I'd like to know—" Max began again, and Angela hushed him patting his arm.

Tadmore walked toward Kent to get his attention. "You had a relationship with Ziola Nutt, didn't you, Mr. Westham." Tadmore said this without preamble. His phone pinged again and this time he took it out of his trouser pocket. He glanced at the device briefly and returned it to his pocket. "Well, Kent?" He looked again at the subject of his interrogation. "Please answer the question."

The other man kept his head down and eyes glued to the hands tightly clenched in his lap. "Is this because of what Hazel told you?"

"No sir. It's from what I've figured out from the testimony of a witness." He regarded the author steadily.

"You had a relationship with Ziola, in the past. You told Hazel it was all over, but something changed lately, and you attempted to rekindle your affair with your business partner. You did a flip flop. What happened to make you want to dump Ms. Dell and reinvolve yourself with Ziola?"

"I don't know what you're talking about." Westham's head came up and his eyes shifted sideways to look out of the window.

This pleased Tadmore, it meant he was making progress. Lies, like liars want to be found out. "The unfortunate thing is, Ziola wasn't interested anymore, was she? She figured out your agenda and she was not going to share her revenue windfall with you. She knew you only wanted to get a share of the money from the video streaming deal. If she let you cozy up to her, you'd press her for a share of the money, Ziola knew this."

Kent merely folded his arms across his chest.

"Or, at the very least, you wanted to receive more of the royalties, am I right? No wonder she hired a new accountant by the way." He lifted his eyebrows at the other man. "I find it odd Ms. Nutt allowed you to stay as an author after she realized you were funneling company money into your own accounts."

"None of that is true." Westham crossed his arms over his chest.

"Of course, it is. When you got wind of the streaming deal, you knew that several of the books in the series were ghost written by other Dunn Wolf authors. After all, you were the accountant. Each of those books are expected to be an episode of the streaming series. Thus, each author is entitled to a share of the media royalties from the half million-dollar deal. Not to mention resale value on other platforms."

This announcement sent a flurry of speculation through the other authors.

"Didn't I say that? I told you," Max said to no one in particular.

Angela hushed him again.

Tadmore raised his voice a notch over the hubbub. "We have your background, Kent. We know how you became involved with Ziola in the first place. You were the original owner of Dunn Wolf Publishing." He paused again as the other authors expressed their shock. Mrs. Roque hushed them as a group.

Kent hunched his shoulders.

"Ziola came into money just at the time your publishing house was failing. Probably because you were bleeding the business dry. You needed an influx of capital in a hurry, so you offered Ziola a sweet deal. If she bought in, she could share in the profits. Did she negotiate a hard deal? Did you give up too much of the company in a bid to let her recoup her investment faster? To keep her interested?" Tadmore shook his head. "Then things began to get out of your control, didn't they?"

"What? You are the other owner of the publishing house?" Bertram spoke for the first time from the corner of the other settee. "Figures."

Tadmore tipped his head to one side as he watched Westham. "No one in this group knew you were the original publisher/owner of Dunn Wolf, did they? Ziola recruited the authors, they thought you were one of them. So did Hazel."

He glanced at the silent woman. She was intently glaring at her former boyfriend. Her bottom jaw jutted out at an aggressive angle. Her breathing was coming in deep gasps as her anger grew, she forgot to hold her side in pain.

The cop turned back to Westham and continued, "As soon as Ziola took public possession of the small press you split the skimmed funds with her, still as a silent partner. That was your trap. Now she was in it up to her eyeballs too, or so you thought."

"The sad thing is, I can see Ziola happily going along with all of this." Bertram rubbed his bald head in frustration. "She wanted recognition so bad she could taste it and would love this scheme." He snorted in derision. "Ziola knew there was no way for an author to know for sure what their sales were. We have to trust our publisher. We don't get to see what the full financial statements look like. We never get full reporting. I doubt she knew how it felt to be ripped off by those you trust." He bared his teeth in disgust. "But I do. I learned the hard way."

The cop waited for Bertram's rant to come to an end. Then he turned back to Kent. "Even after your relationship broke up you two were still partners."

"Partners in crime." Angela interjected and it was Max's turn to shush her.

"Yes," Tadmore gave Angela a nod of agreement. "They were. The lifestyle Ziola lived was much more extravagant than yours, wasn't it, Kent? Did she take over managing everything, even the embezzlement?"

Kent closed his eyes and shook his head. Mute to the allegations, yet his body language was giving him away.

"You were greedy, or you were too much in debt, and still are, according to our forensic accountants." Tadmore tapped the mobile phone in his pocket where he'd been receiving the details. "Your credit card debts are excessive. Collection agencies representing marketing companies are after you. Places which sell book reviews. Especially one such business claims they can promise to get your book on the New York Times best seller list because of their influential contacts." Tadmore shook his head. "And for a hefty fee."

"Then the tables turned on you when Ziola Nutt took control of the publishing business. She forced you to sign a new contract in exchange for cash. Either way, your debts were so massive you couldn't argue. Nothing you, or the other authors, wrote sold nearly as well as Ziola's series. So, you put up with the arrangement." He paused for effect. "For a while."

"We all worked on her books." Max scowled at the cop. "Do you think our illustrious Ms. Nutt could come up with all those unique plots herself? We received pennies for our work. Ziola owes all of us."

Bertram looked at Max and nodded in agreement.

Tadmore stood square in front of his subject. "I'm willing to bet that at some point, your share dried up after the new contract. Ziola decided to keep your cut, didn't she? What could you say? You were just as guilty as she was of fraud, and embezzlement. If you tried to change anything or even thought about reporting Ziola, you'd be right there in it with her. Wouldn't you? No matter what you said to the rest of your colleagues, you also couldn't claim common-law spouse, she was careful to never share living space with you."

"Ziola took advantage of me." The words burst out of Kent Westham. "Just like she did Bertram. He's partly responsible for the success Ziola built and she gave him nothing. She built her success on Bertram's work, and she laughed at him while she took the lion's share of the money and fame."

"I know, and now he stands to make out quite well. As her only relative, Bertram will inherit his sister's assets. So, all ends well for Bertram Nutt, but not for you." Tadmore paused a moment and pivoted to look at Hazel. "And not for Hazel Dell."

"Bertram wasn't in his room when I stopped by, he was in Ziola's room, murdering her." Kent released the stream of words. "He has the contract."

He glared at Bertram. The other man narrowed his eyes at Kent but said nothing.

"Mr. Nutt was down here in the library," Tadmore said. "How did you know the contract is missing?"

The sound of the main front doors opening reached them. Mrs. Roque hopped to her feet at the echoes of voices in the foyer. She briskly walked around Tadmore and out of the room.

Chapter Twenty-Five

TADMORE CONTINUED TO keep his eyes on Kent Westham. "When did you realize you had to come up with a new scheme? It couldn't have been long after Ziola cut you off. And that plan involved Hazel." Tadmore shifted his feet and braced his hands behind his back as he let his stare drill into the other man.

Kent shifted grave eyes to look at the cop. "You know what Hazel did," he said with finality, his tone serious.

"I do and so do you," Tadmore agreed.

"I'm so sorry, Hazel." Kent held out a hand to Hazel plaintively. "I have to tell them what you did."

The woman merely sneered at him. "You got me to break into the bedroom. You begged me to steal something from everyone."

"How did you get my bracelet?" Angela asked, her eye filled with fury.

Hazel had the grace to look apologetically at her friend. "I took it off you before we went upstairs after dinner." She lifted her hand toward Angela, then dropped it in her lap in resignation at the younger woman's anger.

Kent ignored the women's interaction and kept going. "Ziola was horrid to Hazel." He sounded desperate to refocus Tadmore's attention. "She kept promising to publish Hazel's work, but never did. Although that didn't stop Ziola from convincing her assistant to help write one of the books in the series." He pivoted in his chair to look at his former lover. "Ziola pretended to mentor Hazel. Writing the new novel would give her experience. I remember how she laughed at your writing, Hazel, how upset you'd get. Ziola was so cruel to you. Abusive, like she was to me and Bertram." He flung a hand at Maisy and Tiffany. "You heard how Ziola spoke to Hazel at lunch."

Tadmore looked over at the pair of young women.

"Yes, we heard her." Tiffany nodded her agreement.

"It seems to me your publisher spoke to everyone that way. Including me and Tiff." Maisy shook her head. "How can that be enough of a motive to murder someone?"

Mr. Willard entered the room. Everyone's attention shifted to the older man as he carried in an arm load of firewood. He wasn't alone, Constable Winchester and Inspector Zeffler came in behind him.

Tadmore gave the new arrivals a nod.

Willard deposited the load of wood in the log holder by the fireplace. The groundskeeper turned and looked at the group assembled. He pursed his lips and lifted his chin at the cop. Tadmore acknowledged the other man. Willard turned on his heel, but paused to shake Zeffler's hand, then he was gone.

The cop realized Maisy had narrowed her eyes at him. She leaned over and whispered something to Tiffany. They both turned to look at the polished wooden mask on the wall behind the desk at the far end of the room, where he'd been informed the listening screen was hidden.

Zeffler gestured for Tadmore to continue as he and Winchester quietly took up station beside the sideboard near the door.

It was a that point the calico cat reappeared from under the settee where Max and Angela sat. She sauntered over to Maisy and jumped up on the bookshelf.

"Missy, no." Maisy reached over and plucked the cat off the shelf and the feline snuggled smugly against the young woman, the cat's front paws propped on her shoulder.

The constable lifted his chin. "While verbal abuse is a possible motive, I think there was more to it than that." Tadmore looked at first Kent then Hazel. "You both had agendas—"

"Hazel would become so angry, I feared for myself more than once." Kent cut in and looked beseechingly up at Tadmore.

"Stop trying to play the victim card, you snake." Hazel narrowed her eyes at Kent. "You are no victim. You never were." She held her left side again like she was in pain. "I should know."

Kent kept his eyes locked on Tadmore. "It's no wonder Hazel strangled Ziola with her scarf." He continued like the woman hadn't spoken.

"Did she?" Tadmore raised his eyebrows in interest. "Please go on."

"She collected the evidence to be left in Ziola's room to confuse you. Angela's bracelet, Bertram's flask lid, Max's cologne, the lot. She wanted you to think we all could be guilty. Hazel was the clever mind behind this murder, and she strangled Ziola."

"I agree Hazel did have plans to kill Ms. Nutt." Tadmore gave a nod to Kent and held up one hand to forestall any further comment, at least for the moment. "However, you beat her to the punch, so to speak." Tadmore shook his head. "It was after dinner. You went up early, you took Ziola another glass of sherry. She let you in and accepted the drink. Probably as a peace offering." Tadmore shifted his weight to his heels as he spoke. The fatigue he'd been experiencing earlier was now gone with the adrenalin rush of winding up the case. "You were probably up in Ziola's room to plant the evidence, and make sure all was ready. Either way, I think there was an argument, and you lost your temper, strangled Ziola and that spoiled your plan."

"I have no idea what you are talking about. I merely took Ziola a night cap."

Tadmore nodded. The suspect was now confirming information, a good sign.

"Your plan was to have Hazel become so upset, she would end her boss's life. To make her angry enough, you must have told Hazel, Ziola was blackmailing you. You couldn't be together because of the blackmail. You were being forced to dump Hazel, for Ziola, the other woman. I understand you rebuffed Hazel before dinner in the library and then waited on Ziola, paying court so too speak."

"He put my teeth on edge with his sycophantic behaviour." Hazel bared them at Kent. For his part Kent gave her a sniff of distain and turned away.

"Maybe at that moment." The constable glanced at Hazel briefly before continuing. "Then you returned downstairs when the rest began going up to their rooms. You even went so far as to ask Mrs. Roque for a wake-up call so it would look like everyone was going upstairs at almost the same time." Tadmore turned back to Hazel.

"Now it was your turn to enter Ziola's room. You probably knocked and there was no answer so you picked the lock, no challenge for you with your experience, then onto the task at hand."

"I thought I had no choice." Hazel's voice was measured as she stared at her hands in her lap as she clenched them in a white knuckled grip. "He convinced me I had to help him."

"You thought if you wanted Kent back and to have any chance of being published, you needed to set up Ziola's death to look like an accident. How hard could it be you asked yourself? How am I doing?"

Hazel lifted her head and stared at Tadmore. "Kent said it was all over between us if I didn't do something. He couldn't make Ziola stop, she was going to report his embezzlement. He told me if he killed her, the cops would suspect him right away because of their relationship." There was raw hurt and anger in Hazel's words. "I wish I'd kept my past secret from you." She shook her head. "You said we needed to throw the cops off by planting evidence from all of us. They'd never figure it out, you said." Her eyes burned as she looked at her former lover. "You used me," Hazel's words came out in a low hiss.

Tadmore nodded and turned back to Kent. "First you drugged Ziola, probably with something in that glass of sherry you took up to her room. It should have knocked your victim out, but I think you miscalculated with the body index. Ziola was a large woman, her capacity for alcohol, or drugs for that matter, would be higher than you'd guessed. Did Ziola call your bluff? Did she insult you and trigger your anger?"

"Don't be ridiculous." Kent had an ugly look on his face.

"It's all in the initial toxicology report." Winchester stepped forward when he spoke. Tadmore gestured for the other cop to continue.

"The deceased was zonked out on a class three sedative. Which one exactly is being determined. There was no evidence of the drug in her room. The glass found on her night table had been rinsed in the bathroom sink. However, we did find traces of the sedative in the 'P' trap under the sink."

Tadmore shook his head at Westham. "For a writer, you aren't good with details, are you? It takes a few minutes of water running to flush the 'P' trap, but you were in a hurry. Hazel would be coming in shortly. You had to get downstairs to establish your alibi. Still, sometime between when you slipped Ziola the drug and she succumbed to the sedative, you argued."

"You know nothing." Kent shook his head.

"I know strangling someone with your bare hands takes a lot of nerve. A lot of emotion, like anger. When you have nothing else to lose, or fear you are about to lose everything."

"I had nothing to do with Ziola being drugged or strangled," Kent said with almost no inflection.

Tadmore watched him for a moment. "Everyone saw you decline the sherry in the library before dinner, but you did jump to get a glass for Ziola when she came to join you. Is that when you slipped her the first dose?" He took a step toward Kent and leaned on the wing of the chair. "After you killed her, you panicked. Your plan was now compromised." He tipped his head at Kent. "What were you going to do? As the only remaining partner in Dunn Wolf, you could fire the new accountant and go on with the embezzlement. Take full control again, Bertram wouldn't be much of an obstacle especially if you convinced him, you and Ziola were common-law spouses. You'd inherit Ziola's share and owe the whole thing again. Then you could get your life back on track."

Tadmore turned to look at Hazel. Her eyes glittered, it wouldn't be long now. "I don't think you ever wanted to live happily ever after with Hazel, did you? Or publish any of her work." None of this was a question. "Did you have plans to remove Hazel from the picture too? That thought must have cheered you up. You could implicate Hazel as the jealous lover."

The woman's eyes hardened and Tadmore was confident the bond between his two suspects was well and truly broken.

"Are you about to wind this up, Tadmore? We need to get these suspects on the next ferry." Zeffler lifted the lid of the teapot on the sideboard to peer inside. His expression showed disappointment when he found only dregs.

"Just about, sir." The constable shifted his eyes back to Kent.

Westham swallowed. "Hazel came up with the plan to take the publishing house back. I told her I didn't want anything to do with Ziola again." Kent sounded like he was desperate, his words came out in a rush. "She kept on at me, told me I would inherit Ziola's estate as her common-law husband, including all rights and royalties. She said it would be easy to fabricate a renewal of our relationship." The disgust evident in his voice did not ring true. "Hazel is so cold." Kent rounded indignantly on Hazel. "I could never hurt Ziola, I loved her, don't you see? I knew your plan you evil woman. You think you thought if you could convince the cops I hurt you, you'd look innocent. Like I'm the brute who pushed you, that I'm the killer who strangled Ziola." He shook his head and folded his arms over his chest. "Stupid, as usual."

"I am not stupid." Hazel gripped the arms of the chair. "I hoped you could try to reason with Ziola. That's where you went after dinner when she went up stairs. So maybe we wouldn't have to do this, but you never gave me the signal, so I knew I had to take the items and go to her room. Ziola was dead when I got there."

"Indeed." Zeffler interjected. "To sum up, Kent lost his temper when Ziola told him to get lost. Ms. Nutt could cut all of you to the quick." He gestured to the writers with a

circle of his forefinger. "But you most of all, Mr. Westham."
The inspector pointed at Kent. "Ziola Nutt took your
company. She took your ill-gotten gains, cut you out of the
streaming royalties, and she was blackmailing you too."

Hazel laughed dryly at him. "Oh yes, Ziola outwitted
you, Kent. I hated her, but you are not pinning her murder
on me."

Red flashed up Kent's neck as his anger surfaced. "That
woman was a horror show."

Tadmore kept his full attention on his chief suspect. "So,
when you entered the room, Kent, you took Ziola's scarf
and wrapped it around her throat, probably thinking she
was passed out according to the plan. It would look like
she strangled in her sleep. Is that when you realized she was
already dead?"

"Her neck was already red and bruised." Hazel sniffed in
distain.

The cat jumped out of Maisy's arms and stiff walked over
to Zeffler and parked herself by his feet as she looked up at
him.

"That's when it occurred to you, Westham could wrap
the whole thing up and drop it around your neck." Zeffler
leaned down and scratched the cat's cheek.

"I began to doubt Kent and his plan. I realized his
strategy was to have me charged with Ziola's murder. I would
take the fall and he'd be rid of both of us."

"Hazel screamed to get us all in there and make it look
like she had nothing to do with the murder." Maisy spoke up
with a frown at Hazel.

"A belated attempt to protect herself, yes." Tadmore nodded.

"No wonder she locked herself in her own room afterward," Maisy said.

Abruptly, Angela stood. "You both are horrible, horrible people." She walked to the opposite side of the room and stood along the wall beside Tiffany.

Hazel ignored Angela. She glared her hatred at Kent. "Now who's stupid. We've got nothing from all this."

"Nothing but jail time." Winchester's radio sounded. "Jack Birch is here, Inspector."

"Good, ask him to come in here, please." He straightened up. "Tadmore, Winchester, caution our suspects."

"Kent Westham you are charged with the murder of Ziola Nutt." Tadmore took Kent's arm and turned him around to be cuffed.

"Hazel Dell, you are charged with conspiracy to commit murder." Winchester did the same.

Mrs. Roque slipped in quietly with a tray of fresh tea, more chocolate biscuits, and other treats as the constables cautioned their suspects.

The inspector's expression cheered up. "You are a treasure, Mrs. Roque." Zeffler selected a wedge of cake from the plate when the housekeeper put the tray down beside him. He took a healthy bite while Mrs. Roque poured the tea.

The inspector waved at Bertram Nutt and then swallowed. "We'd like that contract, if you please, Mr. Nutt." Zeffler gestured to Tadmore. "Give it to the Constable."

Tadmore gave his inspector a bemused look as he and Winchester escorted Kent and Hazel from the room.

Bertram dug the paper out of his left breast pocket.

THE INSPECTOR TURNED to the housekeeper. "Thank you, Mrs. Roque, a pleasure as always."

The housekeeper's cheeks flushed a pretty pink. "Thank you, Inspector."

As Zeffler climbed into his vehicle, the sun chose that moment to break through the remaining dull clouds.

Tadmore supervised as Westham and Dell were led away to the waiting transport vehicle.

Zeffler glanced at his watch. "You can come in with us to write up your report, Tadmore." He called over to his constable. "I'll have someone drop you at the ferry when you're done."

"Yes, sir."

"Don't worry about Miles, he can stay with us until you get back," Jack said as he watched Patrick close the SUV's back door. "Mari Ann called to tell us she's been called in to work again."

"Thanks, I appreciate this. I owe you."

"No problem, you can help me shingle the café roof this summer. So can Miles, come to that."

Patrick smiled at this. "Sounds fair."

The front door opened, and Winchester came out trailed by Tiffany.

"Are you sure you've got what you need?" The housekeeper asked the cop as Tiffany gave the housekeeper back her master keys. She had used them to open Kent Westham's room for the constable.

"I think so ma'am." Winchester was carrying a clear plastic evidence bag with a large black purse inside. "Ident will finish bagging up the suspects belongings and then we will get out of your hair at least for today. We will be back tomorrow, so please keep the rooms locked."

"Of course." She nodded.

"Where'd you find the victim's purse?" Tadmore asked the other cop. He held a second evidence bag with the creased and wrinkled steaming contract inside.

"Westham's room, between the mattresses."

At that moment, a red Shelby mustang rocketed up the driveway. It slid into the parking area and came to an abrupt halt.

"There she is, finally." Mrs. Roque ghosted up beside Tadmore.

"Who?"

"Miss Sylvia," the housekeeper said.

"Late as usual," Tiffany commented, but still smiled as she walked over to her friend.

Mrs. Roque looked like she wanted to say something, but merely shook her head as she returned to the front step.

A woman in her early thirties dashed from her car, ran past a gaping Tiffany, and up to the entrance, coming to a sliding halt in front of Mrs. Roque. "Is she still here?"

"Who, dear?"

"The publisher? Did she read my manuscript?"

"I'm sorry, Miss Sylvia, Ziola Nutt was overtaken by unforeseeable circumstances."

"Oh, no." Sylvia swung her body away from Mrs. Roque like a four-year-old in a pout.

"Come along and have some refreshment, dear." Mrs. Roque waved one large hand at the younger woman to proceed her.

Dragging her feet, Sylvia allowed herself to be shepherded inside the big house.

Mrs. Roque's mobile phone rang, and she fished it out of her apron pocket.

"That's Alicia's ring tone, isn't it?" Sylvia remarked.

"Yes, it is." Mrs. Roque straightened her spine. "Hello?"

"COME ALONG, MISS SYLVIA, there's quiche for lunch." Mrs. Roque waved the newcomer ahead of her.

"Sounds yummy." Sylvia drifted toward the dining room.

During the housekeeper's call with her boss, Tiffany and Maisy brought Sylvia up to speed on the happenings of the past two days.

She didn't appear to be affected at all by the fact someone was murdered upstairs. Maisy shook her head in wonderment.

"I'll need to put in a call to Jane to invite her family and Gladys for the evening meal. Someone must eat all this food. Too bad Inspector Zeffler had to leave."

The housekeeper took the cardboard box of broken vase and dead flowers with her as she headed in the same direction. Her step was lighter after the call with Alicia Highmere. "You girls are staying for dinner too." Mrs. Roque called over her shoulder. It was more an order than an invitation.

"Yes, Mrs. Roque." The young women answered at the same time.

Then Maisy caught Tiffany's arm and the pair hung back from the housekeeper and the departing guests. Apparently, no one wanted to stay for dinner or overnight now that the ferries were back in operation.

"I can't believe I won't get my deposit back." Angela pouted as she dragged her suitcase out of the front door.

"Did you hear what Hazel said before, when she fell?" Maisy lifted her eyebrows at her friend.

"I did. The cold spot moved again."

"Yep. Either he's trying to make amends for his past sins by exposing a murder plot, or he was up to something worse."

Tiffany shivered. "I think we need to convince Mrs. Roque to get the house blessed and send Mr. Highmere to the light."

"Exactly, except what if there's more than one ghost?"

Epilogue

WHEN PATRICK ARRIVED back at the Birch house the next morning. Arlie met him at the back door in the kitchen.

"So, what's the plan, Pat?" Arlie asked the cop.

"I'll take Miles back to my sister's place." He looked at the kid. "Grab your stuff we have to go."

"Are you taking me home?"

"Yes, your mom's off for two days. I have loose ends to sort out on this case, I have to come back."

"Let me know when Miles is coming for a visit." Jane smiled at the boy as she watched him stuff his belongings back into his pack. "If you're busy, he can hang out with us at the café. I used to do that at his age. I learned a lot." She turned to Patrick and lifted her eyebrows at him and he nodded in understanding.

"What do you think?" Patrick asked his nephew as Miles came to the door to pull on his runners.

"Can I help out, working in the café?" Miles asked.

"Oh, I'll put you to work, don't worry." Arlie looped the backpack strap onto Miles' shoulder. "You were very helpful getting Jack's truck started, thanks again."

"No problem." Miles sounded more adult as he preceded his uncle out of the door. "Jane makes the best cupcakes."

Jane gave Miles a smile. "Thanks."

"Give me a call if you need any help with your 'loose ends.'" Jack wandered across the kitchen to join his family for the departure.

"I might do that, thanks. Any idea where Maisy is?"

"She and Gladys are taking a turn helping at the Community Centre shelter. Mrs. Roque donated the food."

"Okay, thanks." Patrick gave them all a general nod and he walked down the steps. An RCMP SUV was idling at the end of the drive.

"That sounds like unresolved business." Arlie lifted an eyebrow at Jane.

"It does at that," she agreed. They both watched Patrick depart.

The End

Don't miss out!

Visit the website below and you can sign up to receive emails whenever Yvonne Rediger publishes a new book. There's no charge and no obligation.

https://books2read.com/r/B-A-SFCV-EYFOF

BOOKS 2 READ

Connecting independent readers to independent writers.

Did you love *Storm Stayed*? Then you should read *Fun With Funerals*[1] by Yvonne Rediger!

Fun with Funerals
A Musgrave Landing Mystery

Yvonne Rediger
Is it murder without a body?

2

Alicia Highmere is heading home, back to Musgrave Landing after a call from her mother's care home. They said Olivia Frost-Highmere had passed away. But has she? Accompanied by her body guard, Bryce Graham, Alicia won't know for sure until she gets there.

It has been a few weeks since she visited her mother. A suspicious accident prevented her from travelling. For her sister Sylvia, it's been a long time since she's been home, and for her brother James, years.

---

1. https://books2read.com/u/4DqLkk

2. https://books2read.com/u/4DqLkk

Part of the reason the family is estranged, is the fallout from the disappearance of their father some twenty years ago. Allister Highmere vanished without a trace upsetting the family company and leaving the seat of CEO vacant. Uncle Hugo accused Olivia, Alicia's mother, of murder, but is it murder if there's no body?

Read more at blackyvy50.wix.com/yvonnerediger.

Also by Yvonne Rediger

Adam Norcross Mysteries
The Wrong Words
The Right Road

Musgrave Landing Mysteries
Death and Cupcakes
Fun With Funerals
Condo Crazy
Storm Stayed

VIC Shapeshifters
Into the Wood
The Shape of Us
Hell Cat
Trusting the Wolf

Standalone
The Common Touch
Diving In Heart First

Watch for more at blackyvy50.wix.com/yvonnerediger.